The Mesmerist's Muse

EMMA HARDWICK

COPYRIGHT

Title: The Mesmerist's Muse

First published in 2023

Copyright © Emma Hardwick 2023

ISBN: 9798391900801 (Paperback)

The author, and the publisher specifically disclaim any liability, loss, or risk which is incurred as a consequence, directly or indirectly, of the use and application of any contents of this work.

The right of Emma Hardwick identified as the author of this work has been asserted in accordance with the Copyright Designs and Patents Act 1988.

All rights reserved. No part of this work may be reproduced in any material form (including photocopying or storing by any electronic means, and whether or not transiently or incidentally to some other use of this publication) without written permission of the copyright holder except in accordance with the provisions of the Copyright, Designs, and Patents Act 1988.

Applications for the copyright holder's written permission to reproduce any part of this publication should be addressed to the publishers.

The characters in this book are fictional. Any resemblance to persons living or dead is coincidental.

CONTENTS

Unexpected Turns	7
Betty's Bold Move	25
A Fateful Encounter	38
Shadows and Secrets	51
The Widow's Secret	71
Lies and More Lies	85
The Ideal Victim	91
A Problem Shared is a Problem Doubled	97
Mistakes and Missteps	108
Havoc at Highgate	115
The Waiting Game	123
A Spirited Encounter	135
The Charm Offensive	147
The Puppet Princess	152
The Burden of Secrecy	169
Deception in the Darkness	181
The Illusion of Rose-Coloured Glasses	193
Following the Trail	207
The Relentless Pursuit	211
The Plan Comes Together	222
Heartfelt Persuasion	235
Fading Facades	252
Desperate Times	277
In the Hands of Fate	304
Love's Quiet Triumph	326

1

UNEXPECTED TURNS

As Rose's eyes flickered open, a strange sense of anticipation took hold. It was a special day, the birthday of her generous and kind-hearted costermongering employer, Mrs Kelly. To celebrate, Rose had fashioned a humble but heartfelt gift for the occasion, a pin cushion made from bright scraps of fabric and plumped up with sawdust. In the dim light of dawn, it was hard to discern the object from the chaos of the room. Trying not to wake her sleeping brothers, Rose gingerly rose from their creaky shared bed to search for the present. As her fingers finally found the familiar object, perched on the windowsill, a small smile graced her lips. Little did she know that the day's events would soon take a fateful turn, shattering her brief moment of contentment.

The room was dark and stuffy, lit only by a sliver of light coming through the tattered curtain. As Rose's excitement faded, she sighed and rested her head on the pillow, weighed down by the knowledge of her other problems. She frowned at the window as the rain pattered against the glass and the sight of the smog-covered world outside. The dreary weather deepened Rose's slip into melancholy, the greyness a stark contrast to the lush Irish landscape the family had left behind. Memories of emerald green fields and laughter-filled gatherings shared with her father flooded her mind, bringing both warmth and pain.

The cramped tenement was a sorry sight to behold. Upstairs, two modest beds, one against each wall, maximised the limited space in which the family resided. A shared, slim wooden wardrobe stood like a soldier on guard in one corner, while a small, rickety table occupied another, complete with a chipped wash basin and pitcher. The once-cream walls, now stained and peeling, surrounded the family's living quarters, and even when the curtains were drawn, the single, grimy window only allowed a meagre amount of light to filter in.

Despite the room's oppressive atmosphere, signs of love and warmth persisted. The beds were adorned with hand-crocheted blankets, gifts from Rose's late grandmother, which provided comfort and cheer, and were a testament to the family's resourcefulness and determination to make the best of what they had.

Rose's gaze drifted towards her dozing frail, widowed mother. Ellen was surrounded by piles of matchboxes in various stages of assembly on her patchwork quilt. Although she was too ill to leave her bed recently, she continued to work into the early hours of the morning, determined to provide for her children. The strength and resilience of this beleaguered woman were a source of inspiration to all who knew her.

A family photograph of happier times in Ireland adorned the otherwise barren walls, a silent reminder of what they had lost. The image captured the joy that once filled their lives, and now served to sustain them through the dark days.

As Rose stood up from her bed, a gentle voice spoke.

"Good morning, my love. Did you sleep well?"

Rose nodded as she rolled the pin cushion on her hand.

"Mrs Kelly will be ever so grateful for your thoughtfulness," Ellen said, her voice laced with pride and encouragement for her daughter's efforts.

Rose smiled at her mother's words, touched by her unwavering support amidst her own struggles. With the pin cushion cradled in her lap, she wrapped her shawl around her shoulders and sat on the edge of her mother's bed, bracing herself for another day of hard work and sacrifice.

"You do look a bit tired, though, love."

Ellen was right, of course. Sharing a bed with her brothers and standing all day at the market stall in all weathers was exhausting, but it didn't matter. Nowadays, what mattered most was paying the rent and still having enough money for food.

Rose tied up her ragged bonnet strings and secured the lopsided hat with a single rusty pin, then turned to face Ellen.

"Honestly, I'm fine, ma," Rose replied, a hint of weariness in her voice.

As Rose looked in the cracked mirror opposite, she forced a smile at the gaunt face staring back at her. The cracks were a cruel reminder of the impoverished life the O'Shaughnessy's now lived, but Rose refused to let it defeat her spirit. Most days her mother's love and encouragement was enough to help her cope with the harsh world, ready to face whatever challenges lay ahead.

The youngest member of the family, ten-year-old Billy, stirred slightly as he overheard the women talking. A gifted child and always an early riser, he eagerly anticipated his days at school, especially after earning praise from the headmaster earlier in the year for mastering his times tables. Unfortunately, numerous underprivileged families withdrew their children from school, telling tales of illness to conceal their true reason for truancy—earning a crust. Nevertheless, Ellen remained steadfast in her commitment to keeping Billy in school for as long as possible. Recognising his natural talent, she knew the prospect of forcing him into work would crush his spirit.

Ellen sighed heavily as she watched her daughter prepare to leave.

"I'm not sure what we're going to do, Rose. Since your father passed, the meagre amount of money we received from selling his clothes has dwindled, and it won't be sufficient to sustain us for much longer."

Rose's heart ached at the sight of her usually strong and resilient mother appearing so defeated. She squeezed Ellen's hand, offering a reassuring smile.

"We'll figure it out, Ma. I know we will. We always do, don't we? Somehow. Perhaps I can find some additional work to help bring in more money."

"You already work so hard, my dear. I don't want you overworking yourself. I promise, as soon as I'm well enough, I'll find a better-paying job to help support us. We just need to find another solution in the meantime, but I just don't know what that might be," Ellen said, her words laced with exhaustion and worry.

Rose rubbed the rusting buttons on her damp cotton dress, still bearing traces of yesterday's rain. Her mind raced with possibilities, desperate to find an easy solution that could alleviate their financial burden, but nothing came of it, as usual. Considering the dismal weather, she secretly longed to shrink into one of the matchboxes strewn across her mother's quilt and never emerge. Yet, her duty to her family prevailed, and she set aside personal desires to persevere.

Grasping the heavy woollen scarf at the foot of her bed, the last remaining gift from her father that hadn't been sold or pawned, Rose wrapped it snugly around her neck like armour against the trials lurking beyond their home's walls.

Billy's little eyes flickered open, and a broad smile lit up his face.

"Look after ma, Billy. Make her a cup of tea before school, eh?" Rose instructed her younger brother as she went downstairs, her voice tender yet firm.

Billy nodded eagerly, keen to do his part to help their family in any way he could.

"See you later then? I'll try and pop back briefly after the lunchtime rush in case you need anything. Ta ra."

As Rose stepped out into the cold, damp morning, her heart was heavy with worry, but she refused to let it drag her down. Instead, she put on a brave face and strode off in the direction of Commercial Street and Mrs Kelly's market stall.

A sixty-two-year-old with mischievous eyes, thinning grey hair, and a wild sense of humour, Mrs Kelly was a delight to be around. Her ability to entertain the people in her queue when it was busy had been the secret to her success.

Jane Kelly had been a fixture in the area for as long as Rose could remember, always selling her hot coffee no matter what the weather. Rain or shine, she would be there jabbering away, loud and cheerful, greeting everyone with a smile.

No one knew much about Mrs Kelly's past other than she had been born in Ireland, moved to London when she was young and never looked back. She had inherited her stall from her father who perished soon after making the crossing. Everyone knew they could count on Mrs Kelly no matter what, whether it was to buy a hot drink to warm their hearts or just needing a friendly ear to listen.

As Rose approached the bustling market, in her mind's eye she could hear her boss before she saw her, bellowing in her usual booming voice.

> "Come on, love, don't be shy! The coffee's hot and strong, just like me!" she would say waving her ladle around, enticing customers to her stall.

Mrs Kelly would delight in teasing the customers with her witty remarks.

> "A coffee a day keeps the doctor away. No need to suffer through another dreary day without a bit of coffee to perk you up. Look at that lovely mug of yours all glum, sir, you need a sip of my brew to get you smiling again!" she'd say, nodding towards a blushing gentleman customer.

Rose smiled at the familiar scene, grateful for the chance to work with such a vibrant and generous woman. She couldn't help but forget her troubles, if only for a moment. Her heart was lighter as she bounced the pin cushion in her pocket.

As she made her way through the bustling East End market, Rose was immediately engulfed by the noise. Dozens of costermongers competed with each other, shouting out their wares to lure potential customers. The clamour of voices merged with the laughter and chatter of the throngs of people who filled the narrow streets. There was banter and haggling and warning shouts to get out of the way.

The market stalls offered an explosion of colour, with fresh fruits and vegetables piled high. Numerous vendors sold cheap, brightly coloured items, ranging from garishly patterned fabrics to poorly made trinkets, tacky brassware, and crudely carved wooden articles.

But amid the bustling mayhem, the market also had its less savoury side. The scent of decaying vegetables and discarded fish entrails mixed with the odour of horse manure, producing an overwhelming pong that permeated the air. Rose would often encounter a vendor selling unpalatable fayre, such as pickled eels or tripe, which when coupled with the stench, made her recoil in revulsion.

As she elbowed her way through the masses, the pressure of the heaving bodies was suffocating, and the grimy slimy cobblestones beneath her feet required her to navigate between the stalls with caution.

Every so often, she exchanged brief nods with familiar faces. There was a brusque acknowledgement to old Mrs Bridges, who was bartering with a fishmonger over the price of a fresh mackerel, or a forced 'Good morning!' to Sammy the baker's boy as he rushed by with a basket of steaming loaves.

At one point, Rose had to veer aside quickly to avoid a handcart overflowing with wicker crates of shrieking, flapping chickens. She offered a tight-lipped smile to the cart's driver, who tipped his hat apologetically before continuing on his way.

Every so often, she would be forced to pause, either to avoid being jostled by the surging crowd or to stare at the ghastly goods on display. She would run her fingers over the gritty, bruised surface of a damaged apple that had toppled off a stall or the fine edges of a lace handkerchief, all the while trying to ignore the jarring sounds, sights, and smells that made Commercial Road market such an overwhelming, abundant and yet revolting place. Yet, it was amidst this atmosphere, alongside her boss, that Rose felt most alive.

As the young woman approached the spot where Mrs Kelly usually set up her coffee stall, she noticed something was amiss. Instead of the usual bustling activity and the familiar sight of her employer arranging her wares, there was nothing but an empty space which was highly unusual. Jane Kelly was the most punctual person Rose knew. Rose's brow furrowed as she scanned the surrounding area, searching for any sign of the woman. The nagging feeling that something was wrong settled in the pit of her stomach. Could something have happened to her?

"Excuse me," Rose asked one of the nearby stallholders, her voice quivering with concern. "Do you know where Mrs Kelly is today? Her coffee stall is usually here, but it's not."

"I haven't seen her, love. Maybe she's running late?" the man replied, not bothering to look up from his work.

"But she's always here on time. I hope she's alright," Rose said, her worry mounting.

Another stallholder, who had overheard their conversation, chimed in.

"I heard she had some trouble with her hip last night on the way home. Maybe that's why she's not here yet? Got a bit of a peg leg, probably. Nothing too serious."

Rose thanked them for the information and was about to head towards Mrs Kelly's house when she heard a commotion from across the street. She turned to see a stranger jostling for space where Mrs Kelly's stall belonged, attempting to claim the spot for his own. The young, redheaded man with a flat cap and freckled face eyed the area with a calculating gaze.

"Well, I never," Rose muttered under her breath, anger rising in her chest. "He's got no right to take this stall. Not today or any other day."

"Oi! You!"

"Ignore Miss O'Shaughnessy. You set yourself up there, son," the cold-hearted market official instructed, completely disregarding Rose's distress.

"What do you mean, ignore me? Where's Mrs Kelly? Did you make her move to another pitch?" Rose demanded, her heart pounding in her chest.

The market official looked at her with an icy stare, and Rose felt a chill run down her spine.

"No. I didn't. Mrs Kelly is dead, Miss O'Shaughnessy. Folks on her street said she had a heart attack pushing the cart back last night."

Rose felt as if the wind had been knocked out of her.

"Dead? She can't be... How could you be so heartless?" Rose said, her voice cracked with emotion. "Mrs Kelly was an institution here, and you just brush her off like she meant nothing?"

The market official remained stoic, unflustered by Rose's outburst.

"Dropped down like a stone, apparently. Now, if you don't mind, my job is to keep the market running smoothly, not to cater to sentimentalities. The world doesn't stop for the dead, Miss O'Shaughnessy, it continues to turn for the living."

With those parting words, he left Rose to wrestle with her heartache, anger, and the harsh reality that life always marched on, indifferent to human suffering. Her mind was a whirlpool of emotions: anger, sorrow, and above all, confusion. Jane Kelly was so beloved by Rose that the man's unfeeling words felt like a dagger to her heart. Worse still, she dreaded telling her mother that their family's weekly income would be one shilling short if she couldn't come up with a plan to cover the shortfall—and fast.

The young woman trudged on in a daze until well-past eleven, when she decided to seek out Betty Hardacre and confide in her. Whenever Rose was in a pickle, Betty was her go-to confidante. Something of a maverick, Betty always had a talent for devising a plot or a plan to put things right again.

A few years ago, early into their friendship, Rose had found herself in another tricky situation. Walking down an alleyway near the common lodging houses on Brady Street, she was lost in her thoughts. Suddenly, a group of boisterous young lads sprang out from the shadows. They began to tease and bully her, hurling crude remarks about her appearance and laughing raucously.

"Oi, look at the pretty little miss all by herself," one of them jeered. "You shouldn't be wandering around here without a chaperone, darlin'! Anything could 'appen!"

Rose tried to maintain her composure and stand her ground, although her voice quavered slightly as she replied.

"Leave me be. I've done nowt to you," Rose pleaded.

The boys jeered, the gang leader getting ever closer to Rose, until his face was only inches away from hers, his body brushing against her dress, making her fearful.

"Why don't you get lost, eh, mate?"

"Listen to her, lads. Thinks she can talk back to us," he sneered.

Just as Rose began to feel helpless, a strong and resolute voice echoed from the other end of the tenement alleyway. It was Betty, who had spotted the commotion and decided to intervene. With a confident stride, she approached the group, her eyes gleaming with defiance.

"You lot should be ashamed, tormenting a young girl like her," Betty scolded them. "Clear off before I teach you a lesson."

"And what are you going to do, then?" the leader scoffed, trying to maintain his boldness, while his mates smirked at Betty.

Betty's glare intensified, her voice firm.

"Don't underestimate a woman's power, especially when she's defending someone or something she cares about."

Their confidence waned in the face of Betty's determination. With one last insult muttered, they reluctantly began to disperse, leaving Rose and Betty alone in the alley. The lads exchanged uneasy glances. The ringleader cast a final, venomous glare in Betty's direction.

"You'll regret sticking your nose in our business," he warned, attempting to save face in front of his friends.

Betty stuck her fingers up at him in defiance and growled like a rabid dog as the gang melted away.

"Thanks so much for helping me. I don't know what I would have done without you," Rose said gratefully as smiling, Betty shrugged nonchalantly.

"Don't mention it. I can't stand seeing people being bullied like that. We've got to stick together, right? Miss Betty Hardarce, at your service."

As they walked side by side, the two girls struck up a conversation, quickly realising they had a lot in common. From that day on, they would become lifelong friends, their bond forged in that fateful alleyway encounter. They swore they would support and care for each other through life's challenges, each drawing strength from the other. When one girl struggled, the other seemed to be buoyed up. Together they survived. They would take long summer walks in the evening, sharing their thoughts and dreams, and on Sundays, they would treat themselves to a jacket potato from a nearby street vendor and chat for hours. However, now that Rose's father had passed away and money was tight, even those simple luxuries had become a distant memory.

Rose stood patiently outside the bustling seamstress shop on the corner where Betty worked, waiting for her to emerge for her lunch. The distraught girl knew it would be a long wait, but it would be worth it. However, Betty didn't appear at noon. Alone with her burden, Rose began to fret.

The young woman dreaded going back to her lodgings to tell her mother she'd failed to get another job, so she wandered around Whitechapel, passing the familiar rows of brick houses and dimly lit alleyways, hoping to stumble upon a lucky break with another costermonger. She had worked with Mrs Kelly for years, so she knew there were always other small jobs she could do if only someone would only give her a chance. She stopped at a dingy street corner, where a crooked gas-lamp post still managed to cast a shadow on the blackened brick, and observed the hustle and bustle of people coming and going: peddlers hawking trinkets, rag men and their piles of tatty old clothes, little waifs with a basket of rock-hard cakes or withering flowers, and pie sellers with their delicious morsels. Alongside them, cobblers, knife sharpeners, and shoe-shine boys were all striving to make a quick profit. Surely, someone must require assistance?

Despite the evidence of bustling commercial activity, no one could offer any work. Rose ended up wasting time searching for an opportunity that would never come. It was a fruitless diversion, but it was still better than seeing the dread on her mother's face when she confessed her terrible news.

As Rose made her way towards the dressmaker's once more, hoping to catch Betty at the end of her shift, she heard someone call her name from across the street. Looking up, she saw her friend waving excitedly outside Mr Brown's bagel shop.

"Cheer up, Rose, for goodness' sake! You look like someone's died! Guess what! I got a bonus in my wages today for working at the shop for a month and some overtime. My boss, Mrs Ellis, is a soppy old duffer, isn't she? Come on, let's have some fun," Betty said, her dress catching the last of the afternoon light as she gestured enthusiastically.

Before Rose could explain about Mrs Kelly's demise, she found herself being dragged along by the arm with Betty, her tight curls bouncing with each step.

"Where are you taking me?"

"Wait until you see it, Rose!"

"See what?"

"Crendon Pleasure Gardens, of course. It has everything a woman could want—" Betty gushed excitedly. "It's in Chelsea 'n' all!

"—but, Betty!" Rose tried to interject, desperate to tell her friend about her tragic news.

"You'll love it, Rose," livewire Betty continued. "The energy there is infectious. You'll forget all your troubles, I promise. It's the perfect place for people like us to escape reality for a little while on Friday night."

"But, I need to talk to you about something important," Rose persisted, attempting to catch her breath as Betty continued to lead her along at a breakneck pace.

"No time for that, Rose. Tell me on the way, eh?"

Although situated in an upmarket London district, Crendon Pleasure Gardens had a fearsome reputation for bawdiness and spectacle. Its colourful tents, brash music, and nefarious stage acts entertained both rich and poor, with, according to the local parish council's bitter complaints in the newspaper, 'vulgar laughter echoing into the night."

"I really ought to let my ma know where I am before we head off," said Rose, hesitating.

"Don't worry," Betty chirped, digging her friend in the ribs. "Come on, misery guts. I'll get someone to pass a message on to tell her you're going to be late. Your Davy works round the corner from here, doesn't he? We'll pop in on the way. Sorted. You only live once, and on a Friday night, life is definitely worth living, me old mucker!"

As the two girls disappeared into the crowded streets, it was clear to Rose that the evening ahead would be anything but ordinary and how the night would end would be anyone's guess.

2

BETTY'S BOLD MOVE

Amidst the hubbub of Friday night London, the two women felt exhilarated. For Rose, who had never ventured far from Whitechapel, the omnibus journey was an adventure. Her heart still weighed heavily with the thought of poor Mrs Kelly's demise, but she didn't want to dampen Betty's joyous spirit, so she decided to bide her time before broaching the subject.

As they travelled, Rose was captivated by the sights of London: coachmen and footmen in smart uniforms, wiry delivery boys, and bustling pedestrians beneath the towering majesty of St Paul's Cathedral and then the Savoy Hotel along the Strand. Betty whispered to Rose with a mischievous glint in her eye.

"Have you heard the joke about the chimney sweep and the baker?"

Intrigued, Rose leaned in.

"The sweep asked, 'Why do bakers work so hard?'"

"Go on then, why do they work so hard?" said Rose, obliging her.

"Because they knead the dough!"

Betty grinned wildly after telling the punchline.

"Oh, Betty, that's awful. Just awful."

"I know! That's why it makes me giggle."

Several other passengers looked on disapprovingly as Betty continued to gossip and share more witty tales and humorous anecdotes with Rose. The women's laughter filled the air, providing a brief but welcome respite from their daily struggles. However, it was clear that not everyone on board appreciated their frivolity.

They hopped onto another omnibus that followed the route of the north bank of the Thames until they arrived in Chelsea. A sprawling carnival ground greeted Rose, with brightly coloured attractions, seedy bars, cluttered stalls, eccentric entertainers, whirling carousels, towering ferris wheels, smoking-hot food stalls, and a myriad of sideshows. London's elite often looked down on the venue, but it remained beloved by the working class and even drew in wealthy visitors eager to mingle with 'vagabonds and commoners'. For Rose, that night, it was a welcome momentary escape from her troubles and a chance to revel in this new and exciting world with her dear friend Betty by her side. Her eyes widened with wonder as she beheld the scene before her as it unfolded. It was quite unlike anything she had ever seen before.

"Oh, Betty, I want to try everything—do everything!"

Betty smiled at Rose but couldn't ignore their financial situation.

"Woah, Nelly," Betty advised. "We haven't got that much money, so we'd better pace ourselves. What do you fancy doing first?"

Rose's eyes landed on the coconut shy, already picturing the thrill of throwing the ball, toppling the plump coconuts, and winning a lovely prize. However, as she pulled Betty towards the game, she saw the sign: 'sixpence a go'. Her excitement tumbled away. Sixpence was enough for almost a week of nightly fun at an East End penny hop, while this fun would last barely a minute. Sensing Rose's disappointment, Betty comforted her friend by wrapping an arm around her shoulders and giving her a reassuring squeeze.

"Don't fret, Rose," she reassured, "We'll find something else to do that's cheaper. Come on."

As they delved deeper into the decadent atmosphere of the notorious gardens, Rose couldn't help but wonder when the right moment would ever come to share her news about Mrs Kelly and her pressing need for a job.

As they wandered, Betty's eyes lit up with excitement when she spotted the perfect diversion. An enigmatic fortune teller stared at the two women and beckoned them into her small, dimly lit tent, pointing, then curling her index finger.

"What are you doin—?" Rose began to say, but Betty was already dragging her towards the red-and-white striped tent's entrance.

Inside, the air was thick with the sweet smell of patchouli incense. The plump fortune teller, wearing a patterned head scarf and oversized golden hooped earrings, greeted them with a wave. The mystic was sat in the middle, her gnarled hands cradled a mysterious gleaming crystal ball resting on a jet-black stand.

"Come closer, my darlings, and let me read the secrets of your stars," the clairvoyant purred, her velvet voice luring them in.

Rose took her seat with hesitation, eyes wide with curiosity, while Betty flopped down and leaned in eagerly, desperate to begin.

"Tell me everything," Betty said, dropping a few coppers into the woman's outstretched hand. "There's enough there for both of us. Do me first, though, eh?"

The fortune teller began to reveal Betty's destiny in a low, soothing tone, her voice rising in pitch as her vision grew increasingly vivid.

"You will travel far and wide, visit many different places, both in this world and the next. Such a magnificent destiny awaits you! There is still so much for you to experience before your earthly journey ends. My spirit

guide tells me you'll even get a new job in a
West End music hall or theatre!"

Betty gasped in excitement at the revelation, her imagination running wild. However, Rose remained inscrutable, pondering the fortune teller's vague statement. After all, a job in the entertainment industry could also mean a position selling programmes in the foyer or, worse, cleaning the theatre toilets, rather than being a glamorous actress shimmering in the limelight on stage.

The fortune teller winked warmly at Rose.

"Let me reveal your future now, me dearie."

She began her mystical performance once more, her hands dancing above the crystal ball, casting distorted reflections on the smooth surface. Rose glanced at Betty who was gazing into space, probably thinking about being the star turn in an Oscar Wilde play.

"You, too, have significant changes ahead,
young miss," the fortune teller proclaimed,
her eyes suddenly going distant and
unfocused. "I will now channel my spirit
guide again for further insight."

Closing her eyes, she took a deep, slow breath and appeared to enter a trance-like state. The tent's atmosphere grew charged and mysterious, and Rose couldn't help but feel a tingling sensation at the back of her neck. It seemed as though the fortune teller was truly connecting to something unseen, something beyond their world.

Moments passed, and the clairvoyant's expression shifted, as if she were receiving guidance from another ethereal world. Her eyes fluttered open, now filled with a new sense of clarity and purpose.

"A new career in a bustling city awaits you too, miss," she revealed, her voice somehow different, more resonant. "You will work alongside a handsome and charming man, and together, you will bring joy to many people's lives and help them navigate their troubles and find solace."

"Who is he, this dashing Casanova? Betty asked excitedly.

"Your friend hasn't met the gentleman yet, but she will soon," the fortune teller replied.

"Can't be Terry Nolan then, he's already tried to have a dalliance with her and failed," Betty joked, as Rose gave her a cold stare.

The girls said their goodbyes and wandered off, both lost in thought. Rose was still puzzled over the significance of the fortune teller's predictions for herself, while Betty was fantasising about her future as a famous actress. She looked at Rose with wide eyes, excitement radiating from her expression. Little did they know that Rose's future would soon be filled with unimaginable twists and turns, leading both women down a path full of difficult choices.

"I reckon your future with the handsome man sounded just as thrilling as mine, if not more! Then again, just picture it, Rosie. Me. On the stage! Fellas throwing flowers at my feet after belting out one of my songs. Glamorous champagne parties after packed performances. I wonder when it will all happen?" Betty said, her eyes glittering.

Rose bit her lip, torn between wanting to temper Betty's enthusiasm and not wanting to dampen her best friend's spirits. For now, Rose chose to remain silent.

As they walked past a lively game of skittles, the air was filled with laughter, the rolling and clattering of wood-on-wood and the winners whoops of excitement. A little later, they were dazzled by a fire-eater's daring sideshow performance, his breathy flames illuminating the night sky. As the grand finale approached, the man took a final deep breath, his chest expanding along with the audience's anticipation. He took a swig from a metal bottle, then placed one of the flaming torches to his lips and sent a magnificent plume of fire high into the starry night sky with one forceful breath. The onlookers' faces were bathed in a glorious golden glow as they erupted in cheers and applause at each burst of flames.

As the girls continued to explore their attention was quickly drawn to a boisterous crowd surrounding another entertainer. Eager to see what was happening, Rose and Betty made their way through the throng and discovered an elderly man dressed in worn-out patched clothes in the middle of the circle. He was expertly juggling oranges, his hands blurred by the speed they operated under as he maintained an intense focus on his performance. The old man's dexterity was captivating. Suddenly, he changed tack and tossed an orange high into the air, spun around and caught it with ease behind his back. Rose and Betty watched in amazement, admiring his flawless execution and unwavering precision. Once his act was finished, the man took a humble bow. Rose stepped forward to offer her compliments, and the juggler responded with a warm smile, presenting the girls with an orange each. They gratefully accepted the gifts, devouring the sweet fruit before continuing their adventure.

"Here's a penny for your troubles, pal,"
Betty trilled as she pulled some money from
her pocket and tossing it to the performer.

He caught the coin with a flourish, grinning as he flipped it between his fingers. In a playful gesture, Betty placed a segment of the peel behind her lips, flashing Rose a goofy orangy grin that made them both burst into laughter.

Inspired by the juggler's talent, Betty's dreams of life in the theatre were reawakened. She began to talk excitedly about her aspirations once more. Rose was relieved to note that this time, her friend had gained a deeper appreciation for the dedication required to become a successful entertainer and was now considering chasing a more realistic backstage role instead.

> "I reckon I could sew the beads onto dresses for Ellen Terry. How hard can that be? Maybe that's what the wise woman meant when she said I'd be working in the music hall? I don't have to be a diva, do I?"

> "No, Betty. A more modest career could also await you, too. Do you mind if we have a sit-down for a bit? My feet are aching."

> "Come on then, hopalong," Betty said, giving her friend a gentle shove.

As they sat on a nearby bench, Rose tended to her sore feet while Betty observed the lively interactions between the edgier upper-class visitors and their rougher counterparts. Ladies, likely mistresses rather than wives, paraded in rigid bodices and flowing skirts, while gentlemen sported vibrant embroidered waistcoats and top hats. Some couples strolled arm-in-arm, and groups of men puffed on cigars, discussing the day's news, horse racing results, or their latest conquests.

Rose sat twisting her hands in her lap. Taking a deep breath, she turned to Betty.

> "I lost my job today, Betty. That's why I was so upset when you saw me earlier after work."

"But why?" Betty asked, her expression shifting to one of concern. "You didn't do something foolish and let Mrs Kelly down, did you?"

"No, it's not that. It's just that—Mrs Kelly, she—"

"Spit it out!"

"Mrs Kelly's dead, Betty," Rose said as she wiped away her tears. "They say her heart gave out. It was sudden, which is a blessing. I'd hate to think of her suffering. And I daren't tell my ma we don't have my wage. It's all such a bloomin' mess."

Betty took her friend's trembling hand.

"Losing someone you love is never easy, but we'll face it together. And something will turn up jobwise when you least expect it. You'll see."

A defeated Rose smiled weakly amidst the razzmatazz of the fair. Their eyes met upon a troupe of circus performers tumbling down a nearby path. Betty felt a surge of excitement again. She wondered if becoming a professional acrobat was now on the cards! Rose called out her friend's name three times, hoping to tell her more about her work worries, but Betty was far too engrossed to hear a word of what she was saying.

"Right then, Rose. Good to go?

With a nod, they carried on, spotting a sideshow magician who had the audience enthralled with his tricks he performed with an audience volunteer. A member of the crowd shouted out to him.

"Oi, think our young lad here could lend you a hand?"

The flat-capped man pointed to a boy, no more than nine or ten years old, who eagerly approached the stage, then looked nervously at the audience, hoping he wouldn't get anything wrong in front of everyone.

"Up you get then, lad," said the magician, swinging the boy up onto the stage like a gibbon swinging through the treetops, as he grabbed his wiry outstretched arm.

The magician handed the boy a rope and demonstrated how to tie two neat knots in the middle. After a moment of hesitation, the boy followed along perfectly.

"Give them a good tug, son. Make sure those knots are really tight. Pull them hard. Not going anywhere, are they?"

The boy yanked on the knots, shook his head, then handed the rope back to the magician.

With a flash, the magician's white-gloved hand slid down the rope, and as it passed the knots, both vanished! The crowd went wild.

"Were you trying to make a fool of me, son? Were those knots really tight?" the magician teased as the boy's red face nodded vigorously in his defence. "Ah, don't look so worried, pal. I'm pulling your leg. 'Ere, have a gobstopper."

He dropped the sugary treat into the boy's hand, who promptly clapped it into his open mouth. It was so big that it made his eyes bulge like a frog's.

"Right, who's going to be my next volunteer?"

"Me! Me!" Betty shouted, seizing her chance to appear in front of a crowd.

She pushed her way to the front, surprising the magician with her determined stare.

"Alright, err, Miss. Come on up."

In her eagerness, Betty clambered onto the stage like a youth would scale a wall. The magician produced a bundle of gossamer-thin handkerchiefs from his pocket. He formed a loose fist with one hand, and pushed the hankies into the gap with the other. Then he opened his gloved hand to show they'd all disappeared. As the loud 'ooh' from the crowd faded, he slowly moved his hand toward Betty's ear and leaned in as if to whisper a secret. With one final flourish, he pulled out a cascade of colourful fabric from behind her lughole, his windmilling arms teasing out more and more fabric! The audience gasped at the miraculous sight— not least Betty, who stood wide-eyed and open-mouthed as yards of floaty silk swirled around her head.

"Can we have a round of applause for my lovely assistant?"

As Betty bounced down the steps to her rapturous response, she imagined herself treading the boards in the West End again as the star turn and floated back over to Rose.

"Let's grab a drink and finish this night in style, Rose—squiffy!"

Her friend hesitated.

"You know full well I'm not a fan of drinking or being squiffy, Betty."

"Blimey Rose! You can be so dull. I know you've been through the ringer a bit today but you still need to live a little! You asked me to cheer you up, and I will!"

Like a loyal lapdog, Rose trundled behind her friend towards a seedy row of dimly lit tents serving drinks. As they approached one of the bars, a handsome stranger's eyes locked onto Rose and Betty's figures from afar. Unaware of the enigmatic and alluring man observing them from a distance, the girls continued on, blissfully ignorant of the pivotal moment that was now minutes away.

3

A FATEFUL ENCOUNTER

Arm-in-arm, the women ventured in search of the bar with the shortest queue, their steps wobbling with excitement. Soon, they stumbled upon an old wooden stall, its flickering gaslights illuminating a towering display of bottles.

"Two large gins, please, squire!" Betty called to the bearded barman.

Without hesitation, the man filled two glasses to the brim with his own special moonshine.

Rose took a tentative sip and felt the warm liquid course through her body, tingling her senses. Though she'd never tasted anything as strong, Betty's encouraging nods coaxed her into feeling comfortable with it. With each mouthful, Rose found herself becoming more relaxed, a bubbly energy building within her. The gin brought out a side of her she hadn't expected, her cheeks flushing pink. After a few more sips, Betty clapped her hands in delight as Rose shared her thoughts.

"It's nice, but I'm not sure I can finish it all," she declared. "Pass me your glass. You can have the rest."

"You'll do no such thing. Down it, O'Shaughnessy!"

Rose took a deep breath and threw the rest of the liquor down her gullet. Soon, her woozy attention was drawn to one particular gentleman—an imposing figure clad in black, who seemed to have the power to captivate those around him. He stood on a small side stage constructed from rough wooden planks, adorned with red curtains that fluttered gently in the wind. Gas lamps cast an eerie glow over the scene. Above the stage, a vivid painted sign proclaimed, "The Great Vincenzo".

She pulled Betty closer to get a better view. A stout widow, dressed entirely in black, sat on a chair at the centre of the stage. The expectant murmurs of the gathered crowd indicated that something extraordinary was about to happen. As the performer began to speak in a low voice, Rose and Betty shivered with anticipation. The consummate entertainer had woven an invisible spell over the audience. The two friends felt as if their feet were rooted to the ground, unable to move or tear their eyes away from him.

The woman now sat with her chin dipped towards her chest. The man was speaking to her, but they couldn't quite discern his words. With a flourish, he waved his hands over his head in a wide arc, eliciting thunderous applause from those gathered around. The two girls stealthily moved to the front as the mesmerist moved to the front of the stage and began to speak in a hushed tone to the audience.

> "I will now attempt to contact Mrs Morton's late husband, Archibald. Are you ready to proceed, ma'am?" asked Vincenzo, his voice firm and unwavering. Though the woman appeared withdrawn and apprehensive, she mustered the courage to speak.

> "Why aye, yes."

As the area around the stage fell silent, Vincenzo began his ritual, his eyes closed in deep concentration. He called out to the spirit of Archibald, his voice rising with each invocation. At first, there was no response, but the mesmerist persisted, his pleas becoming more urgent and intense as he begged for a sign from beyond the grave.

> "Are you there, Archibald? Do you have any words of love or guidance for your beloved wife?"

Suddenly, there was a loud thud. Everyone gasped in fear as they saw an old unlit lantern tumbling off its hook to the left of the stage. With his eyes burning with intensity, Vincenzo picked up the lantern and opened it. Inside, written on a piece of paper, were four simple words, which he read aloud.

> "I love you, pet."

He cupped his hand on her shoulder and looked down at the widow with a tender expression. The old woman slowly awoke from the trance, rubbing her eyes as if she had just emerged from a deep sleep. She glanced around in confusion at the faces gathered, then let out a gasp of surprise and recognition when she noticed the words.

"Take this note as a sign from your husband.
He wants you to have it."

Everyone held their breath, waiting to hear what she would say. Finally, she spoke, happy tears streaming down her face.

"It's him! My Archie was a Geordie too, and
he always called me 'pet.' I can't believe I
was in the presence of my dear departed!
Thank you so much. It means more to me
than I can say."

"I am honoured to be of service, Ma'am,"
said the man with a bow and a sweep of his
velvet cape. "True love as strong as yours
can cross the thin veil between the land of
the living and the dead. I take great pleasure
in using my gift to reconnect the broken-
hearted with their loved ones, however
briefly."

There was more rapturous applause.

"As you can appreciate, contacting the spirit
world is exhausting. Thus, this is my last

performance of the evening. I bid you
goodnight, friends!"

With another flourish of his hands, he directed everyone's attention away from the old widow, allowing her some peace and quiet to gather her thoughts before helping her off stage. The magnetic aura of the mesmerist lingered in the air, leaving Rose entranced by his presence.

The moment the act was over, the two girls were eager to discuss the spectacle they had just witnessed.

"I wonder if a man will ever love me as
much as Archie loved Mrs Morton, Betty?"

"How should I know, Rose? I suppose it's a
possibility. But from my experience, so far,
all the men I've encountered just don't have
what it takes to be 'husband material'.
Useless lumps, most of the time. Anyway, it
looks like this place will close soon. Let's
have one more drink, then head back?"

Rose, still a bit numbed from the bearded man's moonshine, agreed but wasn't sure it was a good idea. As they retraced their steps to the gin stall, up ahead was the mesmerist, no longer in his cape and top hat, but a well-cut black suit with a crisp white shirt. He moved with purpose and yet every step seemed to be full of grace and poise. In his hand was an ebony cane with a golden handle, which tap-tap-tapped ahead of him. The two girls followed as The Great Vincenzo made his way through the crowded fair. He didn't look back or pay any attention to them. Despite that, Rose couldn't help but feel drawn to him. She noticed his confident swagger and the way he commanded attention from the ladies with his Adonis-like looks.

"Um, Rose?"

"Yes—?"

"I think you have a bit of a thing for this man, don't you?" Betty said as she tugged her friend's shawl.

"Sorry, what were you saying?"

"I knew it. You've got a crush on him, Rose O'Shaughnessy!"

"No, I haven't."

Betty raised her eyebrows.

"Well, alright. Maybe. A bit."

The young woman felt her heart flutter. She couldn't help but notice how he seemed to captivate everyone he encountered. His smile was warm and inviting, and his voice full of charm and panache. His dark hair fell alluringly over his brow and needed pushing away by his rugged hand.

"Gin, Rose? Rose? Do you want another gin? —Jeepers. You stay here. I'll bring the drinks."

Oblivious, Rose watched the man speak to several more ladies before speaking to another chap, who seemed rather animated. She craned her neck and strained her ears, but she couldn't make out what was going on. She wanted to move a bit nearer but was worried Betty might struggle to find her if she strayed. Soon, the entertainer's demeanour had changed. It seemed the chap who had approached Vincenzo was angry about something. She was curious to know what all the fuss was about, but at the same time, she didn't want to get too close and draw attention to herself.

The mesmerist's chiselled face had changed. He was steely and stern, as if he had been caught off-guard by the other man's words. The two continued their heated discussion until, eventually, they parted ways without shaking hands or exchanging any sign of a farewell. Rose gave up trying to understand what the two had been arguing about and decided to focus on finding Betty, who should have returned with their drinks by then.

As the mesmerist walked off towards a man who also looked like he worked at the pleasure gardens, Rose spotted Betty and beckoned her to follow.

"This way! Quickly!" Rose whispered.

The two of them had a quick slurp of gin, then darted over towards The Great Vincenzo, who was now puffing on a cigar as he spoke to the fairground official.

"How's it going, Vinny?"

"Alright, I suppose. Crowd was a bit thin tonight though, Gerry. I think I need to

change up the act a bit. I was considering
getting a female assistant. I'm sure a dolly
bird would attract a few more fellas and put
the women at ease."

Betty looked at Rose. Was this her big chance? A wide grin formed on her face. But before she could say anything, Rose took another a big glug of gin then blurted out:

"I could be your assistant, Mr Vincenzo, sir!"

The artist spun around on his heels and eyed up the attractive young woman in front of him.

"Is that so?"

Betty's eyes narrowed. What a way to be repaid for bankrolling Rose's night out. She should have been destined for the stage, not Rose. The Great Vincenzo stared at Rose, then Betty, for a few moments, seeming to weigh up whether the offer was genuine or not.

"Yes, sir. I would be delighted to help you
with card tricks, rope tricks, escorting
elderly audience members on and off stage.
You name it. And, I can start right away."

Rose kicked herself. If she could start immediately, it meant she didn't have a job to leave. What if he thought she was unreliable? She could hardly ask poor Mrs Kelly for a reference. Had she snuffed out the opportunity already?

"Well, I must say your eagerness shines through, Miss, er?" The Great Vincenzo said, holding out a white-gloved hand as Betty ground her teeth with contempt.

"Miss O'Shaughnessy," said Rose coyly, gazing into his dark eyes.

"Well, miss, I have good news. You are hired. Meet me at the Eagle Tavern, Shoreditch, tomorrow evening at seven o'clock sharp. I shall explain more about your duties."

Rose looked a bit taken aback by his forthrightness and suggesting they meet without a chaperone.

"You can bring your friend if you like?" added the performer, noting Rose's concern.

"I am busy tomorrow evening," said Betty in an abrasive tone.

"Well, that's a pity—"

"It's not a problem. I shall be there, Mr Vincenzo. You can count on me."

"Before you go, Miss, I know it's vulgar to talk about money, but I prefer to be upfront about commercial arrangements. Is two shillings a week enough?"

Rose nearly collapsed with shock and glee.

"You are too kind, sir."

Vincenzo doffed his top hat.

"Until tomorrow then? Goodnight, ladies."

Rose gave a little curtsey and instantly regretted it. Betty was too angry for any pleasantries. They made their way out of the park, towards the river. The night air was cold and damp as the two friends headed for Westminster and on towards the Tower on foot. Betty was livid. Rose had stolen her chance to perform on stage without a second thought.

"How could you do that to me?" spat Betty as they strode along. "You knew how I felt about being on the stage. The mystic said it was my destiny, not yours. And yet you just took my place without a care in the world!"

"I'm sorry," Rose said quietly, hanging her head with shame. "My noggin was a bit fuzzy. I suppose I got caught up in the moment. And you know my family needs the money."

"That's no excuse! I paid for your entrance fee, your fortune to be told, and all your drinks, just to cheer you up, only for you to stab me in the back! Unbelievable. How could you?"

Rose sighed. She knew there was no denying her guilt, but she also felt deeply hurt by Betty's accusations.

"Look, I'll turn down Mr Vincenzo's offer if it means that much to you? Even though I really need the job, you can have it."

Betty looked at her friend with surprise. After a few moments of contemplation, she finally spoke.

"No, it's alright," said Betty slowly. "You should take it. I still have my seamstress work to keep me going."

Rose smiled gratefully at her wonderful friend before throwing her arms around Betty in a tight bear hug. Together they walked back towards Whitechapel with Rose's future filled with renewed possibility. Two shillings was a tremendous sum for such a young woman.

Back at the fair, Gerry Stubbs and his colleagues were patrolling the fairground, ushering out the last of the visitors. Gerry heard shouts coming from the area where Vincenzo's caravan was located. He could see the mesmerist arguing heatedly with another tall, well-dressed gentleman.

"I want you to stay away from my mother. Woe betide you if I find you sniffing around at her house again."

Vincenzo seemed unperturbed by the outburst and calmly responded.

"I'm afraid that is your mother's decision, not yours."

The stranger, obviously enraged by Vincenzo's reply, lunged forward and attempted to give him a right hook. Quick thinking on Gerry's part enabled him to grab the man's fist.

"I suggest you calm down!" Gerry warned as he beckoned his colleagues. "Lads, we've got a problem here."

Realising the situation could spiral out of control if left unchecked, the men pulled the warring couple apart. Vincenzo went into his lodgings and slammed the door shut.

"I'm warning you," yelled the gentleman, leaning forward, straining against the arms holding him back. "Stay away."

The men walked the angry fellow out of the park and shut the decorative iron gates behind him. Back in his caravan, Vincenzo paced up and down the tiny space, wondering what his next move should be. It turned out he didn't have much choice.

There was a knock at his door. Gerry strode towards Vincenzo with a stern expression. His earlier good humour had dissipated.

"Look, Vinny. It pains me to say this, but it's time for you to go," he said firmly. "Your act is causing trouble night after night, and the owner of this place won't have it. The papers are having a field day with all the scandals. Attendance is dropping, fights are breaking out, and the reputation of this fairground is suffering because of it. I told you last month to clean up your act or hit the road. And you haven't, so you can give me your key back and get out."

Vincenzo was left with no choice but to pack his belongings and leave. But as he exited the fairground and headed for Batty Hazlett's run-down Shoreditch Hotel, a sinister smile crept onto his face. This was far from over. He might have lost tonight's battle, but he would win the war.

4

SHADOWS AND SECRETS

The next afternoon, Rose nervously adjusted her best, but plain, dress as she stepped out of her home. The church bell chimed five times as her mother's warbling voice trailed out of the doorway.

"I hope Betty can get you some sewing work with Mrs Ellis, dear."

"Me too, Ma. I'll let you know how it goes."

Rose hated lying to her mother. It only added to her anxiety. She had never met a man unchaperoned before, a fact that made her feel quite uneasy. But the thought of ending her poor widowed mother's descent deeper into poverty compelled her to fasten her bonnet and step out into the London twilight. Two shillings would cover their rent, food, and have a bit left over. This was no time for reticence. It was time to seize the opportunity and find a way to make it work.

The Eagle Tavern was quite a walk away, and every step seemed like an eternity as Rose tried to process all that had happened the day before. Her first trip to the dazzling delights of Crendon and Vincenzo's unexpected offer had come as a complete surprise. She wondered what he would expect from her for such a large sum of money and did her best to ignore the little voice of doubt muttering inside her head. She was relieved that the tavern was a public place at least. Had she been meeting The Great Vincenzo completely alone, she would have been utterly terrified.

With no spare money for an omnibus, the two-mile walk from Whitechapel to Shoreditch took her past Smithfield Market and the Truman Brewery. She could hear the low rumble of fully loaded drays transporting barrels of ale across the city, and the sound of gossiping women chatting on their doorsteps.

As Rose finally arrived at her destination, she took in the impressive sight before her. Taking a deep breath, she stepped up to the entrance of the infamous Eagle Tavern, the sound of laughter and music drifting through open doors and windows.

The tavern's exterior was a striking contrast to the drab lodgings of Brady Street. Its creamy white walls and black bay windows stood out like a beacon in the dark. The gas lamps surrounding the building cast a cheery glow, making it feel like a refuge from the harsh world outside. The scent of roasted meats and pipe smoke wafted through the open door, inviting the innocent young woman in.

As Rose entered the main hall, she was struck by the bustling atmosphere. Patrons from all walks of life, dockers, seamstresses, labourers, clerks, laundry maids, shopkeepers, and more, filled the room. They sat at tables enjoying frothy ales in tankards and hearty meals served on wooden platters. The servers moved with grace and efficiency, their risqué banter mingling with the laughter of the regulars. Rose scanned the crowd for the towering figure of Vincenzo but found no sign of him.

At the far end of the room stood a fiddle player, an old Irish man with a grizzled beard and tiny dark eyes like a snowman's. Next to him was a young boy playing a gleaming tin whistle. Their lively jig filled the floor with couples stamping to its melodic beat. Rose could hardly take her eyes off them as they danced, spinning around in perfect synchronicity, their faces joyous, their hands clapping and heels stomping to the tune. The air was heavy with excitement as more onlookers clapped along to the music, shouting out encouragement to the dancers. The old man bounced on his tiptoes with delight as he played, coaxing every last bit of energy from his violin, the bow leaping over the strings, his fingers a blur. It was clear that everyone in the tavern had gathered for one purpose—to have fun and forget their troubles for a night. Rose noticed it had all the enjoyment of meeting people in the costermonger stall, without having to brave the elements standing outside.

Over to her left, Rose looked on in amusement as three tipsy working-class men argued over a game of dominoes. All of them waved their arms wildly and shouted at the top of their lungs, debating who was the winner and who were the runners-up. One man stood up and raised his fists before him and then took a drunken swing at his chum, missing by a mile. A man and his wife at a nearby table pleaded with them to settle down, but it seemed they were too caught up in the heat of the moment to listen. Rose wasn't sure how much longer they could keep this up before a fight broke out. Just then, a burly man who worked at the tavern swooped over.

"Now listen up!" he bellowed, "I don't want to hear any more of this racket. If you don't calm down, I shall have to ask you all to leave."

The three men grudgingly conceded and mumbled a few protests before returning to their game with less enthusiasm than before.

Rose tapped her toes to the music, gazing over at a wall clock, noticing it was exactly seven o'clock. Where was Vincenzo? She couldn't help but feel a little out of place among the boisterous patrons. She nervously twirled a strand of hair around her finger, eyeing the other customers who were deep in conversation or raucous laughter. Just then, a server approached her with a grin. "What can I get for you, Miss?" he asked.

"Oh, no thank you. I'm fine, really," Rose stammered, flushed.

The last thing she wanted to do was admit that she was feeling flustered by the request, not wanting to drink alone nor spend any money either.

"Alright then," the waiter said with a shrug. "But let me know if you change your mind. We've got the best ale in town."

The main double doors swung open once again, and Vincenzo slipped into the crowded tavern unnoticed, hugging the wall to avoid drawing attention to himself. His sharp eyes scanned the room, quickly assessing the women in the vicinity, and flashing them his charming smile as he made his way towards the bar. However, for the rest of the time, his gaze was fixed on Rose like a hunter stalking his prey.

Finally, he weaved through the crowd, watching her as she swayed to the jig. She was so lost in the moment that she didn't notice him at first, but then her face lit up when she saw Vincenzo standing there, looking at her with a mixture of delight and surprise.

"I arrived just a few moments ago," he replied smoothly. "Forgive me, I couldn't resist the lure of the music."

They fell into an easy conversation, Vincenzo's charisma and wit captivating the young woman.

"My dear Miss O'Shaughnessy, I admire your spirit and your willingness to take a chance on me. I appreciate the trust you have placed in me as your employer."

As they talked, Vincenzo's rapturous smile never wavered, and Rose found herself drawn to him more and more. His subtle yet flirty praise made her feel alive and desirable.

"Why, sir, you do have a way with words," she said coyly, taking another sip of her drink. "I must admit, I am quite enjoying talking to you."

"Ah, but the pleasure is all mine, my dear," he murmured. "I never thought I'd find someone as delightful and intelligent as yourself to share my work with."

The two of them laughed and talked as they watched people dance their hearts out to a few more songs. It felt like all her worries had melted away into thin air. But that wouldn't last for long.

"Shall we take a seat?"

Rose nodded as he gestured to two seats in full view of the other drinkers.

"I expect you want to know more about the work? It is a rather unique opportunity. Some might think it's not above board, but I encourage you to keep an open mind."

Rose started to panic. His suggestion to keep calm had the opposite effect, as she focused all her mind on one thing—how improper her situation was.

"First things first, how do you feel about me referring to you as my sister?"

"I'm sorry?"

"Well, I appreciate that coming out with me unchaperoned creates, hmm, some difficulties for you. And me."

Rose nodded. If she were not so desperate for money, she would have refused his offer to meet up alone in a heartbeat, but hunger played with her mind and weakened her will. And there was that smile of his to consider too.

"Yes. It does concern me that we will be seen alone together in public. I can't lie. Everyone finds out everyone else's business on Brady Street soon enough."

"Well, I reckon that's easily solved if we tell people we are related? If we do, most of those difficulties will go away. Strangers wouldn't be any the wiser."

Rose tipped her head to one side as she considered his suggestion, as the mesmerist's gaze bore into her soul.

"Look at it this way, we both have dark wavy hair and dark eyes. I am sure no one would suspect."

"I suppose not, sir—"

"—Vincenzo, please—," he corrected.

"I know there are lots of working families in the travelling circuses and at the fairgrounds, but I confess, I still feel a little uncomfortable about being deceitful to your audience. I will know the truth."

"Well, needs must. The way I see it, we wouldn't need to lie if it weren't for all the restrictive rules that polite society says we are supposed to follow. We can both benefit from a perfectly proper professional relationship for the sake of a simple white lie. Do you concur?"

"Hmm. Will you put that we are a brother and sister act on your posters?"

"Not exactly."

"Oh!"

"You see, I am planning to give up being a sideshow entertainer. It won't be easy, but I am confident all will be well. I come from a long line of renowned Italian performers, revered for their mesmerism and psychic abilities. My family travelled the length and breadth of Europe and performed for the highest ranks of society, including nobility and royalty, even the Russian court. I had hoped to find patronage with an aristocratic family in England, but it was not to be. I have been a master mesmerist on stage now for some years, and I adapted my skills to entertain the rowdy masses at Crendon. My artistry and abilities are unmatched, and it is only a matter of time before my reputation spreads beyond the bounds of that humble venue."

"But you drew quite a crowd last night? Possibly the biggest of all the side shows?"

"Yes, but I wouldn't be following my calling."

"Which is—Vincenzo?"

"My calling is not entertaining at a mere pleasure garden. It is providing true comfort and solace to the bereaved, to connect their souls to their loved ones once more."

Rose's eyes were wide, and her mouth fell open slightly, her expression one of disbelief and yet delight. When her beloved father, Tom, had died, she would have given anything for one more conversation with him. Could this man in front of her really communicate with the dead? And if he could—could he help her speak to her pa? Her head was swimming with possibilities. Rose had heard talk of Queen Victoria holding séances to try to contact Albert, but she found it all too absurd to be true. She had seen many residents of Brady Street die over the years. No one had ever mentioned seeing their loved ones again—despite hordes of them following many superstitions to the letter. How had this man found the secret to communicate with those who had passed?

Rose shivered, thinking of the strange practices people used to try to contact the deceased. She had heard stories of psychics claiming they could make the dead speak through them, but she had never given them any credence. To think that Vincenzo could actually do such a thing, well, it was both terrifying and comforting at once.

"Can you really talk to the dead? My father passed away a few weeks ago. Do you think—?"

"Do you want me to try and contact him? Will it bring you comfort, Rose?"

She swallowed hard as she nodded. All the raucous noise in the tavern had faded away for her. It was as if time had stood still, and only she and Vincenzo were in the lively tavern.

"Yes, it will. Very much so."

"But you must understand, I can't guarantee success, Rose. I might have a connection to the spirit world, but they must want to contact me too. It's like sending a telegram along a wire. There is no guarantee the recipient will send a message back."

Instinctively, she reached out and grabbed his forearm. She didn't want to risk losing the conduit to her dear departed father—whatever the consequences.

"If you believe it's possible, then I have faith that you can do it."

Vincenzo seemed pleased by her answer, and he beamed at her warmly.

"Very well then," he said with a nod, "let us begin. Do you have anything of your father's with you? A keepsake. A lock of hair?"

"Nothing," she said with a frown.

"Then forgive me, I shall have to open a channel to him through you."

He pulled away then rested his hands lightly on hers as they settled themselves comfortably in their seats. Vincenzo closed his eyes and started to chant softly as he attempted to connect with Tom O'Shaughnessy's spirit. His voice was slow, soft, and soothing. Rose's eyelids grew heavy as she felt her brain slip into a strange mode, not awake yet not asleep either. Her limbs felt like lead.

At first, there was nothing to indicate her father's presence. But after having more of Vincenzo's relaxing words wash over her, Rose thought she heard faint whispers coming from somewhere deep inside her mind which seemed to grow louder as time went on. Eventually, she could make out what sounded like words being spoken by a wonderfully familiar voice — her father's! She used all her willpower to lift her eyelids to see if he had joined them at the table, but they were too heavy to budge. Minutes passed, and it took quite some effort to open them. When she finally did, her father was nowhere to be seen.

Not wanting to disturb Vincenzo from his trance, Rose tried to relish the sweet moment for a few more seconds, but it was becoming increasingly difficult. She closed her eyes tightly once more, desperately trying to recall her father's voice, but with every effort it seemed to become more elusive. Soon, the sounds of the domino players rowing beside them slowly filled her mind again, and before she knew it, she was back in the tavern and nowhere near the spirit world. She opened her eyes and saw Vincenzo staring at her with a look of anticipation.

"Did you hear him?" he asked eagerly.

She nodded, feeling overwhelmed by the emotions raging through her body.

"Yes," she whispered. "I heard my father."

Vincenzo flashed a smile and patted her hand in reassurance.

"That is a wonderful thing, Rose. I'm glad I could help you make a connection. Is there anything specific that he said? Anything you'd like to tell me?"

Rose thought for a moment before replying, trying to remember the exact words of her father's voice from the other side.

"He said—he said he is 'proud of me and that everything that I am achieving'." she replied with tears in her eyes. "He's only been gone a few weeks and it's all so raw.

Vincenzo's expression softened, and his eyes glinted with kindness as he gave her hand one last gentle squeeze before releasing it.

"It seems your pa wants to provide you with some comfort, too," he said gently. "I am so sorry for your loss."

Rose's cheeks shone with the glisten of tears, but she still managed to smile through them. She was grateful to Vincenzo for helping her experience her father's love once more, a treasured feeling that she thought she had lost forever. Now she had it back, it made her heart swell with joy, and she couldn't wait for the curious phenomenon to happen again.

"But why do you want to help people this way? Mediumship is such a strange profession for a gentleman?"

"My motivation to help comes from painful personal experience. My grandfather passed away when my mother was a young girl, leaving my grandmother to raise her on her own. I remember how she struggled with her grief all her life, and how desperately she wished for one last chance to say goodbye to her husband, my grandfather and receive a blessing from him."

He paused, allowing the weight of his words to sink in.

"Knowing how my grandmother suffered with loneliness changed me, Rose. I vowed that if I ever had the ability to help someone like her, I would do everything in my power to give them that chance. That's why I've dedicated myself to mastering this supernatural gift of mine, so I can bring comfort to those who have lost their loved ones."

Rose's eyes welled up with sympathy as she listened to Vincenzo's heartfelt story. It resonated with her own loss, and she could see the sincerity in his eyes. Now, more than ever, she felt certain that she wanted to be a part of his mission.

"Vincenzo, you possess a rare and remarkable talent. It is your duty to share this vocation with the world and I am here to help you. Together, we will ensure you bring people the comfort they need in life's darkest days."

Vincenzo gave her a slow and thankful nod.

"Wonderful, Rose. I was hoping you would say that. Another drink?" he asked, his voice gentle and kind.

"I'm not sure I should," Rose hesitated.

"Shush now. It's my treat. Shouldn't we celebrate your father showing his undying love for you? And I must explain more how you can help me with my work."

Rose felt a whirlwind of conflicting emotions within her, but she offered no resistance as the elegant man snapped his fingers and a bartender appeared.

"A pint of light ale and a large sherry for this lovely lady, please."

Rose had never tasted anything quite like sherry before, and she was struck by its sweet warmth compared with the astringent feeling of the gin. It was like a sip of pure heaven. As they enjoyed their drinks, Rose waited patiently for Vincenzo to unveil his full master plan, captivated by the possibilities it held. Once again, fate had dealt her a hand that meant she had no idea what the future would bring, but whatever happened, she knew it would be extraordinary.

"Now, let me explain how you can help me harness this gift of mine."

Rose leaned in, hanging on his every word.

"Although I have the power to establish a connection between the living and the dead, it's not appropriate for me to visit widows in their homes alone, as I alluded to earlier. I need a companion with me, someone who can pose as my sister or perhaps cousin to put the women at ease and make them feel comfortable with me. This is where you come in, Rose," Vincenzo said earnestly as his underling nodded.

"What do I have to do? Tell me!"

Vincenzo bit his lower lip for a moment before elaborating further.

"You will act as my assistant, helping me set up any equipment necessary for our séances, and answering questions from the family. Most importantly, you must be vigilant in watching for the slightest signs of response from those beyond the veil to the spirit world, and be ready to act on my orders without hesitation or delay. As you can appreciate, every morsel of information we can pass on provides incredible comfort."

He fell silent for a moment. In the stillness, Rose's eyes widened as she processed his words, remembering the recent sound of her father's sweet voice, and the sight of her lonely mother's heartbreak. All of her thoughts multiplied her craving to assist him.

"I am certain that if two individuals who have experience of communicating with those on the other side initiate a séance, the possibility of establishing an effective connection is intensified. It amplifies the energy that has been invited in to connect with the spirits. And since you heard your father's voice, you know you have the ability to make that connection."

"Yes. At least I think so," she said quietly. "Those grieving widows deserve all the support they can get, and I'll do everything in my power to help them—and you."

Vincenzo grinned and raised his eyebrows at Rose, the corners of his light crow's feet deepening with delight. He lifted his mug of ale, silently toasting her, then downed the last of it. Rose smiled back, finishing the remainder of her sherry, then placed her tiny glass on the table.

"Well then! Let us not waste any more time! We have work to do!" Vincenzo exclaimed, his enthusiasm causing him to thump the table so hard with his hands her glass rattled.

"Here's half a week's wages to tide you over," he said excitedly, taking Rose's delicate hand and pressing a cool shilling into it. "There will be more soon. I shall meet you here in two days for our first appointment," he said as he gently led her out of the tavern in search of a cab. "That will be plenty of time for me to find a grieving widow in need of our assistance."

"Two days? Gosh! Are you sure you can find someone to help that quickly?"

Vincenzo flinched at his schoolboy error.

"What I mean is we mustn't let these women suffer a moment longer. I will work tirelessly to find one quickly. Whatever it takes, I will do it."

"Ah, I see. Yes, of course," Rose said with a nod.

A passing cab driver noticed Vincenzo's raised arm and approached them.

"Please take this young lady to Brady Street. This should cover it."

He handed another coin to the driver.

"Right you are, guv."

"Until Tuesday, Rose. One more thing, wear your finest dress."

Vincenzo watched the cab sway away down City Road, Rose's silhouette a blurry shape in the backseat.

As the cab navigated the East End streets, Rose took in the worn cobblestone roads and huddled houses. When the coach slowed to round a corner, she spotted a lonely old, ragged woman sleeping rough in a doorway, shoeless and desperately grubby. The sight tugged at Rose's heartstrings, filling her with deep empathy.

The idea of helping heartbroken widows and possibly resolving her family's financial troubles stirred a mix of anxiety and excitement within her. Opportunities like this were scarce, particularly for an East End woman. And yet, there she was, on the brink of making a real difference. The magnitude of the unique chance both thrilled and intimidated her. As the cab journeyed on, Rose found herself immersed in contemplation, considering the positive impact her newfound work could have on her life and the lives of those around her. She thought of the countless widows in pain and how she could contribute to alleviating their suffering, even in the smallest way.

Rose decided not to share her new venture with anyone, aware that they wouldn't grasp the importance of Vincenzo's mission. Her family and friends would likely think she had a screw loose and fail to comprehend the significance of their work. She would shoulder the burden and responsibility alone. During the remainder of the journey, she fretted over coming up with a plausible cover story for her night-time outings with Vincenzo on his missions of mercy. Explaining her evening absences would be tricky.

As the cab halted at the end of Brady Street, Rose inhaled deeply. She stepped out onto the familiar pavement, knowing there was no turning back now. Whatever challenges awaited, she was ready to face them head-on.

Meanwhile, with Rose now out of sight, Vincenzo wasted no time in returning to The Eagle. The warm tavern glow enveloped him as he entered, with the clinking of glasses and the murmurs of conversation providing a familiar soundtrack. He was struck with a sense of joyous anticipation, the kind that only comes from a cunning plan coming together. Leaning on the rich and robust mahogany bar, he adjusted his elbows to find a comfortable position.

"May I have a large brandy and your finest cigar, please?" Vincenzo asked the bartender.

"Are you celebrating, Vincenzo?" the man inquired.

"Something like that," the cad muttered as his fingers traced along the words of the longest funeral notice in the discarded edition of the London Beacon newspaper before him.

5

THE WIDOW'S SECRET

Two whirlwind days had passed for both of them. Rose returned to the Eagle Tavern once more, a mixture of excitement and trepidation stirred within her. Vincenzo had entrusted her to help him with his mission, but uncertainty still clouded her thoughts about the specifics. Her family's financial woes still loomed large. Plus, she had lied to her mother saying that she was doing some dressmaking work for Mrs Ellis. It was just the beginning of the many awkward lies Rose would have to tell. Despite her qualms, Rose clung to the hope that assisting Vincenzo was the right thing to do.

Vincenzo was already seated at their regular table when Rose arrived at the tavern. He stood up gallantly, his dazzling smile lighting up his face.

"Good evening, Rose," he said, taking her hand and kissing it with an air of sophistication. "You look even more beautiful than the last time I saw you."

Rose blushed at his compliment, feeling a fluttering in her stomach at his refined manners. Vincenzo pulled out a chair for her.

"What may I get for you, my dear?"

"A sherry, please," Rose replied, attempting to conceal her nerves.

"Coming right up," Vincenzo said, waving a hand at the bartender. "So, are you prepared for our visit tonight?"

"Tonight! Golly. That was quick."

"No time like the present."

Rose nodded at him, feeling a surge of determination.

"Yes, I am. Well, I think I am."

Vincenzo leaned in closer, his voice low and conspiratorial.

"Don't fret, my dear. I have a sense that we'll make quite a team, you and I."

Rose couldn't help but smile at his infectious enthusiasm. Despite her reservations, after two days of contemplation she was genuinely starting to believe that they could make a real difference together.

"Shall we go?"

Rose quickly knocked back her sherry and nodded. Vincenzo led her out of the tavern and off to the streets of Highgate, expounding more on his plans along the way.

The address Vincenzo shared with her took them up the stairs of a shabby-looking three-story Georgian building and up to the drab entrance of number thirteen. He rapped lightly on the door, which opened almost immediately. A plump woman with grey hair stood in the doorway, her tired face marked with a look of admiration as she welcomed the duo inside.

As they followed the woman into her small sitting room, Rose noticed several chairs arranged around an old-fashioned dining table. The room seemed to carry a sombre air, as if the grief it had witnessed still clung to the shadows.

"Do you mind if we set up here, Mrs Greaves?" Vincenzo asked gently.

"Be my guest."

Vincenzo placed his smooth black leather briefcase on the white tablecloth. Sleek and luxurious, it looked like something Rose would see in a satirist's political cartoon, not real life. As the psychic clicked the golden locks open, the two women watched in fascination as he revealed an array of intriguing items. The ornate Ouija board, adorned with mystic symbols, caught Rose's eye immediately. She had heard of the strange device, but had never seen one of those in person. Alongside the board, Vincenzo placed a delicate pendulum, several thick squat candles, and a small stack of paper and some sharpened pencils.

"Please take a seat," Vincenzo said as he gestured to the chairs. "We need to be comfortable and relaxed to create the right atmosphere."

"What should I say, Vincenzo? What if I can't speak to him?" Mrs Greaves fretted as she took her seat anxiously.

"How about something simple like 'Are you there? How are you, my dear?' Everyone feels a little awkward at first—it's quite normal," he replied with a reassuring smile.

The widow did her best to settle as Rose watched Vincenzo meticulously set up the rest of the room for the séance. The atmosphere began to shift. The candles flickering flames cast eerie shadows on the walls, creating a dimly lit, otherworldly ambiance. The scent of wax filled the air with an earthy and calming aroma. Rose watched in awe as Vincenzo lit each candle with deliberate care, as if each one held a special purpose in the ritual they were about to perform.

Rose brought a bunch of sage leaves out of her pocket.

"I brought these, dear brother. A local wise woman recommended them. I understand the scent helps cleanse the room and open the way for the spirits to come. Shall I light them?"

"If you like," said Vincenzo, not really caring if she did or she didn't.

The more she watched him, the more Rose was captivated by Vincenzo's exotic presence. He was dressed impeccably in a black suit that accentuated his broad shoulders and tapered waist. His foppish fringe fell just so over his forehead, making him look both mysterious and alluring. When he looked at her it was always as if he could see right through her and into her very being.

He had the appearance of a modern-day Svengali, masterfully leading Rose and Mrs Greaves through setting up the ritual with a confidence and expertise that left both women in awe. His assistant was both allured and slightly afraid of him, but in a way that made her heart beat faster and her senses heightened. It was a feeling she couldn't quite explain, but she knew that she wanted to explore it further. Rose's heart raced. This partnership was far more than she had bargained for on so many levels.

Once everyone was settled around the board, Vincenzo instructed Mrs Greaves to begin by asking questions about her late husband. The atmosphere shifted palpably as they all placed their hands around the Ouija board, with Mrs Greaves looking increasingly anxious as they attempted to make contact. Rose wanted to say something reassuring, but she had lost her tongue.

"Is there something on your mind, Rose?"

"It's nothing, brother. I'm just curious, I suppose. Ignore me. I'm being silly. Sorry," she stammered, embarrassed.

Vincenzo nodded and returned his focus to the board.

"Let's continue, Mrs Greaves. Ask any questions you have, and we'll do our best to communicate with your husband's spirit."

"Ladies, please raise one of your hands and put your finger on the glass. A light touch is all that's needed. That's right. Good. Now, I want you to think of questions only your husband could answer, Mrs Greaves. We need genuine proof so that you can determine whether or not our efforts to contact him are successful. That's the best way I can give you peace of mind that this works, is it not?"

Mrs Greaves nodded. She hesitated for a moment before placing her finger gently on the glass, her hand shaking slightly. Vincenzo looked on intently, his eyes fixed on the glass.

"Focus your thoughts now, Mrs Greaves. Think of your husband and the questions you want to ask him. Think of those happy years together. Imagine him here with us now. Make him feel welcomed."

Mrs Greaves took a deep breath and closed her eyes, concentrating hard. After a few moments, she spoke softly.

"George, are you here with us? Can you hear me?"

The glass remained still for almost a minute, and Mrs Greaves let out a frustrated sigh.

"This isn't working. I don't think he's here."

Vincenzo remained calm, his voice a soft whisper.

"Let's try again, Mrs Greaves. Have patience. Trust the board."

Mrs Greaves furrowed her brow again, trying to think of a suitable question. After a moment, she spoke again.

"George, what was the name of the first pet we had together?"

The glass remained still for a few moments, and then suddenly began to move across the board, spelling out letters, its pace increasing as it travelled.

"R...O...V...E...R," Mrs Greaves spelled aloud, her voice dismayed. "But that's wrong."

After asking several more questions, the glass remained firmly in place. The widow's shoulders slumped.

"This is no use, Vincenzo. It's not working," Mrs Greaves wailed.

Rose felt a pang of guilt and disappointment as Mrs Greaves declared the séance a failure and she couldn't help but doubt the effectiveness of the Ouija board.

"Fear not. There are other methods, Mrs Greaves. All we have to do is find the one that George prefers."

With a flourish, Vincenzo's hand reached for the silver pendulum. He coiled the delicate chain around his forefinger and dangled the device above the board, his eyes fixed on the sterling silver bob.

"I'm going to use my own body energy to charge the pendulum. This will allow us to interact with any spirits that might be present, but in a new way. Different spirits have different preferences. Now, this object is a divination tool that can give us yes or no answers," he explained, "depending on which way it swings."

He demonstrated by asking the pendulum a simple yes or no question and showing Mrs Greaves how it swung clockwise for 'yes' and anticlockwise for 'no'.

"If the pendulum swings in a straight line or doesn't move at all," he continued, "that can mean there's no answer or the spirit is not present. But don't worry, we will keep trying until we get a response. Now it's charged, you try. Hold the pendulum gently and think of a yes or no question to ask your late husband."

Mrs Greaves nodded hopefully as Vincenzo looped the chain over her finger and placed his hand over hers and closed his eyes in deep concentration. The pendulum began to swing in a steady rhythm, and Vincenzo opened his eyes with a look of satisfaction on his face.

"Yes, George is here," he said, interpreting the pendulum's clockwise movement. "Ask your question, Mrs Greaves, and let's see what he has to say."

As Vincenzo reassured Mrs Greaves, Rose pushed her doubts aside and doubled down on her commitment to trust him and his mind-boggling process.

"If you're here, George, give us a sign. Please, George. It would mean everything to your wife."

The glistening pendulum fell perfectly still, and Mrs Greaves looked disheartened yet again.

"Sometimes it takes a while for me to make a strong connection, Mrs Greaves. It's perfectly normal. Perhaps you should ask another question?"

"Do you remember when we first met?" she asked haltingly.

Suddenly, the pendulum flickered and gently swung clockwise. Mrs Greaves let out a relieved gasp.

"At Victoria Park?"

After a few moments, the pendulum began to circle wildly in another affirmative gesture.

For the next ten minutes, Mrs Greaves asked a slew of questions of the pendulum, seemingly pleased with the responses she received. Rose was amazed at the accuracy of the answers. Mrs Greaves had transformed from a melancholic widow into someone brimming with joyous delight.

"Should we meet again like this?" she asked, to which the pendulum replied yes without hesitation. "Then we shall, George, my love, we shall!"

As the widow clapped her hands together in delight, the pendulum bounced like a child's balloon on a string. Rose's heart was melting at the scene. Vincenzo was beaming with pride at his psychic prowess. Mrs Greaves looked on cloud nine and went on to ask George even more questions. Alas, the last few would remain unanswered.

"You must forgive me, Mrs Greaves, but it is rather draining for me to be the conduit with the spirit world. I need time to recover. You do understand."

"Perfectly, Vincenzo. You must protect this special power of yours. Please excuse my greediness."

"There's nothing greedy about wanting to spend as much time with Mr Greaves as you possibly can. A love as strong as yours will never fade."

Rose's heart melted all over again.

"Shall we meet up again in a couple of weeks or so? I should have recovered my strength by then."

"Wonderful, Vincenzo. Would you like a cup of tea?"

"That would be lovely, Mrs Greaves."

The old woman excused herself and shuffled off to the range, leaving Vincenzo and his assistant alone. Rose turned to him, bursting with admiration.

"Your ability to establish such a profound connection with Mr Greaves is amazing. It's truly heartwarming to see the comfort you brought to that poor woman. Your talent is truly remarkable."

Vincenzo smiled modestly, but his eyes sparkled with pride.

"I appreciate your kind words, Rose. This is the second time you've experienced my gift first hand, and I'm delighted you can see this is no fluke."

Vincenzo never expected that his little deception would work so well. 'Mrs Greaves' had played her part perfectly and was utterly convincing that she was speaking with a real spirit. Her ability to appear absolutely enthralled by his aptitude to control the pendulum was something to behold. The mesmerist smiled smugly to himself as he thought of how easy it had been to deceive Rose. He couldn't believe his luck! If he could con Rose this easily, then what about other unsuspecting widows? This was going to be like shooting fish in a barrel. It wouldn't be long before a real widow showed up desperate for answers from beyond the grave, and he would be ready.

He took a deep breath then exhaled slowly as he considered just how much money he could make from this new little venture. It certainly beat scratching around for tips at Crendon.

Just then Mrs Greaves came back into the room with a tea tray in hand.

"I just wanted to thank you for giving me the
chance to talk to my dear husband again.
You have no idea how much it meant."

"It was an honour for my sister and I to
serve you," Vincenzo said kindly, trying hard
not to let his greedy motive show.

Rose noticed a twinge of guilt as she heard him say the word 'sister' again and did her best to squash the discomfort. Mrs Greaves clasped the hand she had used for the pendulum and held it against her rosy cheek.

"Well," said Vincenzo after finishing his tea,
"we should be heading off now. I am sure
you have a lot to think about."

"Gosh, I nearly let you go without paying you your fee. Will you excuse us a moment, Rose?" Mrs Greaves blurted out awkwardly.

The girl watched the two of them disappear into the kitchen, followed by the gentle sound of several coins being shaken out of a metal tin.

"That should cover it," chirped Mrs Greaves. "Thank you again!"

"That's far too much! I couldn't possibly accept all that!"

"No. I insist, Vincenzo. It was delightful to contact my dearest husband. And that was all down to you."

Rose felt a surge of admiration for her colleague at that moment. Despite his slightly dubious methods, Mrs Greaves looked like a new woman, her eyes shining with delight. Vincenzo felt a sense of delight, knowing this partnership with the naive girl was going to be a nice little earner for him.

Later, as they trundled away in their cab, Vincenzo saw Rose looking at him with concern out of the corner of his eye. He put on a fine act, doing his best to look tired and drawn.

"Here's another shilling, Rose. The rest of the money I owe you."

Rose felt a tingle as his hand brushed against hers and she hoped her blushes didn't show—Vincenzo was her new employer after all.

"I think I'll be fully recovered in a week or so, Rose, then we can help another widow find peace in her life. Shall we meet again soon? At the Eagle Tavern at six o'clock a week on Saturday? I know it's rather presumptuous of me, but are you free?"

"Yes! Oh, I can't wait," she replied. "And please do look after yourself and your precious talent."

"Oh, I shall, Rose. You don't need to worry about that."

6

LIES AND MORE LIES

The front door to her Brady Street home creaked softly as Rose opened it, revealing the dim family living space once more. A mixture of the scent of stew from their evening meal and the musty smell of damp walls filled the small room. Throughout her journey home, Rose had been crafting her cover story for the rest of the family, hoping it would be believable. As she ascended the deadly narrow staircase, she spotted her mother sitting up in bed, the soft click-clack of knitting needles filling the air. The flickering flame of an oil lamp illuminated her mother's weary expression, revealing the lines etched by deteriorating health and fears for the family's dwindling finances.

"Evening, ma!" Rose whispered in her ear as she gave Ellen a hug. "Is Billy asleep?"

Ellen's worried eyes looked at Rose and she nodded.

"How was your first shift at the dressmakers? Good?"

"Amazing, ma. I am so lucky. I love my new job."

Rose's eyes showed a hint of guilt as her mind raced to bury the truth when her mother frowned.

"But dressmaking isn't very well paid, is it? Are you sure this is what you want to do?"

Rose hesitated, her heart pounding, but quickly recovered by telling another lie.

"Oh no, ma, this isn't just ordinary dressmaking. It's an express service where wealthy women get their clothes altered at home the night before one of their posh dos. We make the changes in an hour or so, so the clients are happy to pay more. And it's cheaper than buying a new outfit. We can take things in or let them out a little, or add some beads or lace trimmings to give a dress a new lease of life. Mrs Ellis is onto a nice little earner, I reckon."

Her mother's expression softened, but the lingering doubt in her eyes made it clear that she wasn't entirely convinced by Rose's story. Ellen didn't say anything, but she couldn't shake the feeling that her daughter was hiding something. Before her mother could probe further, the door creaked open again as Davy returned from his day labouring as a barrow boy at Fenchurch Street station. His heavy hobnailed boots thudded on the floor. Despite his lazy reputation, he was fiercely protective of his family and didn't mind putting in the long hours if he was paid overtime.

"Well, look who's here, our very own Lady Muck!" Davy said with a sneer, raising an eyebrow as he pointed at Rose.

"What do you mean by that, Davy?"

"I saw you getting out of a Hansom cab on Commercial Road. Why would you need a cab to go to Betty's workplace? It's only a short walk."

Rose's mother tutted.

"Rose, we can't afford to waste money on cabs. Davy walks two miles each way to work. A ten minute one for you is nothing."

Rose felt a bead of sweat forming on her brow as she quickly concocted another lie to cover her tracks.

"The clients pay so much for the alterations that Mrs Ellis includes cab fare for us to visit the lady's house. It's amazing, really. I've been in Kensington tonight. I shared a ride with a couple of other girls working in the same area, so it doesn't cost much. And it gives us more time to get the work done. We can do a couple of client visits in a night that way. Everyone's happy with the arrangement."

Rose hoped her explanation would be convincing enough to end the questioning. Her mother nodded slowly, still appearing unconvinced but not entirely dismissive.

"Well, if dressmaking makes you happy, I support you fully. Just make sure no one takes advantage of you!"

Rose gave a weak nod, eager to escape the interrogation.

"Would you like a cuppa, ma, Davy? I'm parched."

"Oh, that would be lovely, petal. You are a treasure."

Rose was relieved to have an excuse to leave the bedroom and escape the probing questions. As the ever growing list of lies to remember weighed on her conscience, she couldn't help but feel uneasy. Davy, still suspicious, followed her downstairs, his determination to uncover the truth making him clench his fists tighter with every step.

"Tell me more about these wealthy women, Rose. Go on." he asked pointedly. "What kind of clothes did you alter this evening?"

Davy raised his eyebrows. It was obvious he smelled a rat, and Rose knew if he pressed further, her secret might begin to unravel.

As Rose ignored him and focused on preparing the tea, her mind kept returning to her night with Vincenzo and the risks she was taking. Two shillings a week was a lifeline that Rose couldn't afford to give up. As she took a few biscuits from the tin, Davy's doubting eyes seemed to bore into her, a constant reminder of the precarious position she was falling deeper into. Rose felt as though she was balancing on a tightrope, the smallest misstep threatening to plunge her life and her family's fortunes into chaos.

"Are you listening to me, Rose? I want to
know all about this new job of yours."

His sister struggled to keep her breathing steady and her voice calm as she responded to his inquiries, all the while feeling his intense gaze on her. She knew she had to find a way to deflect his attention in the long term. The situation at home was quickly becoming unbearable.

As Rose lay in bed, the guilt that weighed heavily on her refused to evaporate. Her father's teachings about honesty and integrity echoed in her mind, a stark contrast to her increasingly elaborate cover story that needed to be meticulously maintained. The prospect of her family going hungry or losing their home was a constant torment, each lie a desperate attempt to protect them from that fate.

"Hey, Rose. Why don't they just buy clothes
that fit properly in the first place?"

Rose tried to remain calm, but her heart raced. She scrambled for a response that would satisfy Davy's curiosity without revealing her secret.

"Because their bodies change after they've
had a bairn for one thing,"

The mental image of their greedy landlord Arthur Sedgley evicting them and tossing their meagre possessions onto the street made Rose quake. She knew there was no turning back now. Her family's survival hinged on her ability to maintain the charade. Each little white lie felt like a necessary evil, a small price to pay to fend off starvation and eviction.

'What am I doing? How did it come to this?' she thought, even though she knew that she couldn't back out now.

Memories of her father's words she'd heard during her trance in the tavern came flooding back. 'I am proud of you, Rose, and everything you are achieving.' She clung to that thought, hoping that it would be enough to ease her troubled mind. But the feeling of unease lingered, haunting her as she fell into a fitful sleep.

7

THE IDEAL VICTIM

As the first light of dawn filtered through the curtains, Vincenzo roused from his slumber in the shabby confines of one of Batty Hazlett's grotty Shoreditch hotel rooms. Despite a heavy night of drinking, he felt a surge of energy course through him, eager to embark on his search for his next victim. After dressing in carefully chosen attire, he purchased a freshly ironed copy of The London Beacon from the foyer and delved into the obituaries and funeral notices.

Savouring the taste of hot buttered toast promptly delivered by the hotel's room service, Vincenzo's excitement grew as he perused the newspaper. A multitude of funerals and memorial services were listed for the coming week, all celebrating the intricate details of the lives of London's elite. A sly grin spread across his face as he noticed many of the deceased had left behind only their wives, without children keeping a watchful eye over their wellbeing. All those grieving women yearning for consolation, and him determined to provide it in the most cunning and deceitful way.

With glee, he meticulously recorded the relevant details of each service in a small notebook. On reviewing his scribbles, one particular entry caught his attention that was worthy of further investigation. Little did these vulnerable women know that a treacherous predator lurked in the shadows, waiting for the perfect moment to strike. Their polite press notices would unwittingly serve as an invitation for a charlatan to enter their lives and ultimately, their homes.

Vincenzo left his hotel and took a short walk to a pleasant coffeehouse, a favourite watering-hole of the well-to-do. As he entered, he noted the businessmen sipping morning coffee before heading off to work, observing the men closely, learning their mannerisms, clothing, and conversation topics. Being able to mimic them flawlessly would be vital for blending in at the middle-class funerals in his list. He studied each man carefully, making supplemental notes in the back of his little pad.

> "Just a coffee for me, thanks," he said as he settled down on a high barstool by the counter, the perfect vantage point to observe the entire room.

Vincenzo's eyes scanned his notebook, seeking the wealthiest widow who thought would be most susceptible to his charms. As he skimmed through the entries, his gaze came to rest on a name: Mrs Esme Wade, an elderly resident of a rather nice Georgian townhouse in leafy Hampstead, and her husband had been a prominent figure in the city's business circles. Vincenzo's heart raced with excitement as he imagined the wealth and status that he could gain by ensnaring her. He carefully double checked the date and time against the service details in the obituary, imagining himself attending the funeral, dressed in his finest clothing and exuding his usual air of sophisticated charm. He envisioned all the wealthy widows falling under his spell with ease.

The night before at the tavern, the devious man's mind had been hard at work, hatching the perfect plan to make contact with his chosen widows before their husbands' funerals. The beauty of his scheme lay in its simplicity, which made it all the more effective. He would craft short but perfectly written letters of condolence, each one heartfelt and alluding to a fabricated friendship with the deceased husband. Ideally, he would mention a business venture or some philanthropic society or private members club listed in the obituary to lend credibility to his claims.

In Vincenzo's scheming brain, gaining the widows' trust before meeting them face-to-face was essential. It would make the next part of his money-making scheme much easier to carry out. He felt thrilled. This was the chance for him to turn his life around. He had always been ambitious, but his previous plans had never amounted to much. This time, he was sure to succeed beyond his wildest dreams. All he needed was some luck, and he was ready to grab that with both hands.

He drained the last drops of his tepid coffee and made his way to the stationer's to purchase a ream of their finest ivory paper and a squat little bottle of their best blue ink. Upon returning to his hotel room, Vincenzo set to work crafting each letter meticulously. Each one was akin to a work of art. He took the cap off his fountain pen and began to write the best perfectly-personalised and fabulously forged note he had ever mustered.

> Dear Mrs Wade,
>
> I trust this letter finds you in good health, even though you bear the tremendous burden of grief. With a heavy heart, I write to offer my deepest condolences on the passing of your esteemed husband, Mr Wade.
>
> As a close business associate, I can attest to his honourable character. I had the privilege of meeting your beloved husband at the headquarters of Wade's Engineering Company. Each time a new miracle machine was unveiled, particularly the new precision lathes, I was deeply impressed by the speeches he delivered. These launches were always grand occasions, and your husband's steadfast belief in the British Empire's pursuit of ever-growing dominance in international trade left a lasting impression on me.
>
> At the funeral, it would be a great honour to pay my deepest respects to a true titan of

industry. Please accept my heartfelt sympathies during your darkest hour.

If I may be of any assistance or support during this sorrowful time, it would be my privilege to do so.

Yours sincerely,

He signed the letter with a pseudonym, 'Mr Sanders,' adding a flamboyant touch to the signature to enhance its sophistication.

The satisfaction in his enterprise grew as Vincenzo sealed the envelopes to several more letters, feeling one step closer to securing his ultimate goal with each one. Years of performing had perfected his patter, making his written words almost poetic as he expressed sadness at their loss, but also optimism for a brighter future. With a final swish of his pen to address the last envelope, he sealed it, knowing everything was in place for his plan. All that remained was to attend the funerals.

It was all too easy. Mrs Wade, in particular, was the perfect target: elderly, wealthy, and childless. Best of all, she had no close male relatives who might interfere. Vincenzo only needed to ingratiate himself as the spiritual adviser she desperately needed, and everything else would fall into place.

On his way to the Post Office with his precious cargo, he nearly skipped with delight as another thought occurred to him. What if he befriended prestigious local florists and undertakers, wonderful places to discreetly acquire more personal details on the wealthy deceased in the area. All it would take was a subtle backhander to the cash-strapped junior staff.

In the days leading up to Mr Wade's funeral, Vincenzo embarked on a series of painstaking reconnaissance missions, exhibiting a level of skill and precision that would put seasoned spies to shame. Observing from a safe distance, he carefully documented the household's daily routines and the visitors who frequented both the residence and their business premises. He kept an eye on the newspapers in case there were more juicy titbits to be gleaned. He hoped this invaluable information would serve as ammunition for his targeted graveside small talk, particularly when it came to winning the trust of the grieving Mrs Wade, now the sole owner of an expansive Hampstead home. He took great pride in the fact that he had organised it so that Mr Wade's funeral would be the grand finale in his spree, allowing him ample time to perfect his craft as a professional mourner and master manipulator.

8

A PROBLEM SHARED IS A PROBLEM DOUBLED

On Sunday morning, Rose awoke with renewed determination, knowing she had to win over Betty and involve her in the dressmaking deception, and quickly. With the looming threat of Davy uncovering her secret, she knew it was time to act. She hadn't seen much of Betty lately, which usually meant she was angry about something. Rose had a horrible feeling she knew exactly what was troubling her friend.

Taking a deep breath, she left her home and headed straight for Betty's cramped annex room in the common lodging house up the street. The small space, barely bigger than the bed itself, filled with an air of defeat, tugged at Rose's heartstrings, and she couldn't help but feel sympathy for her friend. It amazed her that someone could endure such poverty, live alone and still remain so lively and cheerful. Then again, Betty had always been somewhat of an enigma. But lately, Betty wasn't cheerful. She was livid, having had several days of hard graft to reflect on her glamorous—and missed—on-stage opportunity the fortune teller had alluded to.

"What do you want?" Betty grizzled as she saw Rose's face appear at her door.

"Don't be like that. I need your help."

"I don't see why I should ever help you again, Rose O'Shaughnessy!" Betty yelled. "You stole my chance to be in the limelight, to be on the stage without a care in the world."

"This isn't about being in the limelight, Betty. You've got this job with Vincenzo all wrong."

"I don't think so! If you didn't have something to hide, why have you told your mother I've got you a job with Mrs Ellis? Don't try to hide it, she thanked me for helping you. I felt awful."

Rose didn't dare explain about hearing her father's voice once more and the comfort Vincenzo had given Mrs Greaves during the séance at her home.

"I have this feeling he's up to something. I've heard stories about these sideshow entertainers. Carnival folk going from town to town doing gawd knows what and moving on. Bunch of swindlers, a lot of them. He's up to no good. I can't believe you think this is remotely acceptable. You've lost your marbles. Nothing good will come of this—infatuation."

Rose's face reddened, her fists clenched.

"You don't understand, Betty. Working with Vincenzo is my ticket to a brighter future. You can't say you want to keep bumbling along the bottom with the lowest of society? And he's paying me two whole shillings a week. Imagine what that will do for me? For my family."

"So, you're willing to sell your soul for cash? Two measly shillings was all it took." Betty said, her expression hardening. "Have you stopped to consider the consequences of lying to everyone, especially your family? You're playing with fire! They think you're sewing dresses and you're poncing about on stage with a bloomin' psychic fella."

The more insistent Betty became, the more her friend sank into denial.

"Rose, you're letting this man lead you down a path you know is wrong. What will happen when his scheme falls apart? Do you think he'll stick around to help you pick up the pieces?"

Betty's voice rose with each word. Rose wanted to argue, to defend her choices, but the words caught in her throat. They stood like two generals on a battlefield, each determined to outmanoeuvre the other in their pursuit of victory.

"Please, Betty. I really need your help," Rose pleaded, her voice cracking with emotion. "Since father passed away, we're barely making ends meet. Davy can't hold onto a job with his hot-headedness, and mother is still bed bound after her illness. I don't know how long we can hold on like this. We can't go to the workhouse. If we're separated the heartbreak will kill my ma—and we're like family, too, Betty, aren't we? I wouldn't be asking you to cover for me if I didn't think it was my only chance. I truly believe in Vincenzo's talent. And I can't see any other way out. I just can't."

Betty hesitated before saying something she instantly regretted.

"I can't even begin to agree with your reasoning, Rose, but I understand why you're doing this, so yes—I will help. But you must promise me on your mother's life you'll leave as soon as you've earned enough to top up your coffers and keep your family safe."

It was Rose's turn to utter guilty regret-fuelled words.

"I promise. Cross my heart. I won't let this go on a day longer than it has to."

"So that's agreed," Betty reiterated, her voice heavy with concern. "I'll cover for you and say Mrs Ellis took you on, but I won't lie forever. Let's keep you and your folks out of the workhouse. But I'm warning you. If I find you don't stop working with him the second you can afford to, I swear I'll dob you in to your ma."

"Deal," said Rose, hugging Betty as if her life depended on it, because in a way, it did.

"I'll never forget what you're doing for me."

"You'd better not, missy."

"And, Betty?" Rose said as she loosened her hug.

"Yes?"

"Thanks."

The two young women smiled awkwardly. Rose looked away and saw an enamel plate beside Betty's bed complete with a cracked lump of dry cheese and some bread that looked greener than the grass in Victoria Park.

"Would you like to come over for some food tonight, Betty? Ma said we could make something a bit nicer since it's the Lord's day. Does seven o'clock work?"

"Go on then. Come and pick me up at ten to."

Little did Rose know that Betty's dinner invitation would give Davy the perfect opportunity to interrogate their guest and put both their cover stories to the test.

Instead of damp, that night the O'Shaughnessy's lodgings were full of the smell of boiling cabbage, potatoes, and a faint hint of bacon when Rose arrived home with Betty in tow. She took heart seeing her mother mustering the strength to stand and stir the casserole from time to time. Her two brothers were sitting at the table larking about.

"Why did the bicycle fall over?" Davy asked, grinning. "Because it was two-tired!"

Both lads burst into laughter, holding their stomachs.

"Oh, that's awful, Davy," Rose groaned as she closed the door. "I swear your jokes are worse than Betty's."

All conversation immediately stopped.

"What brings you here, Betty?" Davy asked, his eyes turning into slits. "It can't be the promise of free food, can it? If you are working at the same place as Rose she's earning a packet. Enough for her boss to get her cabs home. It's a bit odd, innit? It'd have Sherlock baffled."

"Watch your manners, young man. Betty is our guest. We'll have less of your rudeness, thank you," Ellen snapped.

Rose's mother smiled warmly at both women and welcomed them to take a seat by the tiny worm-holed dining table.

"Would you like a cup of tea while you wait, Betty?"

"Lovely."

The atmosphere soon deteriorated though and the dinner turned into an awkward affair. Davy kept shooting suspicious glances at Betty, who tried her best to answer his probing questions without giving away Rose's secret.

"I still can't see why you don't do what Rose is doing if you're skint, Elizabeth? And another thing my poor little noggin struggles with is why did Mrs Ellis give a new girl like Rose the more lucrative work, and not offer it to an old hand like you?"

"Oi! Less of the old!" snapped Betty with a smile, hoping to change the subject but failing.

"So, will you get cabs everywhere when you get promoted to the same rank as Rose?"

His mother cut him off.

"What did I say? Enough of that, Davy. Who wants a spoonful of rice pudding for dessert?"

"Me!" yelled Billy, pummelling the table with his fists. "Rice pudding is my favourite."

"I know son, that's why I made it—thanks to Rose's money," Ellen said as she cupped the back of her daughter's hand and gave it a loving shake.

After the meal wrapped up, Betty rolled up her sleeves and attacked the plates with gusto, hoping to deflect Davy's intense questioning.

"Ladies, do you mind grabbing a pail of water for the rest of the washing up?"

The women eagerly agreed and the duo made their way outside to the water pipe. Rose brought up the rear, her stomach churning with anxiety. She could feel the icy tension radiating off Betty, who had clearly been put through the wringer by Davy's relentless grilling at dinner. What started as a friendly get-together had taken a sharp turn into an awkward inquisition. Now, the air was thick with a palpable sense of unease.

"You know I love you like a sister, Rose," she said firmly, "but what you're doing isn't right. I know I'd said I'd cover for you, but I've just had to lie for nearly an hour. Do you have any idea how bad that makes me feel? Your poor mother sucked into all these lies. It's wrong."

Rose stared at the ground, unable to look Betty in the eye. She knew deep down that it was wrong to lie to them all, but fear and necessity were hard taskmasters. There was a good reason for it, she resolved.

"Do you think they'll find out I'm not working for Mrs Ellis from someone else?"

Rose asked nervously, hoping that Betty would have some of the answers she didn't have herself.

"I can't say for sure," she replied honestly, "but I can tell you one thing—Arthur Sedgley knows everyone's business on this street, and it won't be long until the truth comes out about your little scheme. Especially as Mrs Ellis uses the same corner shop as your mother. I'll cover for you for a month, as long as you don't tell anyone else what you are doing, and you're discreet when you head off to see Vincenzo. If anyone asks me directly, I can't promise I won't tell them. I am not good at lying, but you know that. I wear my heart on my sleeve."

"Thank you, Betty. You won't regret it, I promise. I'll get this all straightened out as soon as I can."

"You'd better not let me down. If tonight is anything to go by, I can tell you I'm not enjoying it thus far."

Betty held the pail off the ground as Rose pumped the handle. The thick jet of water sloshed into the bucket, the splashes wetting their boots.

"Is there no way you can tell your mother something closer to the truth? A little white lie perhaps?"

"I doubt it. How do you explain away working with a mesmerist you barely know." said Rose forlornly. "Why oh why did Mrs Kelly have to die? I wouldn't be in this mess then!"

"Perhaps you should get your man Vincenzo to contact her and ask?" joked Betty bleakly, but Rose didn't see the funny side at all.

"Here, give me the pail, Betty. You get yourself off home. I'll see you tomorrow. Spare you another interrogation."

Rose watched Betty skulk home. Alone with her thoughts, she wondered how long she had before everyone knew her business. Her instinct was telling her not long at all.

After helping her mother with the pots and pans, Rose announced she was off to bed, where she lay with eyes wide open yet again as she hid under the treasured crocheted blanket. She was hoping that if she stayed put long enough under the covers, all of her problems would go away. But deep down she knew that wasn't going to happen. She wished that life in the East End could be simpler—that the money worries, secrets, and lies could just go away.

She had put herself in a situation that was now impossible to get out of. No matter how many people Vincenzo helped, there would always be those who were sceptical about his spiritualism and see it as a racket to extort money. She considered asking Vincenzo to channel the spirit of her father for her mother and brothers so they could experience the magical experience of hearing him for themselves? Perhaps that would put an end to their primary concern at least? Then she told herself not to be so daft.

Her dark thoughts were punctuated by little Billy snuggling into bed next to her. His tiny hands wriggled up and around her neck, and he pulled her in tightly.

"Thank you so much for the lovely food tonight, Rose. I am glad you got a job."

Forcing a smile, she softly ruffled his hair then kissed the top of his head.

"My pleasure, " she murmured, although the guilt nearly choked her.

She had to find a way out of this mess, and soon, before her family found out the truth, everything came crashing down. But how? And when? For Rose, it would be another night when sleep proved elusive.

9

MISTAKES AND MISSTEPS

The following day, Rose battled a heavy heart, her mind burdened with the delicate balance she had to maintain. It would be a few days yet until she saw Vincenzo. She decided to stay away from the family home, mainly to avoid Davy, wandering aimlessly as the hours crawled by. As the sun dipped below the horizon, casting a warm glow on the grimy streets of the East End, she longed to make her way to The Eagle Tavern to meet him again. She longed for a time when she could be honest about her profession without fearing the consequences. But would that day ever come?

*

Earlier, Vincenzo was grappling with his own set of challenges. Before him was a cemetery entrance lined with towering trees, their orangy-yellow leaves rustling in the breeze as the weather worsened. The gates, wrought iron and painted black, had ornate gilded filigree designs that hinted at the grandeur within. On either side of the gates, there were towering stone pillars that marked the entrance, engraved with the words 'Kensal Green'.

Upon entering, Vincenzo was struck by the cemetery's vastness. The grounds sprawled out before him, with winding paths and a jumble of elegant and elaborate monuments stretching into the distance. The air was filled with the smell of damp earth from a string of freshly dug graves. The sound of birdsong echoing through the air provided the only bit of cheer.

Vincenzo spotted a gathering and made a beeline for it, striding past rows of grand headstones and decorative marble angels standing on duty, before arriving at a graveside where Mr Mellor's funeral service was about to commence. A small group of heartbroken mourners huddled together, dressed in dark clothes and clutching handkerchiefs.

Observing the crowd, Vincenzo sensed the heavy grief and sadness surrounding them as they wept and consoled one another, while he, the accomplished fraudster, worked hard to hide his excitement.

Silently murmuring under his breath as he stood, Vincenzo rehearsed his icebreaker to begin the conversation with Mrs Mellor. After adjusting his long black coat and matching black hat, he pulled his scarf up to cover some of his face. He took a moment to discreetly toy with the pocket watch chain he had purchased from a Shoreditch pawn shop. Although there was no watch attached to the other end, it was a lovely finishing touch to his gentleman's outfit, perfect for concealing his current lack of wealth. With the chain secured to his waistcoat buttonhole and the other loose end concealed in his pocket, Vincenzo felt satisfied that his look would blend in with the wealthy mourners and create the 'gentleman about town' illusion he desired.

He took a deep breath and slipped into the edges of the gathering, his heart pounding. Scanning the mourners' faces, he searched for the widow while still rehearsing the lines he would use to win her trust. Oh, how he was going to love being her very own trusted Rasputin-like spiritual saviour. Despite the gravity of the situation, Vincenzo felt a thrill as he readied himself for his ruse to finally begin. For the accomplished fraudster, the allure of easy money was irresistible.

He checked a nearby church clock peeping over the treetops. As plump raindrops landed on the path, he pulled up his scarf a little higher. His timing was impeccable. It was 10:30 sharp. The vicar solemnly began reciting the funeral rites over a luxurious coffin, complete with heavy brass fixtures, while Vincenzo observed the grieving attendees: friends, relatives, and acquaintances, all bidding farewell in their own way, shoulders slumped and tears dampening their handkerchiefs. He read the gravestone carefully, hoping the engraving would give him more facts to use in his spiel.

In memory of a much loved husband, father, and grandfather now at eternal rest

"Long may his honesty inspire us and his integrity guide us."

George Williams

30 August 1811 - 6 October 1894

'Williams!' Vincenzo cursed another of his foolish schoolboy errors. How could he have stumbled into the wrong service? Damn and blast. Taking care not to draw attention to himself, he slipped away from the gathering to search for the Mellor service before it was too late. Thankfully, the search would be quick. At a second plot, fifty yards away, he saw another group forming. An ornate glossy black hearse, respectfully pulled by four majestic black stallions, rumbled past guided by an undertaker walking at a quarter of a man's normal walking pace. This was a very wealthy family indeed.

As Vincenzo trudged through the rain towards the group gathered at the graveside, the downpour only seemed to intensify. He made sure to position himself strategically, angling his approach so he could read the headstone without drawing attention to himself. Finally, his eyes fell upon a massive solid marble crypt emblazoned with the Mellor family name, relieved to know he had finally found the right service.

Lowering his head respectfully, Vincenzo let his sodden fringe shield his observant eyes. He was eager to engage Mrs Mellor in conversation, but as he scanned the mourners, he realised he faced yet another hurdle. Three older women stood among the group, each one a possible candidate for the role of 'widow.' It was an unforeseen complication that threatened to throw a spanner in his carefully laid plan. Mentally cursing his lack of foresight yet again, Vincenzo made a note to peruse society columns in the future, hoping to find photos and descriptions of his targets to avoid such a predicament in future. As he prepared to make his approach, the interloper's mouth went dry with nerves. He knew he needed to be suave and convincing to pull off his scheme, but the presence of multiple potential targets did add to the pressure.

As the small congregation gathered around the grave and began to pray, the birdsong stopped and an eerie silence enveloped the rain-soaked cemetery, punctuated only by the occasional stifled sob or sniffle. The vicar delivered his sermon, and soon, only a handful of family members, including the three older women, remained. Still stuck with his conundrum, Vincenzo pondered which one was the widow he sought. Taking a deep breath, he approached the group and respectfully removed his damp hat in deference to the deceased. He hesitated momentarily, unwilling to make any hasty decisions that might later prove regrettable.

"Poor Mr Mellor. Please accept my condolences," he said, as he planned to introduce himself as someone acquainted through past business dealings.

"Excuse me, but who are you?" asked one of the older women abruptly.

Vincenzo felt his heart skip a beat as he gulped, hoping that his guise as a close friend of the deceased would hold up to scrutiny.

"Err, Mr Sanders. You might have heard, I knew Mr Mellor through a partnership we had together within his conglomerate, Devonshire Enterprises," he said, then paused. "We weren't close friends or anything of that sort. Merely workplace acquaintances, I suppose," he added, noticing the sceptical looks from the other mourners. "He always struck me as such an honest man, and his work ethic for fundraising on behalf of Whitechapel's Young Women's Christian Mission was highly regarded at our firm. I did send a letter of condolence to Mrs Mellor, expressing my desire to attend today's service."

"That explains it then," said one of the best dressed grey-haired women.

Vincenzo felt a twinge of relief but it would be short-lived.

"Pleased to meet you, Mrs Mellor."

"Oh no, I'm not Mrs Mellor. I am the housekeeper. Poor Mrs Mellor has been struck down with the same illness as the one that killed poor Mr Mellor."

Irritated and disheartened, Vincenzo took a handful of earth from the mound of soil next to the open grave and threw it onto the lowered coffin where it landed with a dark and contemptuous thud.

"Please give her my best regards. I wish her a speedy recovery."

Vincenzo hastily took his leave. He trudged back to Latimer Road underground station, his sodden clothes sticking to his skin, frustration mounting over his botched mission. As he boarded the steam train, a renewed sense of determination overcame him. He vowed to research his targets much more thoroughly for future endeavours. There would be no more amateur blunders. In the light of his recent experience, he couldn't help but rue his lack of preparation for his next appointment with the all-important Mrs Wade, the most prosperous widow residing in Hampstead.

Vincenzo kept a watchful eye on the passing stations, anticipating his arrival at his next destination: Highgate.

10

HAVOC AT HIGHGATE

At Highgate, thankfully bathed in sunlight, Vincenzo felt a newfound optimism surge through him, invigorating his confidence and brightening his mood. With a few moments to spare, he spotted a group huddled around a graveside, where a lone woman struggled to hold back her tears. She was dressed in a traditional mourning gown of thick silk, adorned with layers of crisp black lace and jet beading, and wore a black velvet hat perched atop her greying hair, its veil cascading down to conceal her face. The elegance of her attire spoke of great wealth. Beside her stood a younger man, his hand tenderly clasping hers. The resemblance was striking and unsettling. Vincenzo was sure the obituary and funeral announcement had made no mention of a son, yet here was another unforeseen challenge. Nevertheless, he steeled himself, battle-weary but still determined to adapt and overcome. The prize was too big to give up at the first hurdle.

Vincenzo cautiously approached the graveside, accompanied by a small group of other mourners. Despite the strategic questions occupying his mind, he tried to remain unobtrusive, maintaining a detached, composed, and courteous demeanour. As he approached,

Mrs Wade looked up, her sad eyes appearing to pierce right through him. Feeling uneasy, he offered a kind expression in return. Then, for the third time that day, Vincenzo listened to the Church of England funeral rites—except, this time, he was at a service where he hoped at least the widow he was targeting was present.

He was somewhat horrified to observe Mrs Wade now seemed to have two sons comforting her, judging by the resemblance. The obituary had been sorely lacking in those important details. *'Rats.'* He estimated that one was around thirty years old, while the other, holding her hand, appeared to be about twenty-five. Based on their posture and attire, he assumed they were professionals of some sort. As Mrs Wade approached Vincenzo after the service, a knot formed in his stomach, and he steeled himself for the upcoming conversation. She looked up at him with tear-filled eyes.

"And who are you?"

"My name is Mr Sanders," he replied gently. "I knew your late husband through his business when he was a manufacturer."

"Which one? He ran a lot of businesses."

"I know, Mrs Wade. He was very talented. It was when he was making railway wheels. I worked for a company that supplied oil for the machines."

Surprised, Mrs Wade's eyes widened, and she let out a small gasp. "That was a long time ago. You barely look old enough to have been working back then."

Annoyed by his blunder, Vincenzo joked, "I attribute my youthful appearance to sleeping well at night."

He then shifted the conversation to her husband's philanthropic work.

"The donation for a new wing at the foundling hospital was very generous. I visited it a week after it opened. It's a fantastic place. Doing excellent work for the youngsters, so I hear."

Mrs Wade seemed to relax slightly, and Vincenzo felt relieved that the second piece of information he gleaned from the obituary helped establish the all-important rapport he needed. As her two sons turned to see who their mother was speaking to, they eyed Vincenzo warily. He could tell the elder son was more suspicious, while the younger brother appeared overwhelmed, focused solely on comforting his mother. Noticing their inquisitive expressions, Mrs Wade attempted to introduce Vincenzo.

"This is Mr Sanders. He used to be one of your father's suppliers many years ago. He's come to pay his respects. These are my sons, Sebastian and Daniel."

Vincenzo noticed from her body language that Mrs Wade was uncertain of both his identity and the nature of his relationship with their father, but she remained polite. The elder son, Sebastian, stared intently, making Vincenzo uneasy, while the younger brother sniffled and nodded respectfully. As they stood together, unsure of what to say next, the sun disappeared behind a thick black cloud once more, and rain began to fall.

Daniel opened a large black umbrella and offered his arm to his mother.

"Let's get you home, Mama."

Grateful, Mrs Wade accepted his assistance and bid farewell to Vincenzo.

"It was a pleasure meeting you, Mrs Wade," Vincenzo said, gently shaking her hand.

"Thank you for your kind words," she replied, nodding slightly. "Perhaps we will meet again one day. I still visit the foundling hospital. I find joy in seeing the good work done there in my husband's name. I have an appointment there tomorrow, something to look forward to during these dark days."

"And so you should, Mrs Wade," Vincenzo responded, charmingly. "I look forward to our paths crossing again."

Sebastian stepped between the interloper and his mother as Daniel guided Mrs Wade towards the awaiting carriage. In the distance, on the footplate, sat a soggy and gloomy-looking driver in his glistening oilskin coat. Vincenzo observed, motionless, as the younger son led the doddery Mrs Wade towards the cemetery exit. He didn't envy him. It would be quite a job getting the frail old thing up several steps and settled in the cab. In the meantime, Sebastian was staring at Vincenzo, sizing him up.

> "You there," Wade said in a deep, authoritative voice that left no room for doubt, "what is your interest in my mother? I've heard all sorts of stories of vultures circling around after a death in the family, vying to take advantage of those left behind. Well, let me tell you, I won't stand for it."

Vincenzo knew his presence there had stirred up suspicion, but he wasn't about to be intimidated by this man's aggressive questioning. He stood straight, looked him directly in the eye, and calmly replied.

> "Anyone has the right to attend a funeral if they are polite and respectful. As I explained to your mother, I'm an old business acquaintance of your father's from many years ago. After reading his obituary, it reminded me what a tremendous fellow he was. I felt I should come and pay my respects. I can assure you, there is no ulterior motive."

Behind them, the gravediggers, eager to get home and out of the foul weather, pulled the brims of their flat caps down and started shovelling the earth into the gaping hole.

Vincenzo paced towards the carriage, but the elder son stepped forward, blocking his path. Sebastian's expression had hardened, resembling a guard dog ready to take down an intruder.

"Leave her alone. Can't you see she's grieving?"

"I beg your pardon? I'm not going to talk to your mother. I need to get to the train station for another important meeting. Step aside."

The son didn't budge an inch. Tall and muscular from playing a myriad of sports at public school, Sebastian exuded a dangerous aura that began to make Vincenzo uneasy, more so when he leaned forward, his nose mere inches away. The mesmerist attempted to barge past.

"I'm warning you. Stay away from my mother. Push off," the son snarled, his eyes narrowing.

With a forceful shove aimed at Vincenzo's shoulder, Sebastian smiled as he watched his opponent stumble. Vincenzo regained his footing, and stood up and smirked at his opponent. Suddenly, with a gladiatorial roar, Sebastian lunged forward, his fist connecting with Vincenzo's face in a powerful blow. Caught off guard, Vincenzo reeled back, his vision blurring momentarily.

Fuelled by adrenaline, Vincenzo retaliated with a fierce combination of punches aimed at the son's belly.

Their breaths came in ragged gasps as they traded blow after blow, their movements fast and brutal. The graveyard became a warzone. The diggers looked over with a mixture of shock and bemusement as the two men battled, neither willing to give in.

Still ushering his mother to their carriage, Daniel looked back in horror. He carefully positioned the umbrella to obscure Mrs Wade's view of the brawl. As the two men stopped fighting, due to exhaustion rather than any kind truce being called, Vincenzo dabbed at the slight split in his lower lip with a handkerchief. He watched Mrs Wade being helped into her carriage and the driver preparing to head off down the winding lane back towards Hampstead. All that remained was the angry son scowling at Vincenzo, daring him not to try bothering his mother again.

Sebastian dusted himself off and straightened his clothes as he strode over to the carriage. Vincenzo slunk off and made for the other cemetery exit on the south side.

He might have failed to have a proper audience with Mrs Wade on that occasion that day, but Vincenzo was determined he wouldn't fail the next time. Instead of heading to the station, he hailed a cab and barked at the driver.

"The foundling hospital. The one with the Wade Wing, my good fellow."

Vincenzo made a note of the route in his notebook, ready to engineer his next 'unplanned meeting' with Esme Wade the following day.

He was delighted to see a tearoom opposite. The long wait for his prey was going to be so much more enjoyable there, especially with all the succulent information to glean from a fresh crop of obituaries and biographical write-ups in the papers.

11

THE WAITING GAME

The following day, after a busy hour perusing the newspaper archives at the British Library Reading Room, Vincenzo stepped off the bustling street and into the serene haven of Rosemary's Tea Rooms. The aroma of freshly brewed tea and warm scones enveloped him, soothing his senses. Golden sunlight poured in through the large bay windows, casting intricate patterns of light and shadow on the dainty floral wallpaper. Vincenzo's eyes darted around, taking in the charming decor and the clusters of cosy tables and chairs. As he made his way to a corner table by the window, he couldn't help but feel a sense of ease wash over him.

"Please, bring me a pot of your finest Earl Grey with milk," he said to a waitress dressed in a smart black and white uniform.

She noted his order in a little book, then gracefully weaved her way to the serving counter. Moments later, she returned with a fully laden tray, complete with a silver teapot and a delicate porcelain cup and saucer. He poured out a cuppa and sipped at it purposefully as he leaned forward, watching the entrance of the hospital intently. Several wealthy-looking visitors entered via the main doors, but not one of them was Mrs Wade.

Almost two hours passed, and there was still no sign of her. The proprietor was losing patience with Vincenzo nursing his drink for far too long.

"Sally, please get the man loafing about by the window to order something else or pay up and go."

Rosemary watched from behind the counter, her arms crossed, as the young girl approached Vincenzo.

"Is everything okay, sir? Do you need some more time to decide? Or shall I bring your bill?"

"Another tea, please, miss," Vincenzo said weakly, his voice quivering. "Thanks for letting me sit here. I'm waiting to pick up my son from the hospital. I get so nervous in waiting rooms. It's silly, I know. It started when my wife passed away at St. Thomas's—"

The waitress, regarded him with concern as Vincenzo offered a feeble smile.

"Oh, you poor thing."

"I left in a rush this morning and don't have much money," he confessed.

What he had uttered was another outright lie. Money was not the problem at all. The last thing Vincenzo wanted to do was to visit the toilet just as Mrs

Wade turned up. He looked at Sally with his best puppy dog eyes, and she gave him a kind smile.

"I'm so sorry to hear about your wife, sir. Why don't I treat you to a ginger beer? You can take your time with that and it won't get cold. It'll be lovely on a sunny day like today and lift your spirits a bit."

"Thank you, miss. What an excellent suggestion."

He had barely touched his drink when he saw Mrs Wade's glossy black carriage pulling up by the hospital, easily identified by its distinctive family crest on the doors.

He threw down a few coins and shot out of the tea shop like a cannonball and then, from a discreet distance, followed his prey inside. As his eyes adjusted to the gloom, he saw a sign advising visitors that the memorial lunch for Mr Wade was due to commence at one. Vincenzo gave a wry smile as he took out a folded copy of that day's London Beacon and settled into a seat near the entrance. Hiding behind the newspaper, he would only peek above it when he heard the delicate sound of a woman's heels clicking on the parquet floor. Finally, his patience was rewarded as Mrs Wade reappeared with some of the other diners.

"Excuse me, Mrs Wade," Vincenzo said, stepping forward with a slight bow.

"Mr Sanders? What brings you here? Can I help you?"

"Actually, I think I can help you. Do you have a moment?" Vincenzo asked, his voice warm and sincere.

"What for?" she replied cautiously. "I don't know you."

Vincenzo lowered his voice. "I have something important to tell you about your late husband."

"Tell me here, then."

"Forgive me, but it's a delicate matter. Might we speak at Rosemary's? It's private there," he suggested, gesturing across the street.

"No. Tell me now or not at all."

"It's about your husband and the local community garden he set up," he said, leaning in.

Mrs Wade's eyes widened.

"How did you know about that?"

Vincenzo tapped the side of his nose and smiled warmly.

"Ten minutes at Rosemary's and I can tell you more. If I'm wrong, you can leave, no harm done."

Intrigued by Vincenzo's knowledge, Mrs Wade reluctantly agreed to follow him to Rosemary's, curious about what would be divulged.

Inside, the smell of freshly-baked teacakes welcomed them once more, mingled with the sound of laughter and light conversation from the other patrons. Vincenzo found another quiet corner and gestured for Mrs Wade to sit down. He caught the eye of Sally again and asked for a pot of tea for two. As they waited to be served, Vincenzo made some small talk with Mrs Wade, trying to put her at ease with his well-rehearsed schtick.

"Mrs Wade, before I say anything, I just want to make sure that you understand that I have nothing but the sincerest respect for your late husband," Vincenzo said earnestly.

"Is that all you wanted to tell me? You said it was important," Mrs Wade said in clipped tones. "I can't have my driver sitting around all day."

Vincenzo took a sip of his tea, gathering his thoughts before he spoke.

"Mrs Wade, I'm sure you have wondered why I have been following you yesterday and today."

"I am a little, yes."

"The reason is that your late husband asked me to contact you a few days ago."

"What do you mean? How could he possibly contact you? He's been with the Lord now for more than a week?"

"Have you seen the advertisements for town halls and assembly rooms around London offering public séances?"

"Yes, but what does that have to do with anything? My sons say mediumship is a load of bunkum."

"I assure you it's not *'bunkum'*, and I speak from years of personal experience. I possess the unique ability to communicate with those who have passed. In truth, I have had this gift since I was a child. Until recently, I was a mesmerist holding séances at Crendon Gardens— attracting a loyal following, I might add. However, as the years passed, I found the increasingly bawdy carnival atmosphere distasteful. Now, I am focused on helping grieving families to contact their loved ones in the privacy of their own homes. After thirty years of marriage, you must miss your husband? I am sure you would appreciate the opportunity to speak to him? You did say you were curious about how I know so much about him. Now you know."

Vincenzo's voice was gentle and sincere as he looked directly into Mrs Wade's eyes. Her own eyes welled up with tears at the mention of her husband's name. How did the man know they had celebrated their pearl wedding anniversary? Perhaps he did have some sort of special power?

"How can I be sure it's him speaking through you?" Mrs Wade asked, her voice wavering with emotion. "It all seems a bit far-fetched."

"Perhaps he might give us a message now?" Vincenzo suggested, his eyes taking on a faraway look as he gazed out into the street.

"Do you think so?"

"Well, we won't know if we don't try."

Vincenzo leaned in, his gaze focused and intense.

"Mrs Wade, will you give me your permission to communicate with him now?"

The widow hesitated for a moment, then nodded, her curiosity piqued. Vincenzo closed his eyes as his pupils rolled up and out of view. He took a deep breath, then began to mutter.

"Mr Wade, if you're with us, please give us a sign. Please? Tell us something only you and your beloved wife, Esme Jane, would know."

As Mrs Wade wondered how he knew her middle name without being told, she watched in anticipation, her breath catching in her throat. Vincenzo opened his eyes and gave her a wild stare.

"Frederick has just mentioned something about—a special song? It might have been the one you danced to on your wedding day? A waltz?"

"Yes! Go on."

"Yes, definitely a waltz," he said, stalling for time as he wracked his brains to second-guess which one it might have been. "I am sensing it was either—'The Blue Danube' by Strauss or Chopin's 'Minute Waltz', or—?"

Mrs Wade gasped, her hand covering her mouth.

"Yes, that's right! 'The Blue Danube'! How did you know that?"

"My powers of telepathy, Mrs Wade. Your beloved also mentioned a fond memory of a holiday you both took. It was somewhere by the sea—"

Mrs Wade gasped again as Vincenzo's eyes rolled into the back of his head and his eyelids fluttered as fast as a hummingbird's wings.

"Yes, his voice is getting stronger now—give me a moment—yes, you collected shells together."

Tears welled up in her eyes as she spoke.

"Yes, that was our honeymoon. We spent hours walking on the beach, collecting shells and pretty pebbles. It was such a beautiful time."

Vincenzo continued, his voice soft and reassuring, delighted with the ease he reeled in Esme. The time invested in his research of their society wedding at the British Library that morning was paying off nicely. The more he deployed his skilful manipulation, the more Mrs Wade was drawn into the deception. He was like a puppet master pulling on her invisible heartstrings.

"There's something else. Frederick is telling me something about a cherished family heirloom. Perhaps a bracelet? Does that ring a bell?"

Mrs Wade looked disappointed. The statement meant nothing.

"Sorry, I am mistaken," Vincenzo said as he raised his hands up to his temples and rubbed them vigorously. "No, he says it's a locket. Yes. Perhaps with a tiny portrait?"

The deep resonance of his voice drew attention from those closest by. Mrs Wade's eyes widened with amazement.

"Yes, it was his mother's locket. He gave it to me as a wedding gift. I wear it every day. It has a picture of her inside."

"Your husband wants you to know he's always with you. He watches over you from the spirit world and feels so proud of how you're coping and caring for your sons."

Mrs Wade glanced around, noticing more onlookers, uneasy about their intrusion on her intimate moment. It was the ideal opportunity for Vincenzo to make his move.

"Mrs Wade, it's not fitting to unleash my full spiritualist powers in such a public place," Vincenzo whispered. "This should be a special, private moment between you and your husband. I suggest we arrange a meeting at your Hampstead townhouse, The, err, Willows?"

"Perfect. We won't be disturbed."

"I think it's best that way. I did notice some tension between you and Sebastian, my eldest. He can get a little over protective of me. Only the household staff will be present on Saturday and I can trust the housekeeper, Mrs Lewis, to be discreet, and keep the rest of the staff below stairs."

"Wonderful, Mrs Wade. And of course, I shall bring a chaperone, my sister Rose, to keep everything firmly above board when we are alone together."

"Thank you, Mr Sanders."

Suddenly, Vincenzo looked up at the ceiling and lightly touched his brow.

"Hang on. I have another message coming through."

"Is he here with us now?" asked Mrs Wade, peering at the empty seats beside them.

"He's not in our realm as such, I'm afraid, but he did ask me to tell you that he will never forget your love and that he can feel its warmth even though he has passed. He hopes you can feel his presence too."

Mrs Wade put her hand on her heart and swooned.

"Yes, I think I can! Thank you so much for telling me," she said softly, her voice trembling with emotion. "You can't possibly imagine how much this means to me."

"He also says to look after his collection of plants."

"Yes, Mrs Sanders, he was the most green fingered of the family with all those orchid awards," she recalled with a fond expression. "Frederick's beautiful orchids were the talk of Hampstead Horticultural Society."

"Now, forgive my forwardness, but there is the delicate matter of out-of-pocket expenses. There is the travel cost and also the cost of the special incense and fragrance oils that attract the spirits—and my time, of course."

"Mr Sanders, do not worry. You will be fully recompensed for your endeavours. Speaking to Frederick again will be priceless. Oh, how I miss him,", she said, fighting back tears of gratitude.

"I'm looking forward to it too, Mrs Wade. Very much so."

12

A SPIRITED ENCOUNTER

Vincenzo pushed open the swing double doors to the Eagle Tavern and led Rose inside, the sounds of lively chatter and clinking glasses hitting them like a wall. The room was packed, filled with people who looked like they were out to forget their worries, even if only for a night. A group of men were singing a bawdy song in one corner, while a trio of women in flamboyant dresses laughed loudly at a nearby table.

Rose followed Vincenzo as he weaved through the crowd, trying not to stare too much at the colourful characters around her. She felt unsure of herself, but Vincenzo seemed confident and in control.

"Remember when you heard your father's voice? That's the kind of special connection we're looking for tonight for Mrs Wade," he reminded her. "Have you been to Hampstead before, Rose?"

"Never."

"Oh, you'll love it. Such a pretty village."

As they finally found an empty table in a quieter corner of the pub, they went over the plan for the séance. Rose chatted endlessly about how Mrs Wade must miss Fredreick terribly.

"How strange it must be for her to know she is going to be able to talk to him again. What kind of questions are you going to ask?"

"We will start with a Ouija board session, I think. If we don't get any response, then we will try a pendulum session," Vincenzo said in a cold tone.

"That's a good idea. It worked very well with Mrs Greaves. Do you mind if we grab a quick bite to eat before leaving?" she asked.

He looked a little irritated but agreed. They ordered drinks as well as some food. As they ate, Vincenzo remained silent, lost in thought. Rose tried to make conversation, but he seemed preoccupied. She reminded herself to stay in character as Vincenzo's sister and not let herself get too distracted by his charm and charisma. They had an important job to do, and Mrs Wade was counting on them. As they got ready to leave, Vincenzo stood up and offered Rose his hand to help her into the cab.

"Let's go and make some magic," he said with a smile.

The young woman felt a flutter of excitement in her chest as she took his hand, the warmth of his skin sending a pleasant tingle down her spine.

Vincenzo and Rose arrived at Mrs Wade's townhouse, a grand and imposing Georgian building with a wrought iron gate that opened onto a pretty cobbled courtyard, divided by a gravel driveway. They were greeted by a middle-aged maid who showed them inside and led them down a long corridor to a large parlour decorated with antiques and paintings.

The room was dimly lit, with flickering oil lamps casting long shadows on the walls. Vincenzo and Rose could hear the sound of a grandfather clock ticking somewhere in the house, which only added to the eerie atmosphere.

As they entered the room, Mrs Wade stood up from her seat and greeted them with a sombre expression, holding a photo of her late husband and playing with his cool gold wedding ring between her fingers.

"Thank you for coming," she said, her voice more of a whisper. "That will be all for now, Mrs Lewis."

Vincenzo stepped forward and greeted the woman, and then gestured to his partner-in-crime.

"This is my sister, Rose, whom I mentioned earlier," he said smoothly. "She is a gifted medium in her own right and will assist me in making contact with your husband's spirit."

Mrs Wade nodded solemnly, and offered them seats at a large wooden table. Vincenzo took a moment to observe his surroundings, studying the room and its contents. He noted the heavy drapes covering the windows, the ornate chandelier hanging from the ceiling, the coverings over the mirrors, and the various trinkets and objects scattered around the room, and yards of leather-bound books on the oak bookshelves.

Rose, on the other hand, was focused on the task at hand. She pulled out her sage smudge stick and lit it, wafting it strategically around the room to help create the right atmosphere for the séance. The sweet scent filled the room, adding to the spooky ambiance.

Vincenzo watched as Rose worked, admiring her attention to detail and dedication to the craft. He knew at that moment she was a valuable asset to his business and that they made a great team. He took a moment to observe his surroundings, until his head suddenly snapped round to the parlour door that was opening.

"Good evening, ma'am. Is everything all right?" the housekeeper asked, sniffing the strange smell in the air.

"Yes, everything is fine, thank you," Mrs Wade replied.

"Very good, ma'am. I just wanted to let you know that the staff have gone out for the night. Mr Lewis will be picking up Sebastian and Daniel from the Dorchester at midnight from their charity dinner."

"Thank you for letting me know. I appreciate it."

"Is there anything else you need before I turn in?"

"No, that will be all, thank you, Mrs Lewis."

"Very well, ma'am. I'll be on my way then. Have a good night," the housekeeper said before exiting the room.

Vincenzo breathed a sigh of relief.

"That's good to hear. We don't want any more interruptions tonight," he said to Mrs Wade.

"No, we don't."

Vincenzo stroked his smart black briefcase containing his séance paraphernalia and smiled. He sensed it was going to be a very productive evening. He looked around the candle-lit parlour once more taking in the family photos and paintings, and began to form a detailed picture of the Wades and Frederick in particular. All of that would come in handy later on when the deceased 'arrived.'

"Let's clear a space on the table, shall we?" Vincenzo suggested.

Mrs Wade immediately took the vase off the table and invited Vincenzo to lay down his Ouija board.

"Can you put out more candles, Rose? I find it helps draw in the spirits more quickly,

Mrs Wade," Vincenzo said, handing her a
box of twelve.

Rose quickly got up and began placing more candles around the room, following Vincenzo's instructions. He neglected to mention that the abundance of candles also helped him see all of Mrs Wade's expressions and body language clearly as he tapped her for information. He watched as Rose lit them with a long waxed taper. When all were flickering brightly, she blew the taper out, and a plume of scented ice-white smoke billowed out of its smouldering tip. Mrs Wade took a seat opposite Vincenzo and smoothed her hair in anticipation of meeting her beloved again.

Suddenly, Vincenzo dropped his head to his chest and began to mumble in a strange language. Frozen to the spot, Rose thought it might be Latin, but she wasn't sure. Looking as if he were possessed or in a trance, it was the perfect addition to his act. Vincenzo then raised his hand like a marionette and placed one of his fingers on the small inverted glass on the board.

"Join me, Mrs Wade," he said, his voice low and almost unrecognisable. "Place your finger here too."

The scent of incense and candles and warm, aged waxed wood panelling filled the dimly lit room. Mrs Wade eagerly obliged, her hands trembling in anticipation as she reached for the glass. Vincenzo looked up at her with a twinkle in his eye and began to explain the process of using the Ouija board.

"The board is divided into two parts," he began. "One part contains letters of the alphabet, the other part numbers. There are two words in the middle: 'yes' and 'no'. The glass comes alive when we use our collective energy to summon your husband's spirit".

Vincenzo spotted Rose still standing like a spare part in the middle of the parlour.

"Pull up a seat and join us, my dear sister," he reassured.

"Now close your eyes, Mrs Wade, relax your body, and empty your mind of all thoughts, except those related to contacting your husband," he said soothingly.

Mrs Wade complied without question as Vincenzo softly recited some incantations to coax Frederick into making an appearance. Rose added her finger to the top of the smooth cool glass. Suddenly, Mrs Wade felt something strange stirring within her mind. She couldn't work out what it was, but it felt like something had shifted in the atmosphere, like something alive and powerful was present.

"Are you there, Mr Wade? Give your lovely wife a sign, please?"

The glass remained perfectly still.

"Please, Mr Wade, Frederick. A sign? Move the glass, make a noise?"

Just then, they heard a loud creaking sound coming from the hallway floorboards, causing the trio to shriek.

"Only me! Sorry!" came the housekeeper's voice. "I just came to check the front door was locked. Goodnight, Mrs Wade."

The three of them slumped back in their chairs and tried to relax, each focusing intently on the glass.

"Please, Mr Wade. There is nothing to be afraid of. Are you there?"

The glass moved a fraction of an inch.

"Wonderful, Mr Wade. Can you do that again for us, please?"

The glass made a juddering start, then smoothly slid to a word on the board.

"Yes!" Vincenzo announced.

Mrs Wade gulped. Vincenzo leaned in closer to the board, his finger still resting lightly on the glass.

"What else would you like to know, Mrs Wade?" he asked gently.

Mrs Wade hesitated for a moment before speaking.

"I don't know. I just want to know that he's at peace, I suppose,"

Vincenzo nodded with feigned understanding.

"Let's ask him then," he said, turning his attention back to the board.

The glass remained still for a moment before moving again, this time spelling out a message: 'I am at peace,' it read. Mrs Wade let out a sigh of relief, tears streaming down her face.

"Thank you, Freddie, dearest," she whispered.

"Is there anything else you would like to ask him?" Vincenzo cooed.

Mrs Wade thought for a moment.

"Yes," she said. "Can he give me a sign that he's still with me?"

The glass remained still for a few moments before starting to move again. It spelled out a message: *'Look for the red carnations.'*

"Gosh!" she said, her voice filled with emotion, as she looked at her framed black-and-white wedding photo with her holding a bouquet of a dozen dark-grey blooms.

"It seems like he's still watching over you," Vincenzo said reassuringly.

"Is he close to God now, do you think?"

The glass slid towards 'Yes' at quite a pace and she smiled knowingly. It was as if she had been expecting such a response, a confirmation that Frederick's hard work and philanthropic endeavours had been rewarded in heaven as promised.

After about an hour of communication, it seemed that both parties were satisfied with their conversation. Rose observed in amazement as the glass spelled out messages from the other side. She couldn't explain how it was happening, but it was clear that something was communicating with them through the board. Vincenzo slipped into a deep trance again and the glass finally seemed to come to a halt.

"Would you like me to use the pendulum, Mrs Wade?"

"No, thank you. Forgive me. I'm not as young as I was. It's quite a lot to take in. I could do with a break. You, sir, are an angel, Mr Sanders."

Rose couldn't help but wonder why Mrs Wade referred to him as Mr Sanders instead of Vincenzo, but she said nothing. Perhaps the poor old thing was tired.

They decided to wrap up their session by sending love and farewells through the Ouija board. Vincenzo said a prayer for his business associate and Mrs Wade made sure to sign off her message with a heartfelt goodbye too. The glass glided back over the board one final time, spelling out: 'Goodbye' before ending on a blank space.

Mrs Wade was ecstatic, feeling as though she had met Frederick for the first time all over again.

"I am truly humbled and blessed to have such a gift," Vincenzo said quietly, his voice tinged with a hint of conceit. "I find such solace in helping those nursing broken hearts."

"I'm beyond grateful, Mr Sanders," she said as she fumbled for her handbag.

"Here, this will cover your expenses and a bit extra for your troubles. Speaking to Frederick again has been priceless. You have made an old woman very happy."

She grabbed a hefty bunch of pound notes and pushed them into Vincenzo's hand. He made a show of declining the money in front of Rose, but he had no intention of doing so. Thirty pounds was an eye-watering sum.

"Thank you, Mrs Wade. You are too kind," he said with a smug smile, then he bowed briefly out of respect.

He had never felt more like a hustler in his life, and he loved it. He packed away his things and counted the money with satisfaction.

Just then, the parlour door swung open, the handle crashing into the wall, and the bulky frame of Sebastian came into view.

"I don't believe it! You again!" he snarled, his eyes narrowing on Vincenzo. "I told you to stay away from my mother."

Even in his drunken state, dressed in a tailored suit and a silk cravat, Sebastian exuded an air of authority and entitlement that intimidated Rose. His cheeks flushed with rage, the furious son lurched around the furniture like an ogre, his eyes wild and bloodshot.

"Leave! Now!" Sebastian roared, hurling a crystal decanter at Vincenzo's head.

The mesmerist ducked as it flew across the room and shattered against the wall, shards of glass and liquor raining down the floral wallpaper.

Much more nimble-footed, Vincenzo and Rose moved quickly, darting out of the house as Mrs Wade, her face contorted with fear and anger, screamed at her son that he was mistaken and to calm down.

"Sebastian! Calm down this instant," she cried, her voice cracking with desperation.

As they ran down the darkened driveway, Rose could hear Sebastian's angry shouts echoing through the night air.

"You won't get away with this! I'll find you!"

Her heart was pounding, and she felt a sense of dread wash over her, the adrenaline coursing through her veins.

"What on earth's going on, Vincenzo?" she asked, struggling to catch her breath.

Rose got no reply.

13

THE CHARM OFFENSIVE

Once they were a safe distance away, Vincenzo turned on his manly charm. He knew the last thing he wanted was Rose asking awkward questions. He decided a tipsy infatuated Rose would be much easier to control, so smiled widely and flashed his well-practised cheeky grin.

"You must think I'm some sort of rascal after that man's outburst," he said as he ran his hand through his dark hair. "But please don't worry about it. I never discussed a price with Mrs Wade, did I? She paid what she felt was appropriate."

Rose nodded her head in agreement, completely taken in by Vincenzo's charm.

"She did give you a lot of money though, Vincenzo. You can see why her son might be angry."

"Perhaps he was angry that she kept the meeting a secret from him? They seem quite a close family?"

As they hopped in a cab back to Shoreditch, Vincenzo used the added privacy to work his Adonis-like magic on Rose once more.

"By the way, it's you who is the angel, not me," he said playfully, reaching out to take her hand in his own.

"I hope I did things the way you wanted, Vincenzo?"

"You were an absolute treasure, Rose. Invaluable, even. I mean it."

She left her hand under his for almost a minute then reluctantly slid it away. In that moment, she would have given anything for Betty's advice on how to handle this strange relationship, but would have to manage without. The couple were quiet for most of the journey back. Rose felt an intimacy with Vincenzo that was unlike anything she had experienced before with a man.

"Can I tell you something, Rose? A secret."

"Of course."

"I was quite terrified by the directness and accuracy of Mr Wade's messages. I am glad you were there to witness it with me, else I might have thought I was going mad. Please say you'll join me for a drink at the Eagle? I need to unwind a little after the experience. And if I am honest, I am a little afraid to be on my own in my lodgings."

"I'll come to the Eagle, but nowhere else! For one thing, it's wrong to back with you, and for another, my poor mother was very ill earlier in the day and I said I'd get back as soon as I could!"

"Crikey! I wasn't suggesting you come back to the hotel with me! Blimey! Just a drink or two, that's all I ask, my sweet. By the way, let's keep our little séance a secret between us. It's better that way. Some people can be so narrow-minded about these things, you know."

At the Eagle, Vincenzo doted on Rose, ordering them both a copious amount of drinks and engaging her in lively conversation that kept her laughing heartily, more so as the sherry flowed. Every now and then, under the table he would secretly brush his foot against hers, sending a thrill through her. She felt like the prettiest princess in the land, lost in the moment and completely unaware of Vincenzo's ulterior motives. The thought of spending more time with him made her heart flutter uncontrollably, and she couldn't help but be drawn into his web of deceit.

The night wore on, and soon it was time for them to part ways.

"I'd better get changed out of this dress. You finish your drink," said Rose.

"I'll walk you back, if you'd like?" offered Vincenzo.

"Thank you," replied Rose, grateful for his chivalry.

As they walked through the dimly lit streets of the East End, Rose felt a sense of adventure and adrenaline once more. She found herself lowering her guard a little more than usual around Vincenzo, perhaps due to the thrill of the night's events, and knowing they would soon have to part.

"Could I beg a kiss off you, mi'lady?" Vincenzo asked cheekily as they arrived at the end of Brady Street. "Only on the cheek, though."

Rose, merry and lightheaded, hesitated for a moment, unsure if it was appropriate, then looked around and gave him a shy nod of approval. Vincenzo leaned in, planting the gentlest of kisses on her cheekbone.

"Would you like to meet up tomorrow, Rose?" Vincenzo asked.

"Gosh, I'd love to!"

"Meet me at eleven tomorrow morning at the junction of Brady Street and Commercial Road," he said as Rose swooned.

As they parted ways for the night, Rose had no idea where this increasingly amorous partnership would end. She knew she needed to be firmer with him with her boundaries and what was acceptable in the future, but for now, she was caught up in the moment.

Vincenzo was excited too but for very different reasons. The séance had been a roaring success, and Mrs Wade's voluntary payment had provided him with valuable information about her considerable wealth. He sensed was on the brink of a very lucrative scheme, and Vincenzo couldn't be happier with how things were turning out.

14

THE PUPPET PRINCESS

"Argh! I have to dash!" Rose explained to her mother. "I've been called into work for an emergency dress adjustment. Err—one of the owner's friends has been invited to a last-minute garden party this afternoon and needs our help. I just found out."

"When will you be back, dear?" Ellen asked. "You're putting a lot of hours into this job."

"I know, but it's worth it. I'm not exactly sure, Ma. Sorry," Rose replied guiltily as she made a point of dropping her wages into the tin.

"But I wanted to play with you today, sis," Billy chimed in, looking disappointed.

"I'm sorry, Bill. I promise we'll play soon," Rose said, bending down and pinching his glum chin.

Davy eyed her suspiciously from the corner of the room, but she ignored his gaze and hurriedly slipped on her coat, waving goodbye through the dull window as she rushed from the house. Davy stuck his head out of the door, but she had already melted into the throng outside.

As she reached the end of Brady Street on the stroke of eleven, a coach squealed to a stop, and a window slid down.

"Prompt as usual, my dear 'sister'. Come on up. I see you have your best dress and bonnet on?"

"Yes, I have. Thank you for noticing. I wasn't sure where we were going, so I thought I should make an effort. Where are we heading, exactly?" Rose asked eagerly.

Vincenzo kept quiet for a moment then told her as the cab lurched into life.

"Up West."

"Seriously? I've only been once, with my friend Betty."

"Yes. I thought you might like a new outfit. Nothing too fancy, but something smart and practical."

"Oh, you really shouldn't spend so much on me," Rose stammered, her eyes as wide as saucers.

"It's nothing," he replied confidently. "Think of it as your work outfit. It will be the perfect 'uniform' for our home visits."

As the cab pulled away, Rose was consumed with remorse.

"I can't let you spend so much money on me," she protested.

"But you've earned it for helping me with Mrs Wade."

"Her son didn't seem to think we were helpful!"

"He was only being protective. It's understandable, given the circumstances," Vincenzo reasoned. "But you saw how happy Mrs Wade was, especially when Frederick mentioned the carnations."

After much consideration , Rose reluctantly agreed, though the lingering guilt of letting someone else pay for her clothing persisted. She decided that in the future, she would buy her own outfits out of her wages.

From their starting point in Whitechapel, the Hansom cab trundled along Ludgate, past the Fleet Street newspaper offices, and towards the Strand, carrying Rose alongside an impeccably attired Vincenzo in his tailored suit and top hat. As they travelled, the dark, narrow alleyways of Whitechapel gave way to wide, bustling streets, lined with grand buildings and enticing storefronts. The stark contrast between the poverty of the East End and the opulence of the West End was striking, with both extremes of London society displayed during their journey.

The cab glided past the ends of streets packed with dark tenement slums, where often the bravest policeman feared to tread. Then came St. Paul's followed by the Strand's theatres, including the Lyceum and the Adelphi, which shone from the cab window, their dazzling lights and posters hinting at many an enchanted evening for theatre-goers. Entering Trafalgar Square, the area teemed with activity, filled with street performers and tourists throwing out seed to feed the pigeons flocking around the iconic statue of Nelson. The imposing facade of the National Gallery loomed ahead, its neoclassical architecture clearly visible from the southern end of the square. Regent Street, a whirl of activity, showcased numerous department stores like Hamleys and Liberty, competing for attention with their eye-catching window displays.

Oxford Street, the sprawling avenue, was packed with well-heeled shoppers eager to find either the newfangled gadgets from the industrial north or classic gifts from around the empire. Tourists from far and wide, paused to admire the elegant architecture around every street corner. Locals shuffled past numbed and oblivious. Chic clothing outlets caught Rose's eye, with their ornate window displays and fashionable mannequins showcasing the latest trends.

The Selfridges building itself was a sight to behold, capturing Rose's attention as the cab came to a stop, ready to usher her into a world of luxury and glamour. Its grand façade was made entirely of white stone, with intricate metal detailing adorning the impressive wood-panelled doors. Inside, ornate chandeliers hung from the ceiling, rich velvet carpets covered the floor, and marble counters were stocked with designer pieces. Rose had never seen a palace, and she assumed that this was the closest thing she would ever see to one.

Everywhere Rose looked, there were smiling customers being served by courteous staff members. Despite her initial guilt, she couldn't help but feel excited at the prospect of buying something from such a luxurious place. She hoped they had a budget-friendly range to choose from. She wondered if it might have been more appropriate for her to ask Betty to make her something, but perhaps Vincenzo thought it best not to wait.

Her benefactor walked her along each aisle, carefully suggesting accessories that he thought would bring out Rose's best features.

"The dresses are on the second floor. Let's go up."

Rose ran her hand along the smooth varnished oak bannister as she walked up the magnificent stairs, taking in her grand surroundings. As she walked higher, she thought the bustling shoppers in the basement below resembled tiny ants.

When they reached the top of the stairs, they were greeted by a kind sales assistant whose gilded name badge read: 'Mrs Harper.'

"Is madam looking for a new dress? Do come this way."

Vincenzo followed the two women watching Rose's head turning left and right, the overwhelmed woman trying to take everything in as she navigated the aisles.

"Something formal for a ball, or day wear?"

"Oh, day wear, I think."

When she got to the right place, the day wear dresses looked exquisite to Rose, never mind the ball gowns.

The assistant helped the woman try on a few pieces until she found the perfect fit and style. Rose was so pleased with her new look, she felt like a proper lady. Gazing dreamily in the full-length mirror before her, it was like an elegant stranger was staring back out.

She peered out from behind the changing room curtain and looked for Vincenzo. He was pretending to be engrossed with the stitching of a pair of men's gloves, but really he was eyeing most of the eligible bevvy of young ladies also visiting the store that day.

"Pssst!" Rose whispered, followed by a frantic wave, but Vincenzo didn't notice.

The young woman stepped out of the changing room, her heart racing. The dress she had chosen was a soft, emerald-green gown adorned with intricate beaded details and delicate embroidery. The high-collared, long-sleeved design accentuated her slender figure while the full, flowing skirt gave her a sense of regal grace. As she looked down at herself, she could hardly believe the enchanting vision was her.

Vincenzo caught sight of Rose as she emerged and twirled, and for a moment, his breathing stuttered. She looked more beautiful than he had ever seen her, every inch a princess. A flicker of guilt crossed his mind as he considered the level of manipulation he was subjecting her to in order to maintain the charade, but he quickly dismissed the thought. Greed had always been his driving force, and it wouldn't stop now.

"Rose, you look absolutely stunning," Vincenzo said, his voice filled with admiration. "You truly are a vision of loveliness, and this outfit suits you perfectly."

Rose blushed under his gaze, feeling like Cinderella at the ball. The weight of the dress, the finery of the fabric, and the way Vincenzo looked at her made her feel as if she had been transformed into a princess. She twirled, watching as the skirt of the gown danced around her, and she couldn't help but feel a sense of awe at the transformation.

"Thank you, Vincenzo," she murmured, her eyes shining with happiness. "I never imagined I could look like this."

As he watched her, Vincenzo couldn't help but feel another pang of regret, but he quickly pushed the thought aside, determined to stay focused. For now, he would continue to charm and deceive, knowing that in the end, it would all be worth it. The mesmerist gave his special smile again, the one that made Rose blush on cue then he took the price tag in his hand and reviewed it.

"And it's a bargain too. We'll take it," he said to the assistant, pulling a large wad of notes from his trouser pocket, held together by an engraved silver clip.

"Do you want to wear it now, Rose?"

"Oh gosh, yes!" she said, pivoting on her heels and gazing at her reflection again.

The sales assistant bagged up her tired old outfit and slipped it in a crisp white paper bag, adorned with the Selfridges name in elegant black writing.

"Where next?" Rose asked.

She could barely breathe when Vincenzo suggested that, instead of leaving as she expected, they should go to the first floor, the home of the costume jewellery.

He brought her another gift: a beautiful necklace made from black velvet ribbon with a mother of pearl and gold filigree decoration at the front. Before he bought it, he stood behind her and lowered the necklace into place. She could feel his breath on her cheek and the soft touch of his hands on the nape of her neck as he did up the fastening. Rose's aching infatuation with Vincenzo intensified.

The shopping trip was rounded off with a visit to Harvey Nichols to buy some new shoes. As soon as they saw the stock, Rose's eyes lit up. The shelves were filled with rows of beautiful footwear in all sorts of styles, from delicate leather button-up boots to regal satin kitten-heeled dress shoes. She felt like royalty as she slipped her foot into each pair and admired the way they hugged her feet perfectly. She was euphoric. Rose might not have gone to the ball yet, but her Cinderella-like transformation had definitely come true.

Opting to choose something practical, she settled on some lightweight leather boots with a small heel, thinking they would work well in the day and at night.

Vincenzo made it known he was very impressed with Rose's choice, which delighted her. He handed over the money with a flourish and thanked the assistant warmly. As they walked to the exit, Rose noticed how much Vincenzo liked looking after her, taking care to ensure that she had everything she needed, and it made her heart soar.

As they left the shop, her beau opened the door for her and gave a little bow, as if he was Sir Walter Raleigh about to use his cloak to cover a muddy path for Elizabeth.

"Are you hungry, Rose?"

"I think so."

"Think so?" he teased

"To be honest, I'm not quite sure what I feel at the moment. It's been quite a day. How does a butterfly feel when it comes out of its cocoon? I think it must be something like this."

"Nonsense, Rose. You are still the kind and thoughtful woman you've always been. All that's changed is the packaging. The lovely person inside is the same. There will be more rewards coming our way for helping more lonely widows. We bring them joy by reconnecting them with the love of their lives, and they bring us joy with their grateful donations. Everyone benefits from our arrangement."

Rose thought back to the comfort they had brought Mrs Wade and tried not to think of the anger her furious son showed.

"Now, which restaurant. Hmm. Let's go to Rules. I'm sure you'll like it there."

"I've never heard of it."

"Well, Miss O'Shaughnessy, if it was good enough for Charles Dickens in his lifetime, it's good enough for us."

Rose's stomach did a flip at that revelation. Charles Dickens had frequented the place. Vincenzo hailed another cab, then he and Rose made their way to the prestigious eatery.

"It's one of the oldest and most beloved West End establishments," he explained, as he made sure his body brushed against hers as they perched on the Hansom cab's narrow bench seat.

As they arrived at the entrance, a smartly-dressed man opened the door and welcomed them inside. The restaurant was richly appointed with dark wood panels adorning the walls, deep red velvet curtains partly obscuring the window, old-fashioned golden chandeliers illuminating the oak tables and weighty leather-bound menus listing a variety of delicious dishes.

Rose gasped in awe as she took in her surroundings. Vincenzo smiled proudly as they were guided towards one of the tables near the windows. The waiter pulled out a chair for Rose and gently pushed it under her as she settled. She'd read about this sort of establishment in books, but never did she imagine visiting one. Vincenzo took his seat opposite, running his hand through his thick dark hair once more, then played with his cufflinks. Rose had barely settled and certainly hadn't opened her menu before the waiter arrived.

"Something to drink, sir, madam?"

Startled, Rose fumbled with what she thought was the wine list. There were pages of thick ivory paper with a myriad of choices. The seconds felt like hours as she looked at the lengthy list—all food.

"Two glasses of champagne, please, my good fellow," said Vincenzo, putting her out of her misery.

Rose was glad she was looking down at the table setting when he said that, else her mouth would have fallen wide open. The waiter soon swooped back with two lead-crystal flutes filled to the brim with the gorgeous bubbly liquid, served on a pristine silver platter. He set them down before his guests, then left them alone once more. Vincenzo raised his flute towards Rose who smiled back at him. Gently, they clinked their glasses together as he made a toast.

"To us. And our wonderful partnership."

Poor Rose was dumbstruck and could only nod. Around her were wealthy businessmen and their preening wives, groups of friends enjoying a pre-theatre feast, and an elderly couple celebrating a milestone wedding anniversary.

"I wonder if we might celebrate like them, Rose?" said Vincenzo under his breath, knowing it was just audible above the clatter of cutlery and buzz of voices.

"Sorry, what was that?"

"Oh, nothing, Rose. Ignore me."

Ignoring Vincenzo was the last thing she wanted to do. Rose couldn't believe how her luck had changed since she met him. Compared with the uncouth men of Brady Street, he was refined, cultured and treated her like a princess. She felt as though she had been given an unexpected gift from God.

Smiling, Rose looked down the menu for something that caught her eye. Out of all the dishes to choose from, she chose one of the specials, pork knuckle with roast potatoes and cabbage. It was the only thing that looked and sounded vaguely familiar. She was glad there were English translations under the French. Even so, most of the translations were still baffling.

The waiter returned with their meals in no time at all and Rose found it hard to contain her excitement as she tucked into the delicious food before her, served on a pristine white plate, edged with gold and a black copperplate 'R' carefully aligned to be positioned at the top. Vincenzo ordered a bottle of red wine to accompany their meals.

"Do you think this is real gold, Vincenzo?"

"Most certainly."

Vincenzo watched her stroke the rim of the plate with delight as he sipped at a large glass of Bordeaux.

"More wine?"

"Are you trying to get me tipsy again, Vincenzo?"

"Would I?" he said as he sloshed out a large measure of the rich and fruity ruby liquid.

After declining the offer of dessert, Rose, feeling very rotund in her new close-fitting dress suggested it was time to head home.

Vincenzo broke their route with two stops, the first being a music hall where they saw a troupe of acrobats, a bawdy female singer, and a strange German businessman-come-armourer who demonstrated his revolutionary bulletproof chest plate on stage thanks to the accurate aim of a bewildered Coldstream Guardsman invited to shoot him at close range on stage. The second stop was at the Eagle Tavern for Rose to change back into her earlier, more understated, dress. Thankfully, the heavy drinkers from Brady Street seemed to have gone to their old haunts nearer to home, and not ventured out to Shoreditch for their evening's entertainment.

Vincenzo checked his new pocket watch and suggested he drop her off to which Rose agreed. In the cab, he gazed at her again with his deep, dark eyes.

"I have a confession, Rose," he whispered,
"I've never met anyone like you before.
You're kind, clever, and beautiful. I can't
stop thinking about you."

Rose's heart skipped a beat. Vincenzo took her hand and gave it a gentle squeeze again.

"I know we've only known each other for a short time, but I feel like I've known you forever. Perhaps we were together in a previous life? Gosh. Ignore me, I'm babbling."

The cab rattled over the cobbles and drains, but the noise seemed to fade away as they talked. They shared their dreams of travelling the world, of growing their business together, of living in a grand mansion with a garden full of roses. Their heads got closer and closer. He leaned in to kiss her then pulled away at the last minute, leaving Rose confused. He did squeeze her hand again, but didn't let her wriggle free this time.

When they arrived back at Brady Street, Vincenzo offered to walk Rose to her door, but she politely declined, knowing that if he did, she might be unable to resist kissing him goodnight. Instead, she thanked him for the unforgettable day and evening and bid him goodnight as he helped her down the narrow metal steps to the pavement. As Rose closed the cab door, Vincenzo leaned out of the open window.

"I'll be in touch soon—as soon as I can. I promise. It might take me a while to find the right person who needs our help. I know I can't come to your house, so please look out for a telegram. I will send one with full details of our next meeting forthwith."

"Alright. Night, then."

"Night, Rose. And thank you for a delightful day."

As his cab trundled away, Rose felt as if her heart was torn in two by their parting. Her internal voice of reason made a rare appearance. *'Stop being silly, Rose. A man like Vincenzo wouldn't settle for a plain Jane like you. This secret romance is all going to fizzle out. Don't let your heart get broken again, like it was by Terry Nolan.'*

Vincenzo's cab ride home was quieter as the city streets emptied. He pulled out a newspaper he had picked up and perused the obituaries, stopping on the names of several wealthy gentlemen who had recently passed. Smiling covetously, he considered how well Rose's new more presentable attire would aid in maintaining their charade with the middle-classes. He contemplated the possibility of marrying her to gain respectability in polite society, with hopes that no one would notice her change in status from sister to wife. It was a risk worth taking to secure her long-term loyalty. There would be widows in other cities, he reasoned.

As he arrived at Batty Hazlett's Hotel, Vincenzo paid the driver and stepped out into the chilly night air. Wrapping his coat tightly around himself, he fumbled for his keys. Out of the corner of his eye, he saw a figure lurking in the shadows across the street looking over, but dismissed it as a mere trick of the light. Keen to be back in familiar surroundings, he stepped into his room and locked the door behind him. He peered through the curtains but couldn't tell if the figure was still there.

Setting his carriage clock alarm for six o'clock sharp, Vincenzo prepared for an early start. He knew that he had three more letters of condolence to write in the morning before he even got to the British Library Reading Room.

15

THE BURDEN OF SECRECY

The seconds felt like hours as Rose waited patiently for Vincenzo to send her his promised telegram. Almost a week had crawled by. She wanted to fill her time with something else, but no matter how busy she tried to keep herself, it only made the time go slower.

At the tiny kitchen table, Rose slumped her shoulders and stared off into the distance, her eyes gritty and bloodshot. Her mother put a comforting arm around her.

"Why do you look so down? Mrs Ellis hasn't fired you, has she?"

Rose wasn't sure how to answer. The more lies she told, the more exhausting it was to maintain the pretence. She decided to pick at her food and shrug instead. Her mother sighed, her tone worried.

"We need your wages, love. Money's getting tight again. See if you can ask for some extra shifts?"

Mrs O'Shaughnessy crossed the small front room to the larder cupboard. She pulled out the rusty metal tin where they kept their savings. Inspecting its contents, she pushed a few coins about its base as she counted them, then returned the meagre kitty to the almost-empty shelf.

"I'll see what I can do. I'm going out for a bit."

Rose trudged down the street, head hung low, feeling worse with each step. Not seeing Vincenzo for a while also meant no income. She was sure he would sort out the back pay owed, but that wasn't much use when they needed the money now. In her dress pocket, her fingers toyed with the pretty necklace Vincenzo had bought her. When she reached Betty's house, she forced a smile and knocked on the door. Betty swung the door open and enveloped Rose in a warm embrace. Rose felt her spirits lift as soon as she stepped across the threshold, but it wasn't enough to conceal her sadness from her friend.

"What's up? Is everything alright?" Betty asked, leading Rose towards the table in her shared kitchen. "Tea? Two sugars?"

Rose nodded as tears welled up, and she choked back an endless wave of guilt and despair.

"I—I think I might have made a terrible mistake," she whispered before clamming up again.

"What sort of mistake?" Betty asked gently. "Whatever it is, we can fix it."

Rose could feel her throat tighten. Swallowing the tea as a delaying tactic was a struggle. Eventually, she managed enough composure to speak.

"I've fallen in love."

"With whom? Please not with Terry Nolan? You know what happened last time."

Rose shook her head then spoke in a whisper.

"With Vincenzo."

"Vincenzo the mystic? From Crendon? You've only known him for two weeks or so!"

Rose bit her lip as she took the necklace from her pocket and lay it on the table.

"He bought me this."

Betty's slender fingers ran over the intricate gold filigree and the pearl inlay.

"Not cheap this, Rose."

"I know.—And he got me a new dress. And some boots. For our act. I've hidden them under my bed."

"Did he now? And this is for working on-stage at Crendon?"

"Erm, no."

As Rose explained how Vincenzo was planning to use his mediumship talents to comfort lonely widows, Betty's mouth fell open.

"I promised I'd cover for you not working for Mrs Ellis, but this séance is something else entirely."

"I know," Rose added meekly. "Please? Will you do it for me Betty?"

*

Vincenzo woke up groggily at six o'clock the clanging of his carriage clock ringing in his ears once again. He cursed softly and stumbled out of bed, rubbing his face.

There were three funerals to attend today, so he took extra care getting dressed, ensuring that his suit fit perfectly and that his shoes were polished to a keen shine. He checked himself in the mirror one last time before grabbing his hat and heading out into the cold morning air. He hailed an empty carriage, giving the driver instructions on where to go first: St Mary's churchyard.

He had learned since his debacle with Sebastian Wade and now cross-referenced the obituaries to double check no one was going to make life difficult for him. Sloppy journalism had caused him a problem he was keen to avoid in future.

As he rode through the streets of London, Vincenzo felt excitement for the earning potential that lay ahead coupled and trepidation about how things might turn out. Though he prided himself on planning things well, there was always a chance that something could still go wrong at the last minute and scupper his agenda. He pushed those thoughts aside and decided to focus instead on making this day as profitable as possible. He poured over the first opportunity from a newspaper clipping and rehearsed his patter to perfection.

> "I'm so sorry for your loss, Mrs Phillips. I remember Mr Phillips from our time together at—"

Vincenzo tutted as looked at his notes to jog his memory for the man's business name. A quick scan of the write-up and a trade directory, and he was flowing again in his best sombre tone.

> "—at his Camden Lock repair shop. His men did a fabulous job on one of my coal barges. He was such a fine man. Irreplaceable. Kind. Witty. Honest. Would you care to share your fondest memories of him?"

He practiced pausing for effect and tilted his head slightly to one side, hoping it made him look more empathetic.

> "You must miss him terribly? I bet you'd give anything to spend another minute with him."

When Vincenzo arrived at the churchyard, he quickly located the likely coffin of Mr Phillips, thanks to the name of the undertaker emblazoned in gold lettering on the hearse. His greed ballooned as he saw the cortege consisting of three immaculate carriages processing behind, along with about a hundred male mourners on foot. Vincenzo guessed they were workers from the dearly departed's boatyard.

Four black stallions with black leather reins and dazzling brass bits between their teeth pulled the ostentatious hearse at a respectful pace. The carriage's glossy black body was accented with deep purple curtains that cradled the casket behind perfectly clear glass. Two exquisite floral bouquets lay beside it, with a smaller arrangement placed on top of the coffin itself. As the procession reached the cemetery gates, both carriages came to a halt, and the occupants slowly emerged.

The two women's faces were partially obscured by mourning veils and hands dabbing eyes with handkerchiefs. The two men, grey-haired and well into their sixties, were dressed in smart black suits. The two groups were having quiet conversations amongst themselves, keeping their upper lips stiff before falling silent as they walked to the graveside. As Vincenzo watched them, he felt his heart clench ever so slightly with the excitement for what was to come.

The pallbearers hopped down from their hearse, looking majestic in their top hats and long-tailed frock coats, shirt collars starched to perfection, their silky grey cravats pinned in place. The most senior-looking undertaker opened up a little hatch and slid the casket forward on its rollers. The pallbearers lined up and slowly raised the coffin up to head height, then all turned in unison and lowered it onto their broad shoulders. The vicar stepped out of the nearby church and took his place in front of them to lead the way, his black cassock billowing in the wind, the sun highlighting the stunningly intricate embroidery on his white silk stole.

Behind the coffin walked the two women, arm-in-arm, supporting one another as they faced this moment of profound sadness. Vincenzo saw them still wiping away tears with handkerchiefs that had long been soaked through. The old men's steps were slow and considered, and they kept their eyes firmly on the coffin before them as they made their way towards the graveside. Bringing up the rear were the workers from Mr Phillips' workshop, a rag-tag bunch of fellows, shuffling along slowly, their grimy leathery hands clasped tightly in front of them. One or two of them were wiping away tears too. Seeing the mourners all united in utter heartbreak made Vincenzo even more confident Mrs Phillips would part with some of her inheritance money even more easily than Mrs Wade who was accompanied by less than a dozen or so well-wishers. The crafty fellow slowly paced towards the gathering, bowed his head, and bided his time.

After the committal, the two old men shepherded the workers back to the boatyard, leaving the two women to grieve alone. Vincenzo delivered his schmoozy pitch perfectly. Securing an appointment with the Phillips' that evening was a breeze.

"That's settled then. I will come to your residence at eight this evening with my sister. I have your calling card. I shall leave you be, now. Farewell, Mrs Phillips, Miss Phillips."

The sombre church bell tolled twelve. Vincenzo bowed his head slightly, awaiting permission to leave. With a nod from Mrs Phillips, he departed. A mischievous smile tugged at the edges of his lips, and once out of sight, his grin spread from ear to ear.

Vincenzo hurried back to his hotel. There was urgent work to be done. He stopped at the concierge desk.

"Can I send a telegram, please?"

He composed the briefest of messages to Rose, requesting her presence at the Eagle that night. It was the first time the concierge had ever been asked to send a message to a Whitechapel tenement. It was all very curious.

*

Across town, Sebastian Wade hurried down Rosslyn Hill, Hampstead, his face flushed with anger and determination. As he approached the small building opposite the Royal Hospital, he noticed the clock tower of Camden Police Station. The constable at the front desk looked up, startled by his abrupt entrance.

"Excuse me, sir. Can I help you?" the constable asked, his tone cautious.

"Yes, I demand to see a senior officer immediately! I need to report a crime—larceny against my own mother," Sebastian said, his voice shaking with a mix of fury and urgency.

The constable quickly gestured for his superior to come over. A tall, mid-fifties broad-shouldered man with a serious expression approached.

"I'm Inspector Collins. What seems to be the problem?"

Sebastian took a deep breath, trying to calm himself before he spoke.

"My mother has fallen victim to a despicable scam artist. He claims to be a psychic and has been preying on vulnerable widows like her. He took thirty pounds from her under the pretence of conducting a séance, but it was nothing more than a con. I fear he'll continue to swindle other innocent women if he's not stopped."

"I see," said Collins furrowing his brow. "This is a serious accusation, Mr Wade. Do you have any evidence to support your claim?"

Sebastian nodded, pulling out a small notebook from his coat pocket. He had been gathering information on the man ever since he realised what had happened to his mother.

"I've taken note of his appearance and his so-called 'sister,' who assists him in his deceit. I also asked about at the golf club and at church and now I have the names of several other widows who might have received correspondence or been otherwise targeted by this man that I think you should speak to. We need to stop him before he causes more harm."

The policeman took the notebook from Sebastian and began to read through the details and noted the sketch of the man's identity which showed a lot of detail. As the officer delved deeper, his expression grew grimmer.

"Do you mind if I keep this for a while?"

"Fine with me, inspector."

"This is indeed troubling. We'll begin an investigation immediately, Mr Wade. I can assure you we'll do everything in our power to put an end to this man's scheming and bring him to justice. He's not the first to pull a scam like this. I'll get our boys to patrol the cemeteries and look out for him, and have a chat with the gravediggers, too."

Sebastian nodded, grateful for the officer's understanding and support. As he left the police station, he felt a mix of relief and apprehension. He knew he had done the right thing by reporting the crime, but he also knew that the man who had preyed on his mother and countless others was still at large. And until he was stopped, no one was safe from his deception.

*

Meanwhile, in her little annex room, Betty decided to try to talk some sense with Rose. They sat on her bed, both staring at the floor. Betty took a deep breath and leaned in closer to her friend.

"I'm telling you, there's something off about him. He's not like any other employer you've had before. When I bumped into your mother she said she was worried about money again. Has he stopped paying you already?"

Rose rolled her eyes and crossed her arms.

"You've said it all before, Betty. I don't see what the big deal is. I appreciate your concern, Betty, I really do. But I know what I'm doing. I've not seen him for a while, that's why I've not been paid."

Betty sighed and shook her head.

"You're not listening, Rose. You're burying your head in the sand like an ostrich. You need to open your eyes and see what's really going on here."

"You don't know anything about this. I'd thank you to stop meddling."

The frosty atmosphere was punctuated by a tug at Betty's curtained 'door'. Rose's little brother, Billy, was jiggling at the threshold, desperate to hand over a slip of paper.

"This came for you."

Rose snatched the note from him and read it. The relief on her face was palpable.

"Eagle seven pm tonight. Please bring smart dress. V."

"I must dash, Betty. Sorry!" Rose said over her shoulder as she left to speed home.
"Come on, Billy. There's no time to waste."

Fully aware of the reason for her friend's abrupt departure, Betty pulled the curtain closed, her heart weighed down by concern for Rose's future. An ominous feeling enveloped the room, leaving Betty to question whether she had done enough to shield her friend from the impending danger.

16

DECEPTION IN THE DARKNESS

Vincenzo and Rose stepped out of the Hansom cab in leafy Islington and surveyed the frontage of the elegant townhouse before them. A slate sign bore the words: 'The Larches.' The streets were lined with tall trees, and the air smelled fresh for London. They made their way up the short but beautifully tiled pathway that led to the imposing entrance. A young maid answered Vincenzo's firm knock.

"Ah, yes. Mrs Phillips is expecting you. She will be with you shortly. She requests that you make yourselves feel at home and start preparing the room."

The curious-looking visitors were ushered into the parlour, the atmosphere heavy with grief. The sweet floral notes of a freshly-cut bouquet of marigolds on the mantle added a little light relief. In the centre of the room, a large table was surrounded by six opulent chairs with ornate carvings on the arms and plush buttoned upholstery. As they walked across the parquet floor, their footsteps were occasionally muffled by the thick Persian rugs.

"Can you turn off the oil lamps, Rose, and I'll get the candles ready?"

Rose visited each lamp in turn, but kept her gaze fixed on Vincenzo. He struck a large household match then lit a series of candles and placed them around the room for dramatic effect.

"Shall I cleanse the room with sage?"

"Please," he said to humour her.

He scanned the room desperately, searching for a glimpse of Mr Phillips' past and knowledge that would be more valuable than the cloying scent as he attempted to channel the spirit of the deceased. The parlour wasn't as overflowing with knick-knacks and mementos as Mrs Wade's had been, but there were enough clues to add plenty grist to Vincenzo's mesmerist mill.

Rose took out her smudge stick, and with a few gentle sweeps of her arm, she felt the air begin to shimmer with spiritual energy. Vincenzo moved the two spare chairs against the wall. Everything was now perfectly positioned, and Rose could feel the power in the room growing stronger.

Mrs Phillips, dressed in black mourning attire, slowly entered the room, her face marked with grief. Her daughter followed, gliding into the room at the same pace. She wore a pristine charcoal grey dress, her figure highlighted by a sombre jet-black silk sash that was cinched in around her slender waist. The two women exchanged uneasy glances before making their way to the seats around the table, where Vincenzo was awaiting them. He extended a handshake to each woman in a gesture of compassion and respect before taking his seat once more. Then, Vincenzo spoke in a low, melodic voice, his eyes fixed on the two grief-stricken ladies.

"Tonight, we will be attempting to contact
the spirit of your late husband and father,"
he said softly. "This is a delicate process that
requires the full cooperation of all present.
Mrs Phillips, you, your daughter, and I must
join hands with my sister and form a chain
of energy that will enable us to establish a
direct link with Mr Phillips' spirit."

The widow and her daughter were so on edge, Rose could sense their apprehension, but Vincenzo's reassuring tone and kind gaze helped to ease their fears.

"Shall we begin?"

The women nodded, and Mrs Phillips gave her daughter's hand a slight squeeze.

Vincenzo's head dropped down, his chin pressing deeply into his chest. He remained still for a few seconds before his head shot back up, jerking backwards. His eyes rolled up in their sockets. When his eyelids flew open, they revealed two white orbs in place of eyes, the irises and pupils barely visible.

"If you are here, Mr Phillips, give us a sign. A tap? A click? Move something. Do whatever you can."

The women all held their breath in anticipation of what might happen. As the ticking of the clock seemed to become louder, the seconds passed by even slower. Suddenly, an icy blast rushed through the room, making the candles flicker ominously and their shadows dance on the wall.

"Can you feel that chill in the air?" asked Rose nervously, feeling as if someone had just walked over her grave.

For her, the sensation was undeniable proof that they were in the presence of something otherworldly. The Phillips women nodded too, but Vincenzo seemed unresponsive, his face still pointing up towards the ceiling. Then he started to speak with a voice that was not his own.

"I am here, my dearest Susan and Elizabeth."

The women gripped hands again. Vincenzo spoke with a measured tone. Each nugget of information he went on to share made the widow and daughter gasp at its accuracy.

"This is the proof we had been searching for," Elizabeth whispered to her mother. "He has to be here with us. There's no doubt in my mind."

They exchanged knowing glances, tears in their eyes. Rose observed the intensity of their response, her head nodding in agreement. At that moment, all three women thought Vincenzo seemed to be more of a miracle worker than a mere mesmerist. A stream of questions followed. Was Mr Phillips at peace now that his physical body was no longer struggling with illness? Was he with Elizabeth's beloved childhood pet dog? Would he come and visit them again?

After thirty minutes, the accuracy of Vincenzo's information began to wane. His body started to droop, and his eyelids began to flicker closed, heavy with fatigue. The women beside him became distraught. The atmosphere darkened with worry that the spirit of Mr Phillips was fading.

"Please don't go, Papa," wailed Elizabeth.

"I am sorry my responses are beginning to lose their sharpness, ladies. As you can imagine, it takes a lot out of me to maintain the connection with the spirit world."

Rose's gaze was wide with amazement. Her worries about Vincenzo's ability to communicate with the dead were erased by the intense raw emotions of the Phillips family, making her confident that he could indeed access the netherworld. After now attending three successful meetings with Vincenzo, she was more certain than ever of his 'gift'. Although she still had no idea how he did it, that didn't matter. She knew that, once again, he had managed to connect the ladies with Mr Phillips that night in some way, and that was what mattered. The room fell silent and still, except for the widow and daughter's tense breaths and the rhythmic ticking of the clock once more. Vincenzo slowly rose from his trance, his gaze coming to rest on their circle of hands, then gently worked his free hand loose. Mrs Phillips went to the mantelpiece and took the thick envelope resting there.

"Our donation. For your fee, Mr Sanders."

"Are you sure, Mrs Phillips? My sister and I can only take the contribution if you truly believe I contacted your husband. My conscience couldn't take it if I felt you'd been deceived."

"You are an angel that walks amongst us. Your insights have been worth every penny. Haven't they, Elizabeth?"

The young woman nodded as she made her way around the room, relighting the oil lamps as Rose snuffed out the candles. Vincenzo sighed with relief and graciously accepted the envelope.

The mesmerist opened his portmanteau and took out his diary, then licked his finger and moved onto the next month's pages, figuring that would give him plenty of time to do some more digging on Mr Phillips. A few pints with some of his workers at the boatyard and a trawl of the London Beacon's business and society pages would provide him with plenty of fresh facts to take inspiration from.

"Shall we say four weeks tonight?"

"Four weeks! That feels like a year away!" shrieked Elizabeth.

The women looked bereft. Having had a taste of spending time with their beloved relative, they were eager to keep up the pace.

"I want to make sure both Mr Phillips and I can recover. I wouldn't want to give you false hope that I could join him again so soon. The connection is not like a tap that can be turned on and off at will. The stars have to align, if you will?"

"You are the expert, Mr Sanders," the women reluctantly agreed.

Mrs Phillips tugged on a thin rope that disappeared up into the ceiling via a decorative brass rose. Soon the maid reappeared and the two house guests were seen to the front door.

Susan and Elizabeth watched Vincenzo and Rose leave, then Susan spoke to Mr Phillips's portrait on the wall as she gripped her daughter's hand again.

"Thank you, my dear. Until we meet again."

As Rose and Vincenzo made their way to the train station to pick up another cab bat to the Eagle, Rose asked him a burning question, one that had been troubling her for some time.

"Are you happy with your move into mediumship and leaving the glamour of working on stage behind you?"

"It seemed like the right thing to do," he said with a shrug. "It allows me to use my skills to help people rather than merely entertain them."

"And you wouldn't want to do a public séance to help more people?"

"Oh no, Rose. I don't think that would suit me at all."

Vincenzo shifted his weight from one foot to the other, his eyes darting about as he fumbled for an excuse.

"I think I would find it too tiring connecting with more than one loved one a night. It is difficult to maintain contact with spirits beyond the grave, especially when emotions run high."

"Yes, it does seem to drain you. Perhaps you're right." Rose nodded.

"Yes. It's like I leave my physical body altogether and I can see myself sitting there. I don't always know what information is coming until it comes out of my mouth, but it seems I can make a genuine connection. There were plenty of details tonight that provided comfort for those left behind after a death in the family. I suppose that's all that matters."

Rose smiled at him. He took her hands and turned to look at her.

"How about you join me for some rest and relaxation at the Eagle, Rose?"

"That would be perfect."

He let her hands slide out of his, pretending to be embarrassed at his show of affection.

"Forgive me."

Rose grinned. There was no need to forgive him. She wanted him to take her hand again. When they were alone in the carriage, she reached for his hand, and once more neither of them pulled away.

Upon arriving at the tavern, a pair of eyes narrowed suspiciously at Rose, dressed in her posh frock and new boots. The eyes belonged to Betty, who had agreed to join Sarah Oakes for a Penny Gaff that night to recover from a tiring week behind the sewing machines. Sarah, always eager for a tipple, had persuaded Betty to have a nightcap at the Eagle afterwards. As usual, Sarah was chattering away, her tongue loosening after a drink or two.

"Have you seen my Terry?" Sarah asked Betty, her voice soft yet slightly strained.
"Not since yesterday," Betty replied, her

gaze darting between Sarah and the newcomers.

"It's not like him to miss a night at the Eagle, Betty. I'm a bit worried. Where can he be?"

Betty twirled her hair round and around her finger while watching Rose.

"Are you listening to me, Betty?" Sarah nagged.

"Er, yes. Sorry. What were you saying?"

Sarah rolled her eyes and began questioning Betty about Terry Nolan's whereabouts again. Rose had disappeared into the privy to change, leaving Vincenzo unattended. Betty was confident he hadn't noticed her observing from across the room. She sighed in frustration, watching Vincenzo eye up other women in the tavern. Was he searching for more sisters to join his peculiar mission, or did he just intend to take one back to his hotel room that night?

"What is he doing? That fella in the posh black velvet suit," Betty conspired with Sarah. "He's supposed to be secretly courting Rose."

"Cor, is he? She kept that quiet—mind you, he is a bit of a stunner! Don't know, though. I've never seen him before," she said flatly, her eyes tracking his leering gaze as it slowly swept over the single women in the room. "But it doesn't look good for Rose's chances with him from where I'm sitting."

"Come on, Sarah," Betty growled. "Let's go before this night gets any worse. Let's look for Terry."

She rose from her chair and headed towards the door. Sarah slurped her drink, eager not to leave a single drop behind. Rose returned, now in her old dress, and tiptoed between the tables to sit across from Vincenzo, who was now waving a pound note in the air to pay for an expensive-looking bottle of wine. Betty noticed Sarah struggling to place her arm in her coat sleeve, the effect of the gin impairing her coordination.

Vincenzo poured Rose a large glass of wine and urged her to take a few generous sips before refilling her glass. Then he led her over to the space in front of the Irish house band, whose lively jig filled the room once more. As they began to twirl and spin to the lively tune, his hand pressed firmly against the small of her back. He never looked away from her eyes, almost as though he was controlling her movements with his gaze. Rose seemed like a puppet in his arms. Realising intervention would be utterly pointless, Betty grabbed her belongings, nearly knocking over a chair in her haste. She took Sarah's arm, shoved it in the sleeve, and roughly pulled at the collar to straighten it up.

"What's the rush, Betty? Has something upset you?"

"It's been a long week, and I just want to get back home."

17

THE ILLUSION OF ROSE-COLOURED GLASSES

On Sunday, Betty longed for a lie-in. Although she believed Rose was old enough to look after herself, seeing her fall under Vincenzo's spell and into deeper trouble bothered her. She pulled her head under her thin eiderdown to escape the worry, but it didn't help. A distraction was necessary. She stepped out into the chilly, foggy air, wrapped her shawl around her shoulders, and headed to the corner store. The street bustled with people carrying out their Sunday morning routines—the usual hawkers, street vendors, ladies with wicker baskets on their arms, and children running errands for their parents.

Upon entering the corner store, Betty scanned for their usual selection of gaudy penny dreadful magazines, but found none.

"You're too late," said Mrs Bates. "All this week's are sold out. Sorry, love."

Betty glanced at the drab front cover of the London Beacon, doubting it contained any sensationalism, even at the weekend.

"I'll take one of these," she said, disappointed.

Little did she know that the sensation that lurked in that particular issue of the Beacon in her hand would soon make her heart race so much more than a penny dreadful ever could.

*

Across the capital, things were heating up in the quaint village of Hampstead, as Sebastian Wade nervously greeted two uniformed police officers at his front door.

"I apologise, Inspector Collins, but my mother isn't here right now. She left this morning on an urgent errand to do with the hospital, and I'm unsure when she'll return."

To Sebastian's relief, the other officer offered a friendly handshake.

"Sergeant Parker, Ted. Pleased to make your acquaintance. We'd still like to have a look around your house, specifically the parlour, if that's alright, with you Mr Wade."

Sebastian led them into the usually inviting room, which now appeared cluttered and disorganised due to the upheaval from the recent events. The cheesy ornaments, keepsakes, and trinkets adorning every surface, made Sebastian feel self-conscious as the officers began their methodical search.

Collins carefully examined the items, donning a pair of white gloves, while Parker jotted down notes. They shared subtle nods and smiles, as if privy to an inside joke. Getting up from the floor after searching under the low chaise longue, Collins came face to face with the sharp beak of a stuffed peregrine falcon perched on a side table, its beady eyes peering at him. He couldn't help but grimace. Meanwhile, Parker grinned at a painting of a rotund tomcat walking on its back legs wearing a top hat and tail.

"My mother has a penchant for these things. Me, not so much," Sebastian said, feeling the need to explain

Collins met his gaze and smiled.

"No?"

"No, I don't!"

The two policemen chuckled, amused by Sebastian's obvious indignation. The maid, carrying a tray of tea and biscuits, blushed as she caught Parker's charming smile from outside in the corridor.

"Tea, gentlemen?"

"Marvellous. Two sugars for me, Miss. None for my colleague. He keeps telling me he's sweet enough already," added Parker.

"Do you have to say that every time, Ted?" grizzled Collins.

"Sorry, sir. Only pulling your leg, sir."

Miss Potts stole glances at the smartly dressed sergeant, admiring his neatly styled hair in particular. It took her an age to dispense everyone's refreshments.

"That will be all, Miss Potts," Sebastian said, snapping the maid out of her daze. "I'm sure my mother will be back soon. Until then, I suggest you get on with your duties."

As the officers continued their investigation, they paused to examine the family's collection of leather-bound books.

"Someone in your family is a reader, Mr Wade."

"Was. My father's collection," Sebastian lamented.

As Collins sifted through the wastepaper basket, Sebastian took a step back, repulsed by the unsavoury items the inspector pulled out. He watched with discomfort as Collins examined old private correspondence, crinkled receipts, sticky sweet wrappers and rather embarrassingly, one of his brother's discarded and decidedly grubby handkerchiefs. Sebastian had to turn away, praying for the ordeal to be over soon.

Suddenly, there was the sound of a pen scribbling furiously in a notepad once more. Parker's expression changed as Collins showed him something. As Sebastian turned back, he saw Collins squirrel the thing away into his pocket before he could figure out what it was.

The officers finished surveying the room, their eyes darting behind curtains and scanning the walls for any final hidden clues or secret passageways. As they ended their search, Parker's gaze landed on a framed photograph of Mr and Mrs Wade on their wedding day. The young bride held a bouquet of carnations, her expression serene and joyful.

"Your parents look so happy then, don't they?"

"Yes," Sebastian replied wistfully. "Mama says it was a beautiful day."

As the search of the parlour concluded, Collins pulled Sebastian aside, revealing the secret item he had pocketed earlier: an empty box of Price's Patent Candles with a price label from The Hoxton Candle Emporium.

"We'll take this back to the station and make inquiries at the candle shop to gather more information. Do you mind?"

"Not at all," Sebastian agreed, his anxiety soaring as the officers prepared to leave.

The maid, still smitten with Parker, escorted the policemen out alongside Sebastian. He frowned at her, but she seemed oblivious.

Once the police left, Sebastian felt his heart race with panic. His mother, a force to be reckoned with, had a fearsome temperament. He recalled the last time she had flown into a rage over a trivial matter, a misplaced spoon from her prized silverware set. The entire household had been on edge for days.

Sebastian and his mother had already had a heated discussion about her involvement with the psychic after the funeral, and he had tried to persuade her to reconsider hiring his services after the man visited their home. But she had been quite adamant that spending money on a mystic was her prerogative. It was this stubbornness and grief that had driven Sebastian to contact the police behind her back. Now that they were fully involved in investigating the séances with a view to halting them, he dreaded to think what her reaction would be to this latest development.

He knew he needed to prepare for her return and find a way to soften the blow of the news. But as he stared at the closed door, he couldn't help but worry about what lay ahead.

*

After brewing a cup of tea and settling back into bed, Betty Hardacre, hoping for a lazy Sunday morning, opened the latest edition of The Beacon, her fingertips brushing over the crisp, smooth pages. The headlines and stories seemed to belong to a world far removed from London's East End, with some more exciting than others.

Foreign War Looms as Diplomatic Tensions Mount.

Prince Edward Opens New Infirmary in Newcastle upon Tyne.

Archie Blake Stands Trial for Manchester Murder.

Council Meeting Approves New Warehouse Development in Ratcliffe.

Audience in Stitches as New Comedy "Charley's Aunt" Debuts in the West End.

Heartless Fraud: Psychic Exploits Mourning Widows.

Betty's eyes lingered on the last headline. She sat up in bed and eagerly read the article.

"Heartless Fraud: Psychic 'Mr Sanders' Exploits London's Mourning Widows"

A fake psychic is reportedly preying on wealthy widows at funerals, charging for his mediumship services and exploiting their grief to gain their trust. According to witness Sebastian Wade, of The Willows, Hampstead and respected Middle Temple barrister at Gibson Dunn Chambers, the suspect approached his mother at his late father's funeral service, offering to communicate with the deceased through a séance.

The man claimed to possess special powers and employed various tricks, including cold reading, sleight of mouth, a wide array of occultist paraphernalia, plus a raft of simple illusions, to convince his victims of his abilities.

Mr Wade stated, "The man, accompanied by an assistant he claims is his sister, left with thirty pounds of my mother's money. I clearly explained the situation to my mother, but she still wanted to meet him again, such was her pain and sense of loss. I had no option but to call in the police. The spectacle clouded her judgement entirely. Clerics, undertakers, and family members need to be vigilant at services until the authorities apprehend him, else their loved one might be next."

The police urge caution. "We are aware of this scam targeting vulnerable women and are actively investigating it," said Inspector Collins of the Camden Police Constabulary. "We ask anyone who has fallen victim to this or similar scams to come forward and report it to us. We also advise the public to be wary of anyone offering psychic services, especially if they are asking for money or offering to visit family homes."

The suspect was described as a tall, lean man in his late twenties or early thirties with dark hair and a penchant for fine fashion. He wore a black frock coat, waistcoat with a gold watch chain, a dress shirt in dark tones and a top hat with a navy ribbon. He sends a handwritten letter of condolence to his prey with personal details he has researched to earn their trust, then engages in small talk at the service, pretending to be a business associate. Mr Wade said the fraudster also stalked his mother as she attended his late father's memorial dinner at a foundling hospital.

The man may turn violent if confronted, and the public should contact the authorities if they encounter anyone matching this description at a funeral or wake.

While the swindler remains at large, the police appealed for information about

> his whereabouts or activities. They are also appealing for the sister to come forward to help with their inquiries.

Betty leapt out of bed, dread rising in her chest. She had to tell her friend the truth before it was too late. The question was how could this be done with delicacy? Rose's heartbreak would be profound. Betty hurried to Rose's home and was greeted by a warm smile and an invitation inside.

"What now? Are you here to lecture me again?" asked Rose.

"I need to talk to you about something important," Betty replied solemnly.

"Is everything all right, Betty?"

Choosing her words with caution, her friend confessed her concerns.

"No, it's not. It's about Vincenzo. He's a fraud, Rose. This whole psychic act—it's all a sham. You must have had your suspicions, surely?"

"Shush! I can't have ma finding out."

Rose's eyes widened as if she'd truly seen a ghost rather than just heard one, and her nostrils flared in anger as Betty produced a newspaper and placed it on the table.

"What's all this kerfuffle?" asked Rose's mother, who had managed to drag her weary bones downstairs, intrigued by their discussion.

"Perhaps you can talk some sense into her, Mrs O'Shaughnessy. Read this," said Betty, jabbing at the piece with her finger.

Rose shook her head in disbelief as she skimmed the report, still unwilling to accept that the refined man who had been so kind to her was a common swindler.

"I don't need to read that," insisted Rose, having to think quickly on her feet. "It must be about someone else. It says 'Sanders' not 'Vincenzo'. I refuse to believe it. He helped me hear pa's voice again. You have to believe me. He does what he promises."

"I know it's difficult to accept," Betty consoled, "but you need to face the truth. He's harming innocent people. You can't stay involved with him. Especially now the police want to bend his ear."

"Betty's right, Rose. You'll end up in prison. You lied to me about working for Mrs Ellis. What else are you lying about? He's taking advantage of you. Turned you into a right little ruffian he has."

Betty and Ellen gazed at Rose, concern etched on their faces. They had no reason to deceive her, but

Vincenzo did, and yet she seemed to believe him over them.

"I saw you two at the tavern yesterday, Rose. I saw you drinking and dancing together. And I also saw him eyeing other women when you went to change out of that fancy dress."

Rose wanted to believe Betty was being vindictive, jealous she had found true love, but there was no point. The article was concerning. Her father had said there was never smoke without fire, and the news article definitely meant smoke.

"Rose, you must know this is serious. I understand you've some feelings for Vincenzo, but it has to stop. You need to go to the police. The article doesn't mention you directly yet, but that will change."

Her mother chimed in, her tone severe. "If the police find out you could have stopped him and you didn't, things will only get worse for you. How could you be so foolish?"

Rose's voice trembled, a mix of hurt and defiance. "Isn't it obvious, ma? I did it for the money. And you don't know him like I do. You haven't seen what I've seen."

Staring at the newspaper article, a whirlwind of thoughts and emotions engulfed Rose. She recalled the joy Vincenzo had brought to the widows he'd helped and the happiness he'd given her. Was the tender, caring man she'd fallen for capable of such deceit? The police's interest was deeply troubling.

But Betty and her mother's voices echoed in her head, cautioning her against believing in fairy tales. East End girls never met their Prince Charming.

Rose felt caught between her love for Vincenzo and her sense of duty. What would become of the widows relying on him if he were exposed? And what of her own heart if she never saw him again? Reporting him would be the ultimate betrayal and surely drive him away for good.

She couldn't ignore the situation, but she needed time to think. She started preparing some potatoes, the menial task giving her a small excuse to be alone.

"I've made a decision," she announced, the rusty peeler in her hand.

"Good, let's go to the police station!" Betty urged.

"No. I'm going to ask Vincenzo to stop before it's too late."

"Are you mad?" Betty retorted.

"Wait and see," Rose said as she tore out the story from the paper.

As she steeled herself for the challenging task ahead, she was unaware that finding Vincenzo again would become a Herculean endeavour. With no knowledge of his whereabouts or how he spent his days or nights when they were apart, she faced an arduous task. Little did she know that her pursuit of Vincenzo's true intentions would not only be a test of her own resolve but would also bring about an unexpected and permanent transformation in her life.

18

FOLLOWING THE TRAIL

Collins and Parker entered The Hoxton Candle Emporium, confident that their visit would prove productive for their investigation.

The shop was a delightful haven of candlelight, filled with every hue and shape of waxen creation. There was the scent of hot wax and burning wick, mingled with the faint homely aroma of spices and fruits from the emporium's comforting scented range. All around there were shelves brimming with tapers, tealights, beeswax candles, thick church candles, cake candles and even a few ornate candelabras. A brass chandelier dangled precariously from a window latch.

Behind the counter, the kindly shopkeeper sat quietly, his white hair neatly combed over to hide his expanding bald patch. Stacked before him were boxes of all sorts of candles, including a decorative display of Price's Patent Candles showcased in a bespoke glass case on the left counter.

The officers approached the man, the sound of their footsteps echoing softly in the cosy shop. The shopkeeper looked up from his ledger and was surprised to see two officers of the law in attendance. "Good day, gentlemen," he said warmly. "How may I be of service?"

"We have some questions about a purchase made from your shop," said Parker, sliding the empty box across the table. "We want to know who came in for a box of these. They're quite a premium brand. I wouldn't imagine you shift many boxes a week?"

"Blimey, lads—I mean, officers—we get dozens of people popping in every day. I can't be expected to remember what everyone takes home with them."

"Well, the chap we think might have bought them is a bit special. Wears a velvet cloak and a top hat sometimes. Tall. Exotic looking. Might go under the name of Sanders. We have a sketch of him. Take a look."

Collins pushed Sebastian's notebook towards the shopkeeper.

"Ah, yes," the shopkeeper replied, "that was the gentleman who made such a fuss when he came in. Most insistent on those particular candles, he was. Wouldn't take another brand."

"Do you remember when he purchased the candles? Does he come in on a regular basis?" asked Collins.

The shopkeeper shook his head.

"I'm afraid I don't remember. Perhaps my apprentice might know."

The older detective glanced at his companion, then nodded.

"Is he here? We'd like to speak to him."

The shopkeeper called out to a young man battling to check in a delivery in the back of the store. He emerged from the shadows, thin and pasty, with a shock of unruly ginger hair.

"Ah good. There you are."

The lad nodded nervously and offered both men a limp handshake.

"Eric, do you remember the customer who purchased that box of Price's Patent Candles? This fellow?" asked Collins, showing him the illustration.

The apprentice nodded.

"Yes, sir. I remember him well. He was here around six o'clock, on the fifth of October, I believe. I remember because I took my brother and sisters to Wilton's Music Hall. I wanted him to hurry up and make his purchases and get off home. Didn't want to miss the start, not at those prices."

"The night Harry Champion played?"

"Yes, that's right, officer."

Collins and Parker exchanged a knowing look, then Parker flipped open his notebook and jotted down the details. The good news was the police now had more to go on. The bad news was it wasn't much.

"Thank you. You have been most helpful," said Inspector Collins. "If he should come back, please let one of our officers on his beat know. All the policemen in the area are aware of this fellow."

"What's he done, exactly?"

"Just let one of our lads know. Best you don't approach him yourself. He has got a bit of a short fuse, as you know."

The detectives nodded in gratitude to the men then headed out of the door, leaving the retailers to their everyday business once more and to worry what their customer might have done to become a wanted man. As the officers stepped out into the street, Collins glanced back at the premises.

"At least staking out the shop in the evenings might be a better bet than the mornings, Parker."

"Aye, sir."

The enigmatic Mr Sanders, the mysterious psychic, might still be eluding them, but at least they were now another step closer to unravelling his secrets.

19

THE RELENTLESS PURSUIT

For three gruelling days, Rose trudged through the bustling streets of Whitechapel, Bow, and Stepney, her heart heavy with worry and desperation. Despite her growing doubts, she clung to the hope that she would find Vincenzo and succeed in appealing to his conscience.

She explored dimly lit taverns, warm and tiny tea rooms, and echoing hotel receptions. She walked through parks, crunching autumn leaves beneath her new boots, and scrutinised countless shops, always scanning the faces of passersby for any sign of her elusive partner.

Alas, Vincenzo was nowhere to be found, leaving Rose to question hers and Betty's judgement and be crushed by the depth of her infatuation. Each day, her heart grew heavier, but she refused to give up, determined to plead with Vincenzo and make him see the error of his ways. But how could she do that when he was nowhere to be found?

As she walked, Rose couldn't shake the feeling that she was being followed. Every time she turned around, there was no one there, but the sensation persisted. She quickened her pace, and sometimes the footsteps behind her matched hers, sometimes not. Fear prickled at the back of her neck. Could it be Vincenzo? Or was it someone else entirely?

Meanwhile, a mere two miles away from Rose's desperate search, Vincenzo sat hunched over the pages of the latest newspapers, alternating between his modest Shoreditch hotel room and the British Library Reading Room with its impressive archive of trade directories, periodicals and old newspapers. The rustling sound of paper being turned as he eagerly scanned the obituaries for precisely the right kind of information filled the place. So intensely focused on his selfish pursuits was he that he had completely missed the news story about his own nefarious activities. The more papers he reviewed, the more his greedy eyes narrowed with determination. Lately, he paid attention only to the death notices and written eulogies, searching for his next perfect prey.

Soon, Vincenzo identified a promising new victim. Out came his fountain pen as he crafted another faked letter of condolence, oozing with false sympathy:

Dear Mrs Worthington,

I was deeply saddened to hear about the tragic loss of your beloved husband, Mr Worthington.

I had the pleasure of knowing him through our mutual involvement in the Osborne Yachting Club on the Isle of Wight. His presence will be sorely missed at Cowes Week, and I can't begin to fathom the pain you must be experiencing.

Please accept my heartfelt condolences. If I can help you in any way, I am, as always, your obedient servant.

Yours sincerely,

Mr Sanders.

Next, with a satisfied smile, he sent a telegram to Rose, utterly oblivious to her nearby frantic search and the emotional turmoil she was experiencing. But the telegram wouldn't be for Mrs Worthington. He had another altogether different target in mind for their next rendezvous.

On the fourth day, while Rose was out on another fruitless search, a telegram arrived early in the evening at Brady Street. Mrs O'Shaughnessy, sensing the significance of the message, sent young Billy to knock for Betty, asking her to come around immediately.

"Should we open it without Rose? It feels wrong, Betty?"

"Now's not the time to lack a backbone, Ellen. Give it here!"

The two women carefully steamed open the envelope and read the note.

"Saturday night. Mrs Wade. See you at the tavern at seven pm."

"He's got a lot of front going back there, Ellen! Perfect!" said Betty, brandishing the newspaper article.

"Back where? What's perfect?"

"We've got the address she's going to, and we've got a supporter!"

"Who?"

"Sebastian Wade. I'm going to tell him I know who Vincenzo is and see if he'll get his mother to invite him without Rose. I'll explain that she's being deceived. I'll take this telegram as proof. Mind if I take a few pennies for the bus fare? And I'll need one of Rose's nice dresses if there's one still upstairs. She told me she's hidden them under her bed. I can't go looking like this."

Before Ellen could inquire about the validity of Betty's ambitious plan, the young woman had already dashed to grab one of the garments from under Rose's shared bed, and pocketed the last of the O'Shaughnessy's money from the metal tin. Then she rushed back to her annex to put on her sophisticated disguise.

Soon, Betty navigated the bustling streets of London by omnibus heading towards Sebastian Wade's house, clutching the newspaper clipping that held the key to putting an end to Vincenzo's deceptions.

As Betty arrived at the doorstep of the Wade residence, she rang the bell, quickly wiped her sweaty hands on Rose's pretty dress, and then waited anxiously for a response. The door opened a fraction at first, then a little more. A maid's icy voice greeted her.

"Can I help you?"

"Yes, please," Betty said, forcing a smile. "I'd like to speak with Mr Wade, Sebastian Wade, if that's possible."

"I'm afraid that's out of the question."

"It's about this story in the newspaper," she said offering it up for inspection. "I know who the man mentioned is—Mr Sanders. And I think I know where he will be."

"I see. And who may I say is calling?" the maid asked in the same frosty tone, clearly unimpressed.

Betty was taken aback by the hostile reception but answered calmly.

"My name is Betty Hardacre."

"Very well, Miss Hardacre. I shall inform Mr Wade of your presence, but I can't guarantee he will wish to see you."

Betty's eyes scanned the affluent street, taking in the ornate gardens and the thick, expensive curtains that concealed the lavish interiors of the grand homes. A few agonising minutes later, the maid reappeared, her expression stern. Betty's heart sank as the maid shook her head.

"I'm sorry, but Mr Wade is not interested in hearing your story. Now, please leave."

Betty, now at her feistiest, refused to budge, standing firm on the doorstep.

"No. I need to speak with him. It's crucial that he knows what I know."

The maid was clearly taken aback by Betty's determination and tried again to make her leave.

"I've told you Mr Wade isn't interested in hearing your story, Miss Hardacre. Please go now, or I will be forced to call the authorities."

However, Betty held her ground, her conviction unwavering. Despite knowing that she was on shaky ground with seemingly circumstantial piece of evidence, she was confident that if she could just have a few moments with Mr Wade, he would understand the gravity of her words. She held out the newspaper clipping for emphasis and declared once again her need to speak with him. The maid huffed in exasperation.

"I said no," she bellowed in her most authoritative voice. "I'm not going anywhere! I'll damn well wait here until he comes back."

A tall figure appeared at the door, his posture commanding and his attire impeccable. He wore a dark suit and seemed a little aloof. She quickly realised that this must be Sebastian. He didn't seem pleased to see her and he wasn't. For him, there had been enough scandal at the Willows the last a lifetime.

"What is all this noise about? You madam, shrieking like a banshee at my front door?" he demanded sternly, his eyes fixed firmly on Betty's face trying to discern her motives.

Betty took a deep breath before speaking with newfound courage.

"I have some information that I believe may be crucial to you, sir."

She handed him the newspaper clipping she had been clutching tightly since leaving Brady Street.

"I know who this man is, and the assistant who helped him. The young woman?"

"How do you know about that?" Sebastian's eyes narrowed with suspicion. "And why not go to the police?"

"Because I know the real truth! It's not as clear cut as it seems, especially with the assistant. Please? Just a minute of your time is all I ask."

Not wanting to attract any more unwanted gossip from the neighbours, Sebastian finally relented.

"So be it. I'll grant your wish. You'd better let this woman in, Miss Potts."

The maid led Betty to a parlour where Sebastian had already taken a seat, his powerful presence filling the room. As Betty entered, she couldn't help but feel a little inconsequential under his cold, hard gaze. Despite her reticence, she squared her shoulders and took a seat at the table, determined to deliver her message.

"What is it that you have to say?" Sebastian demanded gruffly, annoyed she had sat down without an invitation, imagining countless fleas making a home in his plush upholstery.

Betty took a seat, her elegant dress accentuating her figure. As she spoke, outlining Vincenzo's nefarious scheme, Sebastian's mind raced with a mix of anger and fear. He knew his mother's welfare was at stake, but the fact that at least two other vulnerable widows in the area were also targeted made his blood boil. And then there was the matter of the girl, Rose. Betty's account of Vincenzo manipulating Rose left him seething with rage.

"Manipulated, you say?" he growled, his eyes flashing with anger.

"Yes. He knows he couldn't visit women's houses without a chaperone. They pretend to be brother and sister. Rose complies because he's been hinting they have a future together. He recruited her after she saw his mesmerism stage act at Crendon Pleasure Gardens."

"That place is a den of iniquity," yelled Wade, his voice laced with disgust. "The sooner it's closed, the better."

"This Vincenzo fellow is a right charlatan."

"He will answer for his actions, mark my words. Using an innocent girl, luring her into a world of glamour and deception, making her a pawn in a sinister game funded by defrauding widows. Has he no shame? No woman should be subjected to such treatment. We'll put an end to this, once and for all. I'll get a message to Collins immediately."

"I suggest you don't," Betty interjected.

"I beg your pardon?"

"Well, he's coming to see your mother again—on Saturday."

"How do you know that?"

"Will she be free at eight pm on Saturday, Yes or no? Because that's when Vincenzo is due to call. He's meeting the assistant at seven so he can be here by eight. How else would I know when your mother would be alone if not for the message he sent? I've never been here before in my life!"

Sebastian's face contorted as he worked out where he, his brother, the Lewis's, and the rest of the staff would be on Saturday. The woman was right. His eyes widened, and his fist thumped the table when Betty played her trump card and she put the telegram on the table. Sebastian snatched the slip of paper and examined it. His eyes stuck on two words in particular. 'Mrs Wade'.

"I'm pleading with you, sir. We need to report Vincenzo but not Rose. She's guilty of being foolish and infatuated, but she doesn't deserve a prison sentence. I think she's planning on stopping him from coming, but as you know he's got the gift of the gab with most ladies. She's only working there because her old boss, Mrs Kelly, died. It's her two shillings a week from the mesmerist that's keeping her family afloat."

"He steals thirty pounds off my mother and he gives her two shillings? This man really is quite something."

"Let's shadow him, separate him from Rose. He's so greedy he will risk coming on his own. I just know it. I can tell him Rose sent me. I'll tell him something, anything, just to give her a chance."

Betty was fighting for Rose just as she had when she strode down the alleyway to fight off the bullies when they were girls.

"I suppose so," Sebastian agreed begrudgingly.

"Mr Wade, I know it's hard for you to accept, but I think this is the only way to punish the guilty party. I want you to promise me something though—promise me that if things get too hard for Rose and it goes to court, you'll be there to stand up for her. She's young and naive and has been drawn into Vincenzo's trap just like your mother was."

Sebastian let the telegram flutter through his fingers. Betty tucked it down the front of her dress for safekeeping and glared at him. It was crunch time.

"Alright, Miss Hardacre, I promise. If it comes to that, I'll stand up for her in court. But let's hope we can avoid that. It would do my career no good at all. Things would be much easier if we got this cad to plead guilty as soon as possible."

"Shall we go to the station together then, Mr Wade? They're bound to believe you more than me?"

20

THE PLAN COMES TOGETHER

That afternoon, a cold wind blew through the streets of London as Betty and Sebastian sat side by side in the Wade family coach, drawn by two powerful horses, through the streets of Hampstead, guided by loyal Mr Lewis. The dark wood-panelled coach was adorned with gold trim and had the Wade family crest engraved on the door. The carriage's velvet-upholstered seats and intricate interior woodwork showed the fine taste and wealth of the Hampstead family. As they arrived, Betty noted that Camden Police Station, a sturdy red-brick building with elegant arched windows and a large imposing oak door, stood as a symbol of law and order in the area.

Mr Lewis, wrapped in his greatcoat, stepped down from the driver's seat and held the door open for Betty and Sebastian to alight.

"I'll wait here and keep an eye on the coach, sir." he informed them. "Take as long as you need."

Inside the police station, Betty and Sebastian approached the duty officer's desk, where Constable

Bush, a stocky man with a thick moustache, regarded them with a sceptical gaze. It was clear that he didn't expect the likes of a Hampstead lawyer and an East End seamstress to be reporting a case together.

Undeterred by Constable Bush's apprehensions, Betty began to explain the situation involving the mesmerist and his nefarious scheme. Sebastian, standing tall beside her, provided support by occasionally interjecting with crucial details. Constable Bush raised an eyebrow frequently, clearly finding the story somewhat difficult to comprehend.

"You expect me to believe that you know who this fellow is who's swindling widows out of their money by pretending to communicate with their dead husbands?" he asked incredulously.

"Yes, sir," Betty replied firmly, her hands clenched into fists at her side. "I've seen it with my own eyes. He's using his charm and lies to manipulate innocent women like my friend Rose, and he's doing it right under our noses."

"I reported it too to Inspector Collins. You can ask him if you like. In fact, ask him to come and see us. He'll get this straightened out in a trice."

Constable Bush looked them both up and down, noting the contrast between Sebastian's tailored suit and

Betty's more modest attire. The unlikely duo made for an unusual sight in the reception area.

"Inspector Collins is out on urgent business. If you'd like to come back—?"

Betty reached into her pocket and pulled out a telegram, and slammed it on the bench.

"This is the proof we have, officer," she said, handing it over to Constable Bush. "It's a message from my friend, who's caught up in all of this. You need to put a stop to it."

"All right, all right," Bush relented as he read the brief text. "I'll see what I can do."

Just then, Inspector Collins returned the station. Recognising Sebastian from their previous encounter, he approached the man with purpose.

"Good to see you again, Mr Wade. Constable Bush, I'll take it from here," he said, taking the telegram from the duty officer and quickly scanning its contents.

Bush took Collins to one side and whispered in his ear.

"Good luck with these two, sir. I reckon they've been on the gin all afternoon. Right pair of crackpots."

"These two are not crackpots, Bush. I'm not sure what you do during my morning briefings, but it's certainly not listening. This is why policemen have two ears and one mouth. To listen twice as much as we speak. These people have vital information about the counterfeit clairvoyant we're supposed to be apprehending."

"Oh, right sir. The Mr Sanders case. With you now."

"Finally!"

Collins rolled his eyes as he invited Betty and Sebastian to the incident room to interview them. He stuck his head around the door.

"Oh, and Bush—"

"Yes, sir?"

"Get the canteen to bring us some tea."

"On it, sir!"

"Oh, and another thing. Put an ear trumpet on your Christmas list! You might have a better idea of what's going on around here!"

The heavy door slammed behind Collins as he let go of the handle and took his seat.

With renewed determination, Betty and Sebastian plotted with Collins as he began to set his plan into motion.

*

Outside, Mr Lewis realised he'd forgotten to share a vital piece of information he had learned from his brother-in-law during a boozy trip to the horse races at Epsom. Constable Bush took him to the inspector immediately.

"Sir, I just remembered," Mr Lewis said, a hint of embarrassment in his voice. "My brother-in-law mentioned that this boss's household in Islington was approached by someone who sounds like our man. Her husband had just passed, see? I apologise that the details are sketchy, but it might help the police. Not sure of the name. What was it now? Phipps, Phillips? Yeah, Phillips. Anyway, I do know she lives at 'The Larches.'"

Emboldened by his new information, Inspector Collins was determined to uncover the truth about Vincenzo sooner rather than later. He strode to one of the other back offices.

"Get yourself over to The Larches, Parker and interview the widow will you? Get one of the stable lads to sort out a carriage to get you there sharpish. Time is of the essence."

"Aye, sir," said Ted as he grabbed his trusty notepad and stubby pencil.

*

Parker made his way to the Phillips' household, noting another impressive building nestled in one of the quieter avenues of Islington, and rang the little brass doorbell.

A young maid opened the door, her eyes wide with surprise at the sight of the uniformed officer standing on the doorstep. Nevertheless, ever the professional, she quickly recovered her composure and invited Parker inside.

The maid led the sergeant through the grand hallway, and fetched her widowed employer. Parker showed Mrs Phillips the sketches of Rose and Vincenzo, hoping that she might recognise them. As she studied the portraits, her eyes widened in recognition.

"Yes, I've seen both of them," the widow said, her voice wavering slightly. "That man, Mr Sanders, came to our house not long ago."

"Might I ask what for? I appreciate it might be a delicate matter."

Mrs Phillips retrieved a handwritten condolence letter from Vincenzo that he had sent just after her husband's passing. She handed it to Parker, who carefully examined the envelope. He noticed that the printed return address was that of a local London hotel, which he suspected might be Vincenzo's hideout.

"Thank you, Mrs Phillips," Parker said, his voice brimming with compassion. "Would it be possible for me to keep this letter as evidence?"

"I don't see why not."

"And, please forgive my intrusion, but did you happen to arrange a séance to contact your late husband?"

Mrs Phillips hesitated for a moment before admitting that she had, indeed, paid Vincenzo for a session. Just as she confirmed it, her daughter Susan reappeared.

Susan, aware of her mother's vulnerability, stood protectively by her side. Parker addressed both women, asking if they would be willing to contact the police if Vincenzo made any further attempts to reach out to them. Mrs Phillips and Susan exchanged a glance, and both agreed.

As Parker prepared to leave, the women embraced each other, drawing strength from their shared experience. The maid, sensing that her presence was needed elsewhere, quietly escorted Parker out of the house and back to the waiting police carriage.

*

Upon his return to the station, Sergeant Parker presented the condolence letter to Collins, who was visibly delighted with another solid lead. The inspector immediately set about organising a team of four uniformed policemen to visit the hotel listed on the envelope with a view to arresting Vincenzo, while another officer was dispatched to The Eagle Tavern with a sketch of their man in hand to see if anyone recognised him.

In the meantime, Collins continued working with Betty and Sebastian to learn more about the suspects and their methods.

*

Unfortunately, the address on the envelope proved to be a dead end. The policemen returned empty-handed, explaining that it was merely an old envelope Vincenzo had reused and not the Shoreditch hotel where, unknown to them, he was staying. Collins knew they couldn't check every hotel in the city, there were simply too many and promptly gave up with that idea.

However, there was a glimmer of hope. The officer who had visited The Eagle Tavern reported that one of the barmen recognised Vincenzo's sketched face and confirmed that he often came in around seven pm on Saturdays. Armed with this new information, Collins and his team prepared to apprehend Vincenzo and bring an end to his deceit once and for all.

Back in the incident room at Camden, Inspector Collins, Parker, and the other officers huddled around a map of the city, outlining the plan in hushed tones, assigning roles and responsibilities to each member of the team. Betty and Sebastian stood nearby, ready to play their parts in the sting operation. Inspector Collins recapped the strategy.

"Betty, you will shadow Rose from her
house and try to divert her just after the

meeting. One of my officers will keep her safe. Hopefully, the same man will hear Rose pleading with Vincenzo not to go ahead with the Willows visit. That should help with her case at least. The jury will look more favourably on her plight when it comes to trial. You tell her that her mother is gravely Ill and she must return home immediately and offer to take her place at The Willows. I am confident the greedy old goat is bound to insist the meeting goes ahead. Sebastian, you are responsible for outfitting Betty in a convincing enough manner to pass as another of Vincenzo's sisters to chaperone the session so your mother doesn't suspect anything. If she gets cold feet and calls it all off, we're scuppered. Can you organise something between you?"

Betty and Sebastian nodded, as Parker noted down the last of the details.

"Sebastian and I will hide in the servant's corridor. I'll get there at six pm so you can sneak me in without your mother noticing. From there, we will be able to observe the meeting between Vincenzo and Mrs Wade and catch him in the act. Betty can be our eyes and ears in the room in case it's difficult to hear. Sid, Harry, John, Bill, you lot are to wait outside in the bushes in case he makes a run for it. Two at the front, two at the back."

"Yes, boss," they chorused.

Ted Parker stood up, his eyes meeting everyone's turn.

"I know this won't be an easy task. Vincenzo is a master of deception. That devious mind of his can spot something amiss from a mile off. He's got Rose and Mrs Wade wrapped around his little finger. But we can't let that stop us. We've got a plan. We each know our roles. Let's bring this criminal to justice."

Collins took a deep breath and smiled.

"I know we will catch him red-handed. I feel it in my bones. Roll on Saturday night."

"I need to make a move," Betty said to the group, "Rose normally gets home around about now and I need to sneak the telegram back to her so she doesn't suspect anything."

*

As soon as the meeting at the police station ended, Mr Lewis hopped off his coach footplate and rushed over and helped Betty inside.

"Quickly now, Mr Lewis," the young woman said, closing the door behind her. "We must make haste to Whitechapel."

Betty settled into the plush seats, feeling the weight of the operation heavy on her shoulders. She couldn't let her nerves get the best of her, not when so much was at stake. The coach jostled through the crowded streets, weaving through the throngs of people and horses. Betty clutched the telegram in her hand, anxious to get back to Rose's home in time.

Finally, the coach pulled up close by the dingy Whitechapel lodgings. Betty stepped out, thanked Mr Lewis, and peered inside the O'Shaughnessy's lodgings, glad to see Rose was not at home.

As Betty entered the small room where Ellen and Billy were seated, she took a deep breath.

"I need to explain what's been going on with the police this afternoon."

Ellen's eyes widened with concern as Billy looked up at Betty with curiosity. Betty quickly explained the situation with the police and Vincenzo. Billy looked up at her with wide eyes.

"Rose will be alright, won't she?" he asked.
"If she goes to prison, I'll be heartbroken."

Betty put a comforting hand on the boy's shoulder.

"The police know she is trying to stop Vincenzo. I am going to take her place on Saturday," she said firmly. "I'll make sure she doesn't get into too much trouble."

Billy gazed at Betty, reflecting on what she had to say.

"Can I help too?" he asked eagerly.

"Actually, you can," she said. "Before Rose comes back, I need you to go out and look for her. And when you see her, pretend to drop off this telegram again," she said, holding up the folded piece of paper. "That way, Rose won't suspect anything and will think it's a new delivery. Not a word of this to her, promise?"

"Promise," said Billy solemnly as he headed off to carry out his part in the plan.

Ellen turned to Betty with gratitude in her eyes.

"Thank you, Betty," she said. "You're a good friend to Rose."

Betty smiled back, feeling a sense of pride at being able to help her friend and her family. But there was still much work to be done if they were to catch Vincenzo and bring him to justice. Ellen looked worried, but Betty tried to reassure her.

"Let's hope Sebastian can get her a lenient sentence," she said, hoping that their plan would work and Rose wouldn't have to suffer too much.

Just then, Rose burst into the room, clutching the earlier telegram in her hands. Thankfully, she ignored discussing the telegram and the conversation moved on.

"How's your day been, love?" her mother asked wryly.

Rose gave a convincing cover story and didn't breathe a word about her real reason for being missing all day hunting for Vincenzo yet again. Betty breathed a sigh of relief, knowing that they still had a chance to catch the charlatan and clear Rose's name.

As Saturday approached, Betty couldn't help but feel nervous. The plan was tenuous at best, and everything hinged on their ability to outsmart a man blessed with almost unrivalled cunning. Would they be able to pull it off? Only time would tell.

22

HEARTFELT PERSUASION

Upstairs in the cramped shared bedroom, Rose carefully folded her finest dress and placed it into a worn, yet serviceable, bag. Her pulse quickened as she prepared to leave for her meeting with the enigmatic Vincenzo. Although she wasn't entirely certain if the psychic performances were genuine or fraudulent, she knew that the men from the widows' families were growing increasingly suspicious.

Rose's heart was torn with conflicting emotions as she prepared to meet Vincenzo. On one hand, she feared losing the love of her life if she were to confront him about their séances. On the other hand, she knew that the consequences of continuing to fall out with the widow's powerful wealthy son would be dire. As she silently rehearsed what she would say to him, her voice trembled. She knew that this was a pivotal moment that would determine their future together, and she hoped that Vincenzo would listen to reason and abandon their dangerous enterprise.

Downstairs in the cramped front room, Ellen shuffled the deck of playing cards with trembling hands, while Betty, Billy and Davy exchanged fleeting glances filled with worry. Ellen cleared her throat.

"Who's up for a game of Snap?"

As the trio engaged in the spirited game, their laughter gradually grew more genuine, and the sharp claps of their hands slapping the cards on the rickety table filled the room with energy. Focusing intently on the game, they hoped their animated distraction would be enough to keep their concerns hidden from Rose.

"Right. I'm off to work," Rose announced, trying to conceal the bag with the dress behind her. "Don't wait up."

"Take your coat love, it looks like rain," said her mother.

"Yes, ma. Stop fussing! Bye."

Betty watched intently from the window as Rose stepped out of the house and began to make her way down the narrow street.

"Quick, Ellen, help me get changed," the young woman said, her voice barely above a whisper.

Together, they hurriedly dressed Betty in the outfit Mr Lewis had dropped off. Ellen adjusted Betty's hat and gloves, giving her an approving nod.

"You look the part, now go and be careful," Ellen urged her.

Betty took a deep breath, put her tatty old coat over her posh frock and slipped out the front door, her heart pounding in her chest. She hurried along the cobblestone back-streets, careful to keep a reasonable distance between herself and Rose. As she moved stealthily through the bustling city, she couldn't help but feel a sense of dread knowing that the success of their plan depended on her ability to shadow Rose, and then persuade her that her place was by at her sick mother's bedside.

With her keen eyes focused on Rose, Betty followed her from a distance, blending seamlessly into the crowd, her old coat allowing her to become just another face in the throng of people that filled the busy streets of London. As Rose moved forward, Betty expertly darted from one alcove to another, using the various nooks and crannies to conceal her presence.

As she shadowed Rose, Betty's heart raced with anticipation and anxiety. She knew the importance of remaining undetected, and her instincts and agility served her well. The streets were teeming with activity, yet, Betty's determination and focus never wavered as she continued to pursue Rose, remaining a silent and invisible guardian in the crowded city.

*

As Rose neared the place where she was to meet Vincenzo, her heart fluttered. The powerful pull of love clouded her good sense, momentarily causing her to forget the perils that accompanied their secret rendezvous. Nonetheless, she steeled herself, intent on persuading him to abandon the séance that evening. Deep within her heart, Rose harboured a steadfast belief that Vincenzo's affections for her were genuine. She couldn't help but imagine a life shared with him, a life unburdened by the hazards and duplicity that presently beset them. With each step she took towards their fateful encounter, her resolve to safeguard their love and ensure their future together only grew stronger.

Betty, determined to keep pace with Rose, found herself struggling against the increasingly bustling crowd and the onslaught of obstacles that impeded her progress. At times, she narrowly avoided collisions with pedestrians, delivery lads with sack barrows or carriage traffic while crossing the busy streets. Relief washed over her as she finally caught up, just in time to see Rose disappear into The Eagle Tavern.

With a dry mouth and clammy palms, Betty scanned the surrounding area before spotting a side entrance to the establishment. With a deep breath, she prepared to slip inside, her eyes filled with both concern and determination.

What a shame it would be that Inspector Collins's plan would soon begin to fall apart at the seams.

The Eagle Tavern was a dimly lit haven, filled with the heavy scent of tobacco smoke and the boisterous laughter of patrons. The lively melody of soprano singing bawdy bar room songs accompanied by an excited pianist filled the air once more while servers deftly navigated through the crowds, bearing steaming plates of food and frothy mugs of ale.

Rose's heart raced with excitement and anticipation as she spotted Vincenzo seated at a secluded table in the back. His charming smile lit up his face as he greeted her with outstretched hands, his eyes sparkling with affection.

"My dearest Rose, how lovely to see you," he exclaimed. "I've been eagerly awaiting our meeting."

"—me too," Rose said, hesitating for a moment, her mind racing with thoughts of the danger they faced.

She was flustered and looked in her bag for the newspaper clipping about the fake mesmerist but it was gone. She fidgeted, cursing under her breath. Vincenzo's warm gaze and gentle touch on her hand put her at ease, and she took a deep breath before unburdening herself.

"Vincenzo, forgive me, but could we call off the séance tonight," she said, her voice trembling with concern.

"What do you mean, 'call it off', my dear? We cannot simply abandon our plans. Mrs Wade is expecting us, and our reputation as professionals is at stake," he replied, his voice low and measured.

"Her son was livid last time he turned up.
Don't you think it's too risky? What if he
goes to the police? What if he already has,"
Rose pleaded, her eyes filled with worry.

Vincenzo's expression softened as he listened to her as she rifled through her bag again, but he remained resolute.

"My dear, I understand your concerns, but
we cannot let fear rule our lives. We must
press on and do what we do best. I have no
doubt that everything will go smoothly, just
as it always has. You know firsthand how
wonderful it is to hear a loved one's voice
when they have passed. And there was Mrs
Greaves and Mrs Phillips, and Susan.
Sebastian is jealous of the trust Mrs Wade
puts in us. It is her decision not his."

Although Rose's attraction to Vincenzo was deepening, she couldn't help but feel like they were playing with fire.

"Vincenzo, please reconsider," she insisted, her voice shaking. "I'm begging you, let's not go."

Vincenzo's smile faltered for a moment, and Rose could see a flicker of annoyance in his eyes. Betty, watching from a distance, felt a knot form in her stomach. She had warned Rose about Vincenzo's unscrupulous nature, but it seemed her friend was too smitten to listen.

"Rose, please don't be so dramatic. We've done this plenty of times before, and everything has gone without a hitch," he replied, his voice growing more stern. "I am sure Mrs Wade will have made sure her son stays out all evening this time."

Not wanting to alienate thr girl any more, Vincenzo's expression softened once more, and he took her hand in his.

"My dear, let us not dwell on such unpleasant thoughts. We are together now, and that is all that matters. Let us enjoy each other's company and worry about the rest later," he said, his voice gentle and reassuring.

As they spoke, noses inches away from each other as they leaned in, Rose failed to notice a group of rough-looking men nearby, their attention clearly focused on their private conversation. Vincenzo, sensing Rose's apprehension, gently placed a hand on hers once more. Betty's teeth ground together.

"Now, my dear, let us focus on the séance for now. We can discuss your concerns afterward. I promise."

Rose reluctantly agreed, silently promising herself that she would confront him later. Given the amount of time he seemed to spend pouring over details in the newspapers, she thought it was rather odd he didn't spot last week's article.

As the evening wore on, another shadowy figure slipped into the tavern, eyes trained on Betty from a distance. Unaware of the mysterious watcher, Betty remained focused on the task at hand.

After a while, Rose excused herself to change into her outfit for the séance. Vincenzo, too, made preparations to leave. Once they emerged from the tavern, Betty resumed her pursuit, intent on finding a moment to interrupt and to fib to Rose about her mother's grave condition. However, fate had other plans.

The skies opened up, unleashing a torrential downpour that sent people scurrying in every direction, seeking shelter and clamouring for cabs. The chaos of the rain-soaked streets made it nearly impossible for Betty to keep her eyes on Rose and Vincenzo.

Amid the confusion, Rose and Vincenzo slipped away, vanishing like shadows in the stormy night, leaving Betty standing alone, drenched and frustrated. Little did she know that the other pair of eyes was still watching her as she stood defeated and deflated in the busy street.

Betty's heart sank as she watched Rose and Vincenzo disappear into the waiting cab, her plan to interrupt their meeting thwarted by the sudden downpour. The rain was coming down in sheets now, making it difficult to see and move quickly.

As she hurried through the streets, Betty's senses were bombarded by the sights, sounds and smells of the bustling city in the rain. People jostled for space under awnings and umbrellas, their hurried footsteps echoing against the slick pavement. The pitter-patter of raindrops hitting the ground, the hissing of carriage wheels on wet cobblestones, and the distant rumble of thunder combined to create a symphony of sound.

Betty's mind raced with worry and frustration as she tried to keep pace with Rose and Vincenzo. She knew that time was running out, and that any delay could jeopardise their entire plan.

Suddenly, Betty collided with a passer-by, causing him to stumble and nearly lose his footing. The man turned to her with a scowl, his face twisted in anger.

"Watch where you're going, you clumsy oaf!" he spat.

Betty could see the man's flushed face and bulging veins, the raindrops falling from his hat and the mud splatters on his coat. Her heart sank as she realised that she had lost sight of Rose and Vincenzo, the delay and the passer-by's anger causing further frustration and delay.

Just as she was about to continue on her way, Betty bumped into someone else, and this time she recognised him. It was Davy, Rose's brother. Betty could see that Davy was soaked to the bone, his hair and clothes plastered to his skin. Water dripped from his nose and chin as he glared at her with narrowed eyes. She could also see the anger and worry etched on his face, and could feel the tension radiating from his body.

"What the blazes are you doing here?" Davy growled, his voice low and menacing. "You should be at home, out of this blasted rain!"

"I'm trying to follow Rose and Vincenzo," Betty explained, her voice trembling with emotion. "But the rain and the crowds are making it difficult."

Davy's expression softened slightly as he realised the situation.

"Did you see where they went?" he asked, his tone now more concerned than angry.

Betty could see the raindrops clinging to his lashes and the dampness of his clothes, the sound of the rain making it difficult to hear each other. She shook her head.

"No, I lost them in the crowds. But I have a plan to follow, we need to go to The Willows."

"I don't care about the plan," Davy said stubbornly, his voice rising with frustration. "I need to sort this out with Sebastian, man to man."

Betty knew that interfering with the rest of the sting was not an option.

"It's too late for that, Davy. We can't interfere with the rest of the plan. All we can

do now is testify to Rose's good character.
Leave it to the police."

Davy looked like he was about to argue, but then hesitated, sense finally prevailing over spite..

"You're right," he said, his voice softer now.
"I just—I can't lose her too. First, our losing father, and now our sister facing prison. It's too much."

Betty put a comforting hand on Davy's shoulder.

"I know," she said, her voice gentle. "But we'll get justice for Rose. I promise."

*

Inspector Collins arrived at the Wade's Hampstead townhouse, hoping to catch the con man Vincenzo in the act. The lawman felt a sense of unease as he was led to Wade's cluttered parlour. Like the Mona Lisa, the beady eyes of the stuffed falcon watched him as he walked to the sofa and took a seat.

Mr Lewis appeared at the hidden servants' door, closely followed by Mr Wade himself. The door creaked open further and Mr Lewis gestured for the man to enter and hide from view. Mr Wade and Collins quietly slipped into the hidden servants' corridor, which had a secret peephole that allowed them to observe the parlour without being seen. Collins' heart raced as he considered the high stakes of the case and the possibility of finally apprehending Vincenzo and his accomplices in the act.

The staff, including the head of the household Mrs Lewis and the maids, observed the strange behaviour of Mr Lewis as he let Mr Wade and the detective into the hidden corridor. They exchanged confused glances but knew better than to inquire about the situation. They continued to go about their duties, acting as if nothing out of the ordinary was happening to avoid arousing suspicion with Mrs Wade, who was getting ready in her bedroom.

Mrs Wade descended the grand staircase, her grief momentarily lifted by the anticipation of the upcoming séance. She entered the cluttered parlour, adorned with various trinkets and photographs of her late husband, Frederick. She walked over to his portrait, hanging proudly above the mantelpiece, and gazed lovingly at it.

"Oh, Frederick, my love, I miss you so much. But tonight, I feel like you're here with me again. I can't wait to hear your voice and feel your presence once more," Mrs Wade murmured, her voice soft and tender.

She paused for a moment, as if listening for a response, before continuing.

"Do you remember the first time we met? You were so handsome, so charming. I knew from that moment that we were meant to be together. And we were, weren't we? We had such a wonderful life together. All those happy years."

As Mrs Wade spoke, her eyes filled with tears and her voice trembled with emotion.

"Oh Frederick, I miss you every day. I miss your laugh, your touch, your scent, endlessly complaining about your orchids. But tonight, with Mr Sanders' help, I'll be able to hear your voice again. I'll be able to tell you how much I love you, and how much I miss you."

At the mention of 'Mr Sanders', tucked away in their hiding place, Sebastian and Collins exchanged a knowing glance. Sebastian's annoyance was palpable, but he knew better than to voice his concerns out loud. Instead, he exchanged a tense glance with Inspector Collins, who made a quick 'shh' gesture with his finger to his lips. They both knew that any noise could give away their presence and blow the entire operation.

The grieving widow reached out a hand to touch the photo, as if trying to bridge the gap between life and death.

"I know it won't be the same as having you here with me, but it's something. It's a chance to feel close to you again, if only for a little while."

*

Meanwhile, as eight o'clock loomed, Vincenzo and Rose arrived at The Willows in Hampstead, the rain still coming down in sheets. The wheels of the heavy cab splashed through the deep puddles as they pulled up to the gravel drive, the water streaming down the coach's windows like tears.

Rose clutched Vincenzo's arm, a look of apprehension on her face as they stepped out into the stormy night. As they approached the door of The Willows, Rose's heart was beating fast. She couldn't shake off the deep sense of unease about the séance they were about to conduct.

"Please, Vincenzo, can't we just leave? I have a really bad feeling about this."

Vincenzo smiled reassuringly and took her hand.

"Rose, my love, you worry too much. I promise you, everything will be fine. Mrs Wade is a willing participant. We bring her solace in her hour of need. Trust me."

Rose did her best to squash down the feeling that Vincenzo was perhaps driven by money more than genuine psychic ability. She was distracted, lost in thought about how she could make him see sense, but she was not really listening. She wanted to tell Vincenzo about her deep feelings for him, but she worried that it would ruin their relationship, which, up until this point, had been platonic with just a hint of clean romance.

As they stepped up to The Willows, the old Georgian house seemed to come alive with a sense of mystery and intrigue. Rose felt a knot form in her stomach as she walked down the dimly lit driveway. She knew that they were walking into uncharted territory and still couldn't shake the feeling that something was amiss. Vincenzo, on the other hand, appeared to be in his element. He carried himself with an air of confidence, and his well-groomed appearance and fashionable clothing gave him an air of sophistication. As he rapped on the door, Mrs Lewis answered and welcomed them into the parlour.

"Ah, Mr Sanders, so good to see you again," she said, offering a warm smile.

Vincenzo returned the smile, then turned to Rose.

"You remember Miss Sanders, Rose, my assistant."

Mrs Lewis gave a polite nod before leading them into the cluttered parlour. Mr Lewis joined the police man and Sebastian as they watched on. The trio looked on agape after jostling to look through the peephole, all three shocked to see that Rose had accompanied Vincenzo instead of Betty!

As Vincenzo opened his briefcase, the sound of its thump echoed through the room, and Mrs Wade turned to him with anticipation.

"Shall we begin?" he asked eagerly. "Please, set out the candles, Rose," he said, gesturing towards the table.

Rose nodded, turned down the oil lamps and and took out the candles, setting them up around the room on various pieces of wooden furniture, the crisp strike of the match on the box preceding each springing wick to life. She then took out her smudge stick, lighting it and using the smoke to cleanse the area.

"Thank you, Mr Sanders . I'm so grateful for your help," Mrs Wade said, her voice cracking with emotion. "I am so sorry about my son last time, crashing in like that and ruining everything. You don't think that debacle will frighten off Frederick?"

"Absolutely not," the mesmerist said, putting his fingers on his temples. "Frederick's spirit is here with us tonight, and he is eager to communicate with you."

"I just want to hear his voice again. Do you think he'll speak to me directly?" she asked.

"He will definitely communicate via the ouija board or my pendulum. Of that I have no doubt. Some questions about the afterlife, or things left unsaid between them would be a good place to start, Speak from your heart, Mrs Wade. He will hear you," he said in a soft, soothing tone.

"Yes, yes, of course. I just want to tell him how much I miss him and how much I still love him," she confided, her eyes filled with tears as Vincenzo nodded in fake agreement.

"That's a wonderful sentiment, Mrs Wade. And I'm sure he'll appreciate hearing it."

"I'm so grateful for your help in this matter," she said, her voice quivering with anticipation as she prepared for the séance to begin.

Vincenzo slid the small glass for the ouija board in between the yes and no boxes and pulled a small silver pendulum out of a black velvet bag.

"Shall we begin, ladies?" he said darkly. "It is time for us to reach out to the spirit world once again."

Collins couldn't help but feel a sense of unease as he watched from the hidden corridor. With Rose's unexpected appearance, he knew that the night was far from over, and he found himself wondering what else would not go to plan.

21

FADING FACADES

Sebastian and Inspector Collins stood squashed up side-by-side in the dimly lit servant's corridor, their eyes fixed on the small peephole that allowed them to observe the séance taking place in the Wade's lavish parlour. They leaned in closer, straining their ears to catch every word spoken within the room.

In the parlour, the air was thick with tension and the waxy scent of burning candles. Vincenzo, ever the mesmerist, manipulated Mrs Wade with his convincing psychic act with ease, which grew more spectacular as the séance progressed. The flickering candlelight cast eerie shadows on the walls, and the room seemed to hum with an otherworldly energy, as if the late Frederick Wade was indeed present among them.

Seated around a polished mahogany table, Vincenzo, Rose, and Mrs Wade held their fingers on a glass, which rested on a ouija board. The board was a beautiful and haunting artefact, its inlaid wooden letters and symbols gleaming in the candlelight. Mrs Wade, her eyes wide with anticipation, began to ask questions.

"Frederick, my love, do you remember the name of the hotel we stayed at for our honeymoon?" she whispered, her voice shaking with emotion.

The glass moved with a slow, deliberate motion as Vincenzo gauged Mrs Wade's response as the glass moved towards the letters. Knowing they had visited Brighton for the honeymoon, he began with a guess at 'T-H-E.' Mrs Wade's smile broadened. He pondered Royal or Grand, for the next word but plumped for Grand and deftly slid the glass towards 'G' which made Mrs Wade nod gently. From there it was plain sailing to complete the reply.

"So, he's telling us 'The Grand Hotel.' Is that right?"

"Yes, that's right! Oh, Frederick, I miss you so much," Mrs Wade gasped, tears filling her eyes.

Encouraged by the seemingly accurate responses, she continued with her questions.

"Can you tell me the name of your favourite bird?"

Again, the glass moved, spelling out 'F-A-L-C-O-N.' Mrs Wade nodded, her face a mix of sadness and wonder.

"Yes, such a sweet majestic creature."

As the séance went on, Mrs Wade's energy began to wane, and she appeared increasingly tired and emotional. She thanked Vincenzo profusely for bringing her solace. Vincenzo, sensing the opportunity for more information, asked Mrs Wade one last question.

"Just one final thing? Did your husband ever consider becoming a policeman? I'm getting a very strong feeling about something to do with the police?"

"I don't think he ever mentioned it, no," said Mrs Wade, shaking her head, puzzled.

Rose looked horrified at Vincenzo's playful questioning, especially in light of the newspaper article stating the authorities quest for him.

Inspector Collins and Sebastian exchanged nervous glances. The tension between them heightened when, in their shock, Collins' elbow accidentally hit the servant's door, causing a loud thud to resonate through the parlour.

"Are you sure? Frederick seems to be telling me that he would have had a great deal of fun protecting the city from criminals. Make of that what you will," Vincenzo joked, as the two men in the corridor glared at each other, their bodies aching from their hunched-up viewing positions.

Sebastian secretly raged as he watched his mother being manipulated so easily by the devious Vincenzo. The tension in his jaw and the white knuckles betrayed his simmering fury. Knowing the charlatan was taking advantage of his mother's grief was one thing, watching it happen in real time was something else entirely.

As Vincenzo took the sizeable payment, greed flashing in his eyes, Collins and Sebastian burst from their hiding place. The abrupt intrusion shattered the séance's sombre atmosphere, and Vincenzo's face transformed from calm assurance to panic as he realised he had been caught.

Stunned, Vincenzo was grabbed by the strong hands of the police officer and ably assisted by Mr Wade, his protests and struggles futile against their firm grasp. Rose, her eyes wide with shock and disbelief, froze as the officers arrested the man she had trusted—and begun to love. Mrs Wade, her face a mixture of confusion and anger, shrieked for the men to leave Mr Sanders alone, unable to comprehend the scene unfolding before her. The chaos and emotional turmoil in the room escalated as the séance attendees grappled with the gravity of the situation in the real world.

Vincenzo's face contorted with rage as he was forcefully handcuffed, the cold metal biting into his wrists. He glared at Inspector Collins, his eyes burning with fury and betrayal. The once calm and collected mesmerist was now a cornered animal, desperate and unpredictable.

Rose's heart pounded in her chest, her emotions a whirlwind of fear, heartbreak, and disbelief. As Inspector Collins turned to her, she felt her knees buckle, the world around her blurring as tears welled up in her eyes. She could hardly breathe, her chest constricting as if an iron band were wrapped around her. The image of Vincenzo, the man she had trusted and even loved, being arrested was too much for her to bear. She felt faint and struggled to remain standing as the policeman approached her.

Mrs Wade, meanwhile, was utterly confused by the sudden turn of events. Her eyes darted from the arresting officers to her son Sebastian, and back to the sobbing Rose. Anger simmered beneath her confusion, as the realisation that she would not be able to contact her late husband again began to sink in.

The séance was drawing to a close as Vincenzo, his face a mask of exhaustion, announced that he was feeling drained. In truth, he had exhausted the seam of intuition he gained from his careful examination of the room and its contents, mining every clue and detail to weave a compelling narrative for the grieving widow. With feigned regret, Vincenzo's voice took on a tender tone.

"I'm afraid Mr Wade's presence is fading now," he said, his gaze locked onto Mrs Wade's tear-filled eyes. "But before he goes, he wants you to know that he is happy and at peace. Most importantly, he loves you, his dear wife, with all his heart, and that love transcends any distance between this world and the next."

Mrs Wade, overcome with emotion, reached for her handbag that lay near the French-polished table. The handbag, adorned with intricate embroidery and a delicate silver clasp, spoke of her refined taste and social standing. Her hands trembling, she opened it, lightly licked her thumb and began to count out a generous number of pound notes, their crisp edges rustling softly as the pile grew higher on the table.

As Vincenzo reached out to take the payment, Inspector Collins and Sebastian suddenly burst out from their hiding place, catching him off guard. In a single swift move, Vincenzo was grabbed and apprehended, leaving Rose frozen in shock at the sudden turn of events. Meanwhile, Mrs Wade began shrieking in protest, pleading for the men to leave Mr Sanders, as she knew him, alone. But it was too late, justice had finally caught up with the fraudulent mesmerist, and his misdeeds were now exposed for all to see.

Outside The Willows, Betty and Davy arrived breathless and soaked to the skin, having run through the rain to catch up with the arrested duo. Officers staking out the place darted from the bushes to support Collins. Betty and Davy watched helplessly as Rose was roughly marched towards the waiting Black Maria. The police vehicle loomed ominously, its dark and foreboding presence adding to the weight of the situation.

"Please, sir!" Betty pleaded with the policemen, her voice shaking with emotion. "Rose is a good person! She's innocent in all this!" The officers exchanged glances, unmoved by her pleas. "It's for the courts to decide, miss," one of them replied curtly. "Now move aside, please."

As the police looked on with anger and determination, Betty and Davy couldn't help but worry about Rose's fate. The reality of the situation was sinking in, and the two friends felt a deep sense of dread for what lay ahead.

Vincenzo fought, twisted, and dodged as he was forcibly moved along by an officer holding either arm. He was bundled into the other Black Maria, with its dark interior smelling of damp and stale tobacco smoke, a testament to the countless criminals who had been transported in it before.

On the doorstep, Sebastian seemed smug, proud he had achieved his goal and was now rid of Vincenzo for good. He stood with his arms crossed, watching the scene unfold before him. Betty approached Sebastian, their expressions fierce and determined.

"You better use your legal skills to defend Rose, as you promised. She doesn't deserve to be punished for that rogue's greed."

Davy's face flushed with anger, his demeanour reminiscent of a vigilante ready to fight for justice and protect his loved ones, whatever the personal cost. Sebastian looked at them for a moment, his eyes narrowing.

"I'll do what I can to help her. But you need to understand that the law must take its course."

Keen to avoid any more local gossip, he slammed the door in their faces as the two Black Marias disappeared into the distance, leaving the Betty and Davy on the doorstep to hope that Sebastian would keep his word.

As Vincenzo and Rose were escorted to the imposing Camden Constabulary, the damp smoky air clung to their clothes. These ever-present London street odours served as a constant reminder of the world they were now leaving behind, and the life they once knew, now crumbling before them.

In the processing area, dimly lit by the steady glow of gas lamps and their noses assaulted by the smell of stale tobacco and pungent disinfectant, Collins sternly warned both of them.

"Now listen here," he said, his voice cold and firm, "you best do as you're told if you don't want things to get unpleasant."

Vincenzo's eyes flashed defiantly, his jaw clenched, but he remained silent. Rose, on the other hand, looked crushed and terrified, her delicate features drawn with anxiety, her once bright eyes clouded with fear.

They were escorted to separate cells within the bowels of the Camden Police Station, left alone amidst the damp and dreary confines to reflect on their actions. The cold stone walls and sparse furnishings offered little comfort to either of them as they contemplated the consequences of their deceitful deeds, a heavy weight upon their hearts.

An hour later, the heavy metallic door to Vincenzo's cell creaked open, and a stern-looking policeman stepped in. Vincenzo sat up, his heart racing at the sight of the uniformed official. The officer motioned for him to follow.

"Collins wants a word with you," the policeman said gruffly, his tone indicating he wouldn't put up with any backchat or surliness.

Vincenzo sweated, memories of earlier in the evening flooding his mind, as he reluctantly complied with the officer's demand. The policeman noticed Vincenzo's hesitation.

"You'd better comply, old chap, or you'll get cuffed. Understand?"

Vincenzo nodded mutely and followed the policeman out of his cell, his heart thumped as he panicked about the possibilities of what would happen next.

Collins and Parker began their interview with Vincenzo by recapping his plan to defraud grieving widows with fake séances, presumably preying on the wealthy women he found from their illustrious husbands' obituaries. The very idea of his plan made their blood boil, their anger palpable in the room. Collins raised an eyebrow, a hint of disbelief in his voice.

"So, let me get this straight. You're saying that Rose was the mastermind behind this scheme, and you were just following her lead?"

Vincenzo nodded eagerly, his eyes wide with desperation.

"Yes, that's exactly it. She was the one who convinced me to go along with it. I never would have done it on my own."

Collins leaned forward, his tone icy and disdainful.

"And yet, we have evidence that suggests otherwise. Letters in your unmistakable handwriting, receipts for candle purchases for your séances, and several witnesses who can place you at the scenes of the crimes."

Vincenzo's bravado faltered, his voice quivering.

"Well, yes, but that's because Rose made me do those things. She was very—persuasive."

Parker finally spoke up, his eyes narrowing.

"Persuasive how, exactly? Do you really expect us to believe that a fragile young woman like Rose could have manipulated you, a strong-willed mountain of a man, who is a skilled mesmerist with years of experience?"

Vincenzo spluttered, his hands shaking has he pleaded with the men.

"I'm telling you the truth! She used her feminine wiles to make me do her bidding! If you get my drift?"

Collins stood up, his face a mask of fury.

"Enough. It's time for you to start taking responsibility for your actions, Vincenzo. You defrauded vulnerable widows and preyed on their grief for your own gain. You needed Rose to add a thin veil of legitimacy to your shameful operation. It's time for you to face the consequences. Attempting to pin this on Miss O'Shaughnessy will fail. I can tell you that now. Shall we start again?"

"But, I am telling the truth!" Vincenzo protested, his voice barely a whisper.

Parker held out a piece of paper in front of his suspect, his expression unyielding. It was Mrs Phillips' letter of condolence in Vincenzo's own handwriting.

"Care to explain this?" Parker asked, his voice cold and measured, as effective as a blade against Vincenzo's throat.

Vincenzo looked down at the paper and swallowed hard, his heart sinking as he realised that his fraudulent activities were finally catching up to him. The rogue attempted to stutter out an excuse, but Parker cut him off with a dismissive wave of his hand.

"Save it. We both know what you've been up to, and it's time for you to come clean."

Vincenzo's shoulders slumped in defeat, his spirit crushed as he realised that he had nowhere left to run.

Taking a deep breath, Vincenzo began weaving the most masterful sleight of mouth session he had ever conducted, using every ounce of his skill to pin the blame squarely on Rose as the mastermind. There was no way he was going down without a fight.

"I was quite content working at Crendon Gardens. I was one of the highest-paid sideshow acts in the place. I rued the day I met her and she persuaded me to leave a perfectly good job and abuse my talent."

"Go on," said Collins, his voice dripping with disdain, as he watched Parker sharpen his pencil, poised to scribble every morsel of the interview in his little notebook.

*

Later, Rose was escorted down the same narrow tiled corridor with its damp walls and flickering gaslights, the sound of her footsteps echoing ominously around her. As she neared the interrogation room, she could hear the raised voices of Collins and Parker, their words indistinct but filled with menace. She could feel her heart pounding in her chest as she was pushed through the door and into the room, where the two detectives were waiting for her. Collins immediately began to berate her, his words biting and cruel.

"We know you're involved in this little scam preying on vulnerable old ladies," the inspector said, his voice low and dangerous.

Parker tried to calm him down and appeal to Rose's conscience.

"You might as well tell us everything now. We're here to help you," he said with respect. "But you need to start telling tell us the truth."

Collins looked at his colleague, wondering why the man had gone soft in the head. Fraudsters deserved no mercy. If men like Vincenzo worked hard in proper, respectable jobs, Collins felt his own would be a lot easier.

*

Rose tried to protest her innocence, but she could feel the weight of their suspicion bearing down on her, the tears stinging at the corners of her eyes as she tried to keep her composure.

Collins leaned forward and fixed his piercing gaze on the distraught and lonely young woman.

"We think you know he was a fraud. You'd better start telling the truth," he said in a firm voice.

Rose's mind raced as she tried to figure out how much Collins knew. She couldn't afford to reveal everything, not yet anyway. She was still trying to protect Vincenzo, even though she knew deep down that he was a con artist. She wondered how Collins had picked up on her doubts and hesitations.

Collins slid a newspaper clipping across the table towards Rose. "We found this in your possession. It was concealed in the lining of your bag," he said. "Looks like you're not being entirely honest with us, miss?"

She knew that she was caught, and that the only way out was to confess.

"It was all Vincenzo's idea," she said finally, her voice barely above a whisper. "I just went along with it because—because he bought be things, promised me things, told me we were really helping the widows deal with their grief."

Collins snorted derisively, but Parker's tone was more supportive.

"It's alright, Miss O'Shaughnessy," Ted said. "You did the right thing by telling us."

She took a deep breath and began to explain her role in the deceit, starting with the moment she had discovered Mrs Kelly's death and needed to find work desperately.

"Initially, I believed in Vincenzo's powers after making contact with my father, but gradually I became more disillusioned, especially after the fight with Sebastian Wade and the newspaper clipping. I had tried hard to persuade Vincenzo to call off the visit to the Wade's at the Eagle Tavern, but he had refused to listen. I'd been weak and foolish to go along with his plan. I swear I never intended to hurt anyone. The widows seemed to derive some sort of peace of mind from his antics, which played on my conscience. If they felt relief, was it really so bad?"

Collins listened to her story with a mixture of scepticism and sympathy. He could tell that Rose was genuinely remorseful, but he also knew that she had played an active and willing role in the fraud. He pressed her for more details, trying to uncover any critical information that could lead to Vincenzo's conviction.

As the interrogation continued, Rose felt like she was trapped in a nightmare from which she could not wake up. She had never imagined that her love for Vincenzo could lead her down such a dark and dangerous path. Now, she could only hope that Collins and Parker would be able to secure a conviction that was harsher for Vincenzo than her.

As she was led down the dimly lit corridor by Constable Bush, the flickering gaslights casting shadows on the glazed-tile walls, Rose's tear-stained face and hunched posture spoke volumes about her distress. Her sobs and mournful cries echoed through the cold, damp corridor, the weight of her guilt crushing her as she lamented ever getting involved with the smooth-talking con artist, Vincenzo. Her mind was consumed with remorse as she considered the impact of her actions.

Parker felt a pang of sympathy as he peered out of the investigation room and watched Rose being led back to her cell. She looked so sad and broken, still crying and hunched over in the pretty dress Vincenzo had bought her. He wanted to do something to help, but he knew there was almost nothing he could do personally without risking the trial. He turned away and busied himself with his interview papers, the scratching of his pencil against the notepad filling the sombre room.

Rose sat in her cell, lost in her own thoughts, when she suddenly heard a voice wafting through the small window in her cell door. At first, she couldn't recognise the voice, but as she listened closely, it hit her. The voice belonged to Mrs Greaves, one of Vincenzo's victims. Rose bolted towards the door and saw the woman's face peering across from her cell, her hair dishevelled and her face streaked with dirt.

"I'm so sorry for what's happened to you,"
Mrs Greaves said sympathetically.

Rose's blurry eyes filled with tears as she looked out.

"I was such a fool," she said. "I can't believe I
fell for Vincenzo's lies."

Mrs Greaves' expression turned serious.

"It wasn't your fault, Rose. Vincenzo planned everything. He even hired me to pretend to be a widow so that you would believe in him."

"I have been such a silly fool," Rose whispered as her heart sank.

Mrs Greaves leaned closer still to the window.

"You have to tell the police everything, Rose. You have to clear your name and stop Vincenzo from taking you down in his place. You can be sure he'll be spinning them coppers a right yarn with that clever tongue of his."

Sally's voice was barely a whisper as she leaned closer to the cell window.

"He's going to try and make it look like I'm your accomplice. You mark my words, else why am I here? I was in on it. You have to tell the police the truth, Rose," she said urgently. "I'll say he approached me when they feel my collar, I promise."

Rose nodded numbly as Mrs Greaves' words sank in. She tried not to think about what would happen to her if the woman reneged and said she was Rose's stooge not Vincenzo's. She got the feeling Sally would say anything to the police to get herself off the hook, and then she might consider the consequences of her evidence for Rose.

As Sally's ominous words echoed in her mind, Rose wondered how she could have been so blind and naive.

The thought made her sick to her stomach. Her heart shattered all over again as she realised once and for all that he manipulated her from the very beginning, playing on her financial vulnerabilities and her desire for love.

Parker paced down the corridor, his appearance snapped Rose back to the present.

"Thank you" she mumbled, as he passed a small tray of food through the door window.

He watched her as she nibbled on the meal but the taste of the bread and cheese soon turned to ash in her mouth. She set the tray aside, her appetite gone. His concern for her welfare grew. He knew that he had to tread carefully and not breach his professional code, but he couldn't help worrying about her. He decided to keep checking from a discreet distance. All he could do was offer her a bit of kindness in a bleak and frightening situation until a better plan surfaced in his brain.

For hours, Rose sat on her cold, hard bed, her mind still reeling from her conversation with Mrs Greaves. She felt betrayed and manipulated by Vincenzo and Greaves. Who else betrayed her? As she tried to make sense of it all, her eyes began to droop after her sleepless night.

They soon sprang open the next morning when she heard a woman's heels followed by a familiar voice wafting in from the corridor.

"Rose! Oh, my dear, what have they done to you?" Betty exclaimed as she was let into the cell.

She looked horrified at Rose's condition, her eyes puffy from crying, her complexion grey and her once-lush hair now tangled and dull.

"I'm fine, Betty," Rose said weakly, trying to sound stronger than she felt. "I just need to clear my name, then I'll be fine."

'Just' was such a small word to say, and it did a good job of obscuring the monumental difficulty that came with facing the task ahead.

"That's the spirit, Rose!" Betty said, her voice rising with enthusiasm. "You need to fight back with everything you've got. We can't let Vincenzo get away with this."

Rose nodded, her determination growing as Betty spoke.

"I knew I needed to take control of the situation and make sure Vincenzo pays for what he had done."

Betty put her arm around Rose's shoulders and squeezed her friend so hard her bones nearly cracked.

"Betty, you did tell the police I'm innocent, didn't you?" Rose asked, hoping for some reassurance.

"Yes, I did," Betty replied, putting her hand on Rose's shoulder. "I told them you were naive and lovestruck, but not a criminal. And they believed me. I know it. Especially Sergeant Parker."

Rose breathed a sigh of relief, grateful for her friend's support. She knew she couldn't do this alone. Betty explained how the sting was supposed to go, that she had followed Rose to the Eagle and had hoped to get Vincenzo to agree to swap places. Rose looked stunned.

"Yes, I came here a couple of days ago to talk to the police, along with Mr Wade. I was at home when the telegram was delivered talking about visiting Mrs Wade's again. I went to see Sebastian to try and convince him to use his house to trap Vincenzo."

Betty took her friend's hand.

"We had a plan, me, him and the police. I was supposed to take your place that night. I followed you to the tavern, but I lost you when you left. I am so sorry."

"You'd do that for me? Gosh. I don't know what to say."

"Oh, Rose, you silly thing. I've always stuck up for you, haven't I? Did you know Sebastian's a top-flight lawyer?"

"No! Cripes."

"I did a deal with him. In return for telling him when Vincenzo was due to visit his mother again, he was to defend you in court. And he only went and agreed. Well I think he agreed."

As they talked, Parker walked by, overhearing their conversation. He knew he shouldn't get involved, but he couldn't help feeling a sense of empathy for Rose.

Touched by Betty's unwavering loyalty to Rose, Parker knew that he had to do everything in his power to help her. That's why he ended up waiting outside the Willows for hours, hoping to catch a glimpse of Sebastian. Parker was relieved when he finally saw Wade leaving on foot, striding with purpose in his best frock coat, top hat and striped grey trousers. He followed him to Hilltop Lodge, which was a well-known unofficial haunt of the local freemasons. Wade paced up the marble steps and disappeared inside.

As Parker approached the entrance, the doorman stopped him.

"And you are?"

"I am here in a semi-professional capacity," Parker warned as he dug out his police badge from his inside suit pocket.

After some initial reluctance, the doorman allowed him to enter. Parker found Sebastian sitting in a private room off the main reception area with several other well-dressed men.

"Sorry to interrupt, Mr Wade. Might I have a word?" Parker asked.

Sebastian looked irritated by the interruption but agreed to speak with the officer.

"What's the meaning of this, Parker? Why are you following me when I'm going about my business?"

The two men paced towards the far corner of the room.

"I just want to make sure that you will help Miss O'Shaugnessy, Mr Wade. I haven't seen you since the night of the arrest. We did make a deal, did we not? I've had it confirmed by the undercover officers on the night that Rose was trying to stop Vincenzo from defrauding your mother on that second visit, but he overruled her. She is naive and foolish, but not a hardened criminal. She needs your help. I trust you will help her prepare her case, as you agreed with Betty."

Sebastian hesitated.

"But I am a respected barrister. Why would I defend a Whitechapel slum angel? I have a reputation to uphold. I'll be a laughing stock," he protested.

"Because it's the right thing to do, and you know it. You practice to fight for justice and

uphold the Queen's laws and not just fight
for the clients who have the deepest pockets
to pay your fees? Yes?" Parker said firmly.

Sebastian reluctantly agreed.

"You have my word, Sergeant Parker."

"Good. I shall expect to see you visiting Miss
O'Shaughnessy soon then?"

"Yes, of course," Wade confirmed with an
awkward nod.

"I'll leave you to your evening then, Mr
Wade," Parker said, slipping out of the room
before his presence was noted further.

As he walked away, he heard Peter Jenkins, the owner of a huge collection of Limehouse bonded warehouses quiz Sebastian.

"I've seen him before. Sergent Parker isn't
it? What was a copper doing here," asked
Peter suspiciously

"It's nothing, Peter. Now, who's round it is.
Don't tell me it's mine again," Sebastian
joked, changing the subject.

Time marched on and a date was set for the trial—two weeks hence. Parker kept checking on Rose's wellbeing, and even sneaked in a few comforts in the form of a book and a warm blanket. Rose was grateful for the kindness, but Parker could see that her spirits were low, and that keeping her hope alive was more and more of a struggle since Sally Greaves was freed until she needed to testify.

One day, while working with Collins on the case, Parker couldn't help but ask if Wade had visited Rose yet, since Parker had heard not talk of it. Collins looks up from his paperwork

"I haven't seen him around here lately, Parker, no. But that's not really his job, is it?"

"We had a deal, sir. Miss Hardacre gave us the telegram on the understanding that we would protect Rose from the fullest extent of the law, due to her diminished responsibility because of his grip on her. And Sebastian agreed too. You were there. We are here to protect the innocent and pursue the guilty, aren't we?" Parker argued.

"All right, stop badgering me Parker. I'll look into it. Now can we carry on preparing the evidence for the prosecution now? Or do you want to keep idling and gossiping like an old fish wife?"

"Sorry, sir. I just felt it was important to—"

"Enough, Parker, Enough!"

As the trial approached, Parker's worry for Rose grew. Despite the support from her friends and family, on the day of her questioning, she would be alone in the dock. Her mental state seemed to deteriorate by the day, despite her brave face. He prayed his clandestine visits and small acts of kindness would keep her hopeful. But with the trial looming closer, Parker feared his efforts wouldn't be enough to save her from a bleak future. Wade barely made one or two appearances, and they were brief, according to his colleagues at the constabulary. As the weight of the situation bore down on him, he wondered if it was too late to help her fight for her freedom in court. Being held before the trial was one thing. It was a few uncomfortable weeks, but he feared a lengthy prison term would be the death of her.

23

DESPERATE TIMES

After a few gruelling weeks spent in the dank, dimly-lit cells of the Camden constabulary, a place with the lingering scent of damp and despair, the legal proceedings against Rose O'Shaughnessy were set to begin.

As they were escorted through the bustling streets of London, they arrived at Bow Street Magistrates Court, a formidable brick building with grand windows. The rattle of the wheels on the cobbles filled the vehicle, followed by the clang of heavy wrought iron gates slamming behind them.

They were quickly transferred into the waiting area and then brought into the courtroom by the ushers, with Rose two steps behind Vincenzo. The courtroom was imposing, with dark wood panelling and uncomfortable wooden seating. The walls were lined with faded tapestries and heraldic emblems for the queen. The judge's bench loomed high above the rest of the room, its ornate carvings testifying to the power of the law.

As Vincenzo took his place in the dock, he looked smug and self-assured, his shoulders back and his head held high. Rose, on the other hand, looked terrified, her eyes darting around the room as she clutched at her simple grey shift dress. The weight of the situation bore down on her, and she could feel her heart pounding in her chest. She could feel Vincenzo's gaze burning into her, and she wondered how they had ended up like this. The trial was about to begin, and Rose knew that her fate hung in the balance.

As Rose lowered herself onto the cool wooden bench, she scanned the gallery above her, searching for the familiar faces of her family and friends. To her dismay, she found only curious onlookers and spectators, no one she held dear. Loneliness washed over her, abandoned and vulnerable, the reality of her situation hitting her hard. Would she have to face the harsh consequences of the trial alone, without the support and comfort of those she loved? The thought left her feeling defeated, and her heart heavy with the weight of the unknown.

In contrast, Rose couldn't help but notice Vincenzo's air of confidence, and she surmised that he must have chosen to represent himself in court. He had always been cunning and persuasive, and she wondered if his talents would be enough to sway the judge and jury in his favour. She was correct. Vincenzo was indeed acting as his own counsel, but only because he had no other choice since all his money had been confiscated by the police during their investigation. Despite his dire financial circumstances, Vincenzo still managed to present himself impeccably, dressed in a finely tailored suit that accentuated his tall, lean frame. His appearance was a testament to his resourcefulness and determination, and Rose couldn't help but feel a twinge of unease at the thought of facing the accomplished performer in court. Her panic soared as she looked towards Vincenzo, catching his icy stare, filled with contempt and malice. He clearly blamed her for confiding in Betty, revealing the secret they were supposed to share only between themselves. In his opinion, none of this would have happened if she hadn't blabbed. He was a genius when it came to covering his tracks and he believed, on balance, he would have fared better without her meddling.

As Rose sat in the courtroom, feeling alone and vulnerable, the O'Shaughnessy's appeared in the gallery, their faces tense with worry. Rose's heart leapt with relief at the sight of them. She knew that they would stand by her, no matter what. Collins and Parker were also in attendance, their expressions stoic and unyielding. It was clear that they were there to observe and take note, rather than to offer any support or comfort. Despite this, Rose felt a small sense of relief knowing that she wasn't completely alone in this ordeal.

As the judge entered the courtroom, the bailiff called for everyone to rise. The judge was an imposing figure, wearing a long, flowing robe and a snowy white wig perched on top of his head. He moved with an air of authority, his piercing gaze taking in the assembled audience. Behind him, two clerks hurriedly took their places, carrying sheaves of paper and luxurious fountain pens. They appeared nervous, their hands shaking slightly as they adjusted their spectacles and arranged their papers on the bench. The judge took his seat on the high bench, and the light murmurs in the courtroom faded away to silence. His eyes scanned the jury, the defendants, and the assembled audience, before finally settling on the prosecutor.

> "Let us begin," he intoned, his voice echoing through the room as a hush fell upon it.
> "Ladies and gentlemen of the court, we are gathered here today to hear the case against a Mr Vincenzo Rossi and Miss Rose O'Shaughnessy on charges of grand larceny. Specifically, it is alleged that the defendants have defrauded numerous widows out of significant sums of their inheritances and life savings through a series of clever and premeditated schemes relating to Mr Rossi's fabricated psychic ability. How do you plead?"
>
> "Not guilty," Vincenzo boomed, as he puffed out his chest with confidence.
>
> "Not guilty," Rose added with a much quieter tone, her heart sinking as she looked around for Sebastian Wade, but he was still nowhere to be seen.

Vincenzo fiddled with his cufflinks and straightened his tie. In the gallery, Parker, Betty, Ellen, and Davy whispered amongst themselves, wondering where Wade could be. Betty was especially angry, feeling betrayed by the barrister's broken promise to defend Rose. The four of them looked towards the door expectantly, hoping that Wade would still show up, but he didn't.

"Proceed, Mr Rossi."

Vincenzo, now acting as his own counsel, oozed arrogance and self-interest as he laid out his version of the events surrounding the charges against him and Rose. His voice dripped with disdain as he painted Rose as the mastermind behind the entire operation.

> "It was all her idea," he proclaimed, as he thumped the top of the dock. "She devised these elaborate schemes, luring innocent people with false promises of contacting the deceased, and shamelessly betraying their trust. Playing on me with her feminine charms. She set up the appointments, spinning a right yarn to the women. She even hired a contact of hers to pretend to be a widow. That was the level of deceit she had resorted to."

As Vincenzo continued his tirade, Rose could feel the weight of the allegations bearing down on her, her shoulders slumping under the pressure. She looked around the courtroom, her eyes pleading for someone to see through Vincenzo's lies. Yet, she saw only judgment and contempt in the faces of the spectators and jurors.

How could she defend herself against Vincenzo when he was determined to succeed at all costs in getting himself off the hook, even if it meant sacrificing her for the crimes they had both been a part of? The courtroom seemed to close in on her, and she felt like a small, helpless creature trapped in his thick web of deceit.

As Vincenzo wrapped up his testimony, a smug expression crept across his face, clearly revelling in the damage he was inflicting on Rose. The poor, downtrodden woman, feeling the heavy burden of her predicament, knew she had to find a way to reveal the truth of Vincenzo's treachery and clear her name, even if it seemed like an insurmountable challenge. Her determination to fight for justice began to flicker within her like a small, resilient flame.

He leaned back in the dock, a sly grin playing at the corners of his mouth, knowing that he had covered his tracks well and was confident that he could talk his way out of this mess. But Rose could see through his bravado and noted he had not witnesses to support his claims. She hoped Mrs Greaves would not renege on their earlier discussion. Rose knew that they were in deep trouble and that Vincenzo would need more than his silver tongue to get out of this debacle.

Just as the judge was about to give up calling for the defence, Sebastian Wade burst into the courtroom, his face flushed with exertion. The judge glared at him disapprovingly as he hurriedly took his seat. Sebastian flapped about looking thoroughly disorganised, and

Rose couldn't help but wonder if she was in even more trouble than before.

"Please don't make a habit of this, Mr Wade. I expect better of you. I am almost minded not to let you speak at all."

"My sincere apologies, Your Honour."

Wade addressed the court with confidence, quickly regaining his composure.

"Your honour, esteemed members of the jury, I submit to you that my client, Rose O'Shaughnessy, is a young and naive woman who was completely unaware of the fraudulent activities of Vincenzo Rossi. She only began working with him out of necessity, following the sudden death of her previous employer, a coffee-selling costermonger, Mrs Jane Kelly. I ask you to consider this as we delve into the complexities of this matter."

Rose felt a little more confident, as she watched the faces of the jurors follow Sebastian around the courtroom floor as he spoke.

"I implore this court to consider the facts," the barrister said, his voice resonating with conviction. "My client was not a willing participant in these fraudulent activities. She was deceived by Mr Rossi, made to believe in the validity of his claims, and was exploited for his own gain. It was only after the truth was revealed, by virtue of a humble newspaper article about the self-proclaimed mesmerist, that she understood the gravity of the situation. Rose's involvement in this scheme was minimal, and she had no knowledge of this rogue's true intentions until a few days before her arrest. I urge you to see her as the victim she is, just as much as the widows, and to consider her innocence in this sorry tale."

The courtroom listened intently, eager to hear Wade's arguments and the unfolding story behind the case.

"I call Constable Pickles who heard a conversation between the two defendants, or the night they visited Mrs Wade."

The constable was called to the witness box, his eyes scanning the courtroom as he stepped up to testify.

"Constable Pickles," Wade began, "can you please describe to the court the events of the night in question at the Eagle Tavern?"

Pickles nodded, recalling the night vividly.

"Yes, sir. I was working undercover at the Eagle Tavern, under the orders of Inspector Collins. He wanted me to keep an eye on Mr

Rossi and Miss O'Shaughnessy. During their conversation, I overheard Miss O'Shaughnessy say, 'Let's not go,' when the subject of the fraudulent activities arose. Specifically, it was in reference to their second visit to Mrs Wade at The Willows in Hampstead."

Wade pressed on, seeking to clarify the situation.

"And did you hear her make this request more than once?"

Pickles nodded solemnly.

"Yes, sir. Miss O'Shaughnessy asked at least twice for them not to go through with the visit to Mrs Wade. It was clear to me that she was hesitant and didn't want any part in the scheme. It seemed as if she had found her own moral compass, but Vincenzo's influence was overpowering, and pulled her off course."

Sebastian Wade's eyes flicked across the room, observing the jury's reaction to the testimony before turning his attention back to Constable Pickles. It was crucial to establish Rose's reluctance to participate in Vincenzo's fraudulent activities, and he hoped the jury would consider the weight of the constable's testimony.

As the cross-examination began, Vincenzo confidently approached Constable Pickles, a sly smile playing on his lips.

"Constable, you mentioned that you overheard the conversation at the Eagle Tavern, a rather lively and noisy establishment, if I'm not mistaken," Vincenzo began, his voice dripping with condescension. "In fact, there was a band playing that night, wasn't there?"

Pickles nodded, his brow furrowing.

"Yes, that's correct."

"Considering the volume of the music and the general din, can you truly say with confidence that you overheard every word of the conversation between Miss O'Shaughnessy and myself?"

Despite the challenge, Pickles stood firm in his response.

"Yes, I am sure. I was close enough to hear their conversation clearly."

"And what else was discussed during that conversation, Constable? Can you remember?", Vincenzo asked, his eyes narrowing.

Pickles hesitated, scratching his head as he tried to recall the specifics. He struggled to come up with a satisfactory answer, feeling the weight of the courtroom's gaze on him. Sensing Pickles' difficulty, Vincenzo smirked and dismissed him.

"No more questions, Constable."

As the officer left the stand, he looked at Rose and Sebastian Wade with a hint of remorse, hoping his wavering memory hadn't jeopardised Rose's chances at proving her innocence.

Next, Wade called Betty to the stand and the courtroom hushed as she took her seat. He resumed his line of questioning.

"Miss Hardacre, could you please recount the circumstances under which Vincenzo first asked Rose to work with him?"

Betty sighed, recalling the fateful night.

"We had gone to Crendon Gardens, where Vincenzo was working as a stage performer. We saw a Gypsy Rosa Lee style of fortune teller. She said that I was destined for a glamorous life in the West End. Rose was going to met a handsome man who was going to change her life."

There was much sniggering in court, which irritated Betty.

"Afterwards, we saw a few side shows, had a drink, and watched Mr Rossi's act. We bumped into him after he'd come off stage and he said to one of his friends he was looking for an assistant. We presumed he meant at Crendon Pleasure Gardens. Rose blurted out she could help. I remember arguing with her on the way home, feeling jealous because I believed that glamorous life should have been mine, not hers. But it was clear that Vincenzo wanted to work with Rose, not me."

"And what happened after that?"

"Later, I showed Rose a newspaper article about the police closing in on a fraudulent mesmerist in the area," Betty explained, her voice shaking slightly. "Earlier, she had confessed to me she wasn't working on stage and things had changed in their working relationship. She was expected to pretend to be his sister during private séances instead. She also said she was becoming attracted to Mr Rossi. He can be a bit of a charmer, let's say."

There were some guffaws in the gallery which threw Betty off her stride.

"Carry on, Miss Hardacre," Wade urged gently.

"I begged her to stay away from Vincenzo, but she didn't listen. She did, however, promise to confront him the next time she saw him and planned to tell him to stop his séances and go back to the carnivals as a sideshow entertainer. I think he had convinced her they had a real future together. She told me she thought he might propose soon. I think she was hoping he would quit the deception and be a law abiding citizen and they'd get married."

"And did she do that? Look for him with a view to calling off the visit to The Willows?" Wade asked.

"Yes, she did," Betty replied. "Rose spent four whole days searching for Vincenzo around the streets of Whitechapel, Stepney, Bow. She didn't know where she lived, you see. Finally, she found him at the Eagle Tavern on the night of the final offence. I supposed it was too late to stop him by then. He would have been blinkered by his greed and done everything to sway her. He can be very persuasive."

Wade nodded, satisfied with Betty's testimony.

"No more questions, Miss Hardacre."

As Betty took a breath, Vincenzo was seen furiously scribbling notes, his face a picture of anger. He got ready to stand, but his plan was scuppered.

"It's almost one pm," the judge interjected. "I suggest we have a break for lunch. Let's reconvene in an hour."

Murmurs filled the courtroom as the judge and his assistants turned to leave. The atmosphere was tense, everyone discussing the morning's proceedings and anticipating what was to come.

*

After lunch, the attendees filed back in, and Vincenzo leaped to his feet, eager to discredit Betty, beginning his cross-examination with a confident stride, and his eyes fixed on her.

"Might I ask why didn't you stop Rose from going to the Eagle if you were so concerned about Mrs Wade and your friend? Why not get her burly brother Davy O'Shaughnessy to keep her at home?" Vincenzo asked, a hint of disdain in his voice. "May I remind you that you are under oath, Miss Hardacre."

Betty, flustered by the question, blurted out her response.

"I had a deal with the police where I would swap places with Rose at the last minute to help lessen her sentence in return for securing a conviction. The plan was for me to beg you to bring me along instead as your chaperone, so I could help the police catch you in the act."

The court was in uproar. Betty's posture crumpled as she bit her lip and looked at Mr Wade. Vincenzo's eyes widened, seizing upon the opportunity to exploit Betty's revelation.

"So, Miss Hardacre, you admit to conspiring with the police to entrap me? How very interesting," he said smugly, turning to the jury. "Ladies and gentlemen, it appears that Miss Hardacre here was not only aware of the alleged criminal activity but also actively tried to participate in it. How can we trust anything she has said in her testimony?"

The judge banged his gavel, calling for order in the courtroom.

"Mr Rossi, please proceed with your questioning."

Vincenzo nodded then paused for effect.

"Miss Hardacre, why did Rose fail to confront me? She had ample time to confront me, yet chose not to. It seems to me that Miss O'Shaughnessy was not as reluctant to participate in her fraudulent activities as you claim."

Feeling cornered, Betty snapped back at him.

"Rose was infatuated by you. She was scared of losing you. She told me you were about to propose. And she didn't know where to find you! You never told her where you lived so you could carry on attending more funerals and fing more victims. She spent four days trying to track you down, and by then, it was too late, you had already made another appointment!"

"She could have stood me up though, Don't you agree? If she really wanted an end to our professional relationship. Yet there she was, turning up again and again. Surely being a law abiding citizen is more important that acting on a crush, a dream, an infatuation, with a man you are claiming she considered a fraudster?"

"But!"

"No further questions, Your Honour," Vincenzo said dismissively, returning to his seat with a satisfied smirk.

Sebastian Wade, assessed the damage done to their case as he rolled his pencil up and down his notepad to hide his unease.

In the courtroom, tension was palpable as Vincenzo called upon Mrs Sally Greaves. As she stood in the witness box, a sense of unease settled over the room. Vincenzo, confident in his plan, addressed her directly.

"I'll be brief, Mrs Greaves. You agree you were present at a séance conducted by myself and Miss O'Shaughnessy?."

"Yes, I was."

"But unbeknownst to me, Rose had recruited you to masquerade as a grieving widow. The plan was to deceive me and prove the validity of Rose's scheme to extort money from vulnerable ladies using my showmanship skills. You were Rose's stooge, were you not? Admit it."

Sally's face contorted with indignation, and she vehemently denied his accusations.

> "No! You're wrong, Mr Rossi! It was your idea. I was following your orders. Rose had never met me until the night when we met in the fine apartment you hired to set her up. You showed me the room and told me what to do in the afternoon hours before the séance."

The crowd gasped, shocked by the revelation. Vincenzo struggled to hide his fury, feeling the eyes of the courtroom on him. He had been caught off guard by Sally's complete betrayal, and his carefully laid plans were beginning to unravel.

> Mrs Greaves continued her confession, exposing her role in the deception by posing as a bereaved widow under Vincenzo's detailed instructions.

> "Why are you lying, Mrs Greaves."

> "I am not. I've told the police everything just like I told you now. I only helped you because I was desperate for money. I didn't fancy meeting up with strange men behind pubs to make ends meet if you catch my drift. You came along waving your cash and took advantage of me. But Rose—she was an innocent victim in all of this."

The courtroom murmured, and Vincenzo's anger boiled over. His usual silver-tongued eloquence seemed to have temporarily abandoned him, leaving him struggling for words. The room was charged with emotion as everyone awaited the next development in this unfolding drama, with Sally Greaves turning the tables on Vincenzo and fighting for Rose's innocence.

Sebastian got up from his seat and began to cross-examine Sally.

"Mrs Greaves, please tell the court about the payment you received from Mr Vincenzo for your participation in this scheme."

Sally sighed, looking remorseful.

"He paid me ten shillings to fake the séance and convince Rose that he had a natural talent for contacting the spirits of dead husbands. If I had known how much trouble it would cause, I would never have agreed to it. I'm ashamed to say the money swayed my judgement. I just did it as a one off. I didn't expect him to prey on so many poor ladies."

She welled up with tears as she looked directly into the eyes of the jurors, pleading for understanding. The courtroom was silent, save for the sound of Vincenzo scribbling as he seethed when Sally Greaves left the witness box. He could not believe that his plan had been so thoroughly dismantled by this woman's testimony. Vincenzo stood up, his voice shaking.

"Your Honour, I have no more evidence to present."

"Mr Wade?"

"Your Honour, I would like to call my final witness, Mrs Esme Wade. For full disclosure, Mrs Wade is my mother. May I proceed."

"This is very unusual, but you may, Mr Wade."

The frail woman slowly made her way to the witness box, shuffling her hand along the smooth handrail as she stepped up. She seemed both nervous and determined as she prepared to share her side of the story, hoping to bring the truth to light and secure justice for Rose and see the cad who had exploited her get his just desserts. Mrs Wade cleared her throat and began her testimony. She looked directly at the jury, her voice firm.

"During Mr Rossi's séances, Rose was always quiet and unassuming. It seemed to me that she, like myself, was taken in by his scam, genuinely thinking he was contacting the spirit world. I am certain that Mr Rossi, or Mr Sanders as he called himself to me, was the ringleader in this scheme. I don't know how he did it, but he was able to convince me that my dear Frederick was speaking to me. I was so grief-stricken, I just wanted to believe it was true. I am sure my behaviour made Miss O'Shaughnessy believe he was offering some sort of real solace to me. I can understand how easily she could be deceived my this cad. I was."

As the trial continued to turn against him, Vincenzo couldn't contain himself any longer.

"But I do have a gift, Your Honour! That is why Miss O'Shaughnessy hired me. I implore you, ask Detective Inspector Collins about a message I received about the police during the séance at Mrs Wade's house!"

The judge looked sternly at Vincenzo.

"Mr Rossi, I must warn you, if you continue to interrupt the proceedings, you will be held in contempt of court. Be silent!"

Undeterred, Vincenzo persisted, pointing at Inspector Collins.

"He was there, Your Honour! He heard me talk about the police! I do possess some psychic abilities! And Sebastian Wade over there, who was listening in with him in the servant's corridor, can attest to that as well!"

The judge lost his patience

"If you could predict your future, Mr Rossi, I suggest you would not have been in the parlour at all that evening and thus avoided arrest! Now, be quiet."

The courtroom erupted in giggles, gasps and whispers, the attendees shocked by this unexpected development. Collins and Wade exchanged awkward glances, clearly uncomfortable with the attention Vincenzo's outburst had drawn upon them. The judge banged his gavel.

"Silence in court. You may proceed, Mr Wade."

"Might I ask how much money you gave Mr Rossi for his services? I appreciate this is an embarrassing question, but it is an important one."

"Thirty pounds on the first visit, and twenty on the second."

The disapproving murmurs grew louder in the courtroom reflecting the staggering sums involved.

"That's all Mrs Wade," Sebastian confirmed, sensing his mother's intense discomfort.

Mrs Wade, terrified by the outburst and the ordeal of testifying, appeared even more frail and shaken. A court usher quickly escorted her away, offering his forearm as support as she took the steps down from the witness box. Rose stared at Vincenzo who was slumped on his seat in the dock with his head in his hands.

Sebastian Wade called his final witness. Gerry Stubbs, the official from Crendon Gardens, to testify.

"You were Mr Rossi's former employer where you not? Can you tell the court more about that please?"

"During Mr Rossi's employment at Crendon Gardens, he had multiple altercations with strangers over money. These incidents only served to further damage our reputation as a respectable place for entertainment."

Some members of the gallery sniggered again as Stubbs sighed, clearly frustrated.

"The negative newspaper stories were relentless, and the owners of the carnival acts found that fewer respectable patrons were visiting the pleasure gardens, while more unsavoury characters like Mr Rossi were taking their place. It was shortly after Vincenzo's dismissal from Crendon Gardens that it seems he set up his fraudulent mediumship service. He was obviously desperate for money at that point. I reckon his stage act where he pretended to get messages from the dead to share with the audience would have been perfect training for his deceit with people like Mrs Wade. I can see why he would be tempted to try it. He was such a genius at observing people's body language and asking them leading questions. He was the most skilled in the business at mesmerism. Pity he used his skills for evil rather than a light-hearted stage act."

"That will be all, Mr Stubbs."

Then, Wade in his role as the defence lawyer began his summing up of Rose's case.

"Ladies and gentlemen, it is abundantly clear that Vincenzo was the master manipulator, the devious puppeteer pulling the strings in this despicable scheme. He engineered a fake séance with Sally Greaves.

Rose, on the other hand, is as much a victim as the widows who were cruelly deceived. In fact, she bravely attempted to put an end to Vincenzo's machinations before their second visit to Mrs Wade's home."

Vincenzo, unabashed and cunning, countered the defense's claims with feigned sincerity, skilfully casting doubt on Rose's innocence.

"Esteemed members of the jury," he implored, his eyes wide, "I beseech you to consider the possibility that Miss O'Shaughnessy and I were not a double-act, working in tandem to defraud unsuspecting widows. Rather, I was an unwitting pawn, ensnared by her wicked web of deception. She arrived in Crendon with malicious intent, seeking a victim to manipulate into aiding her treacherous schemes. She observed then preyed upon my unique stage skills and my sixth sense, which allowed me to connect with the spirit world, and twisted them to serve her cold-hearted pursuit of profit. And forgive me for the language, Your Honour, but Sally Greaves, a common prostitute from the St Giles area is hardly a credible witness. She would do and say anything for a few pennies."

The atmosphere in the courtroom grew tense as the jurors absorbed the conflicting testimonies, their faces a mixture of uncertainty and concern. Whispers of doubt and speculation filled the room, as the audience awaited the jury's verdict with bated breath, the fate of Rose and Vincenzo hanging precariously in the balance. The courtroom was tense as the opposing arguments were laid out before the jury, each side presenting their case with conviction. The fate of Rose and Vincenzo now lay in the hands of twelve ordinary citizens, who would decide whether justice would be served.

As the judge began his own summing up, he addressed Rose sternly.

"Miss O'Shaughnessy, although there are mitigating circumstances in your testimony and witness statements, it is evident that you were complicit at some level in this nefarious scheme to defraud vulnerable widows. Mr Rossi, you have shown yourself to be a hot-headed impatient man who delights in his own self-confidence and delights in forging his own way in this world."

He paused, looking at the jury.

"I trust that you will reach the right conclusion in this complex case and ensure that justice is served. It is now time for you to retire and deliberate on the verdict. The court will reconvene in two days at ten am for your verdict."

With that, the jury members filed out of the courtroom behind the foreman, their expressions inscrutable. The room was filled with an air of anticipation, as everyone else in the gallery made their way outside.

As Rose was escorted from the courtroom, her hands trembling and her eyes downcast, she barely registered the supportive waves and whispered encouragement from her friends and family. She seemed to be in a state of shock, the weight of the trial and the uncertainty of her future bearing down on her fragile shoulders.

Vincenzo, usually the picture of self-assuredness, appeared less confident than normal. His trademark swagger had vanished, replaced by a tense, uneasy expression as he too was led away to the cells.

Outside the court, Inspector Collins and Sergeant Parker met Rose's family, their faces etched with concern. Collins, a man of few words, merely offered a solemn nod. Ted Parker, however, took it upon himself to speak to the family about the potential outcome of the trial and the consequences that would come with a guilty verdict.

> "Rose's fate now lies in the hands of the jury," Parker said, his voice laden with worry. "We can only hope that the evidence in her favour is enough to sway them. But with Vincenzo's manipulations and the seeds of doubt he's sown, nothing is certain."

As the family made their way home, they clung to each other, fear and worry gnawing at their hearts. The uncertainty of Rose's fate cast a heavy cloud over their thoughts, and the once-vibrant streets of London seemed to take on a more sombre hue.

Parker re-entered the dimly-lit courthouse by the back stairs, showed his badge to the guard and descended the worn stone steps to the cells where Rose was being held. The pungent smell of damp and despair filled his nostrils as he made his way through the narrow, dank corridor. Upon seeing Rose, his heart ached at the sight of her tear-streaked face, and the utter emotional turmoil that seemed to consume her.

"Rose," he said softly, placing his hands on the cold iron bars, "I have faith that justice will be served. I've seen good people acquitted many a time. The judge overseeing your case is known to be fair and impartial."

Rose found his voice was gentle and reassuring, and his gaze held a sincerity that offered a glimmer of hope.

*

Meanwhile, in the jury room, twelve men and women were engaged in a heated debate, their voices echoing through the high-ceilinged chamber. They pored over the evidence presented during the trial, struggling to reach a unanimous verdict.

The foreman, a stout, middle-aged man with a pompous air about him, was adamant about Rose's guilt.

"She's from the East End, one of those poverty-stricken rabble," he declared disdainfully. "She must have been complicit in this vile scheme. Easy money, innit?"

Another juror, a younger woman with a compassionate expression, countered the foreman's prejudice.

"Vincenzo made a career from being a master manipulator who took advantage of Rose's dire financial situation," she argued, her voice full of conviction. "He used every trick in his arsenal to deceive her and make her an unwitting pawn in his fraudulent activities."

The other jurors listened, some nodding in agreement, others remaining unconvinced.

As the jurors deliberated for two long days, Rose remained in her cold, damp cell, the weight of uncertainty pressing heavily on her. She paced the small space, wringing her hands as her thoughts raced, consumed by anxiety and fear about the outcome of her trial. Each minute felt like an eternity, the silence broken only by her second guessing the jury's impassioned discussions. With each passing hour, her hope waned.

24

IN THE HANDS OF FATE

It was the day of the verdict and the trial reached its climax. Onlookers crammed into every corner of the opulent courtroom. An atmosphere of anticipation permeated the air as the anxious crowd awaited the conclusion to the proceedings. The polished wooden benches groaned under the weight of the tense spectators, and the sun's rays filtered through tall windows, casting a solemn golden light over the proceedings.

With an air of authority, the judge, clad in his flowing robe and white curled wig once more, addressed the foreman of the jury.

"Have you reached a verdict for both defendants?" he asked, his voice echoing in the hushed room.

"We have, Your Honour," the foreman replied, projecting an air of calm determination, despite the gravity of the situation.

"The charges against both defendants are fraud, embezzlement, and grand larceny," the judge reiterated, his words a sombre reminder of the seriousness of their alleged crimes. What is the verdict for Mr Vincenzo Rossi?"

All traces of Vincenzo's previous arrogance had vanished. He stood in the dock, his face pale and his hands shaking. He seemed to shrink under the judge's scrutiny, his once-confident demeanour replaced by an overwhelming sense of vulnerability.

The foreman took a deep breath as he gazed at the jury and pronounced the fateful word: 'Guilty!' The declaration rang loudly in the air, a palpable force that seemed to send a shockwave through the courtroom. A small cheer and a round of applause broke out among the crowd. The clamour was short-lived, however, as the judge's glare brought silence back to the courtroom.

Rose, standing in the dock, was horrified by the events unfolding before her. Her family, looking down from the gallery with dread, peered over the edge, their eyes fixated on her. Her mother gripped her brother Davy's leg, her fingers digging in, as they all awaited Rose's fate.

The judge, his face a picture of solemnity, turned his attention to Vincenzo and addressed the swindler harshly.

"Mr Rossi, your selfish and greedy deeds at
the expense of vulnerable women are
deplorable," the judge said, his voice
echoing through the courtroom, capturing
the full weight of his words. With an air of

finality, he declared, "You are hereby sentenced to twenty years in prison."

The room held its breath as the judge's attention shifted to his co-defendant.

"Have you reached a verdict for the defendant, Miss Rose O'Shaughnessy?" the judge asked the jury foreman, his voice carrying the weight of authority.

The foreman stood, his voice steady despite the magnitude of the moment.

"Yes, Your Honour. We find the defendant, Miss Rose O'Shaughnessy—not guilty!"

The tension in the room evaporated in an instant, as waves of relief washed over Rose and her family, there spirits instantly lifted.

Vincenzo, however, was livid at the announcement. With a guttural roar, he leapt at Rose across the defendant's box, his hands outstretched, intent on throttling her as he screamed like a madman. The courtroom erupted into chaos as onlookers gasped and shouted, the atmosphere a whirlwind of shock and disbelief.

Acting with lightning speed, the guard, clad in their smart black uniforms, sprang into action and apprehended the frenzied Vincenzo. As they struggled to restrain him, the judge pounded his gavel with a thunderous crash, striving to restore order.

"Enough!" the judge bellowed, his voice echoing through the chamber. "Take him down, and charge him with contempt of court as well!"

Vincenzo was dragged away, still kicking and screaming, in a vicious scuffle with the courtroom guards. The heavy oak doors slammed shut behind them with a resounding thud, and the courtroom fell into an uneasy silence, the lingering echoes of Vincenzo's fury a stark reminder of the drama that had just unfolded. The judge then turned his attention back to Rose, his gaze stern.

"You are very lucky in this instance, Miss O'Shaughnessy. I trust you will take this experience to heart and be more cautious in your future dealings."

Rose, her voice barely audible, meekly acknowledged her admonisher.

"Yes, Your Honour," she replied, her eyes downcast as she contemplated the tumultuous events that had just transpired.

As Rose stepped out of the courtroom, she was immediately met by the warm embrace of her family. Their excitement and relief were profound as they rushed towards her, their arms outstretched, eager to envelop her in their love and support. Like a protective cocoon, they surrounded her, their faces radiant with happiness, and their eyes glistening with gratitude. The burden of the trial had finally lifted, and in its place, a newfound sense of hope and unity blossomed amongst them.

In that tender moment, the trials and tribulations of the courtroom felt like a distant memory, replaced by the certainty that they would face whatever challenges lay ahead, together.

Meanwhile, back in the gallery, Tanner Carlisle, a prominent London journalist at the Beacon, feverishly jotted down her thoughts in her trusty notepad, determined to capture every detail of the dramatic conclusion to the trial. With a sense of urgency, she dashed off to the newspaper's head office, keen to get the sensational news hot off the press and into the hands of the nation.

Outside the courthouse, a boisterous crowd had gathered, drawn by the spectacle of the high-profile trial. As Rose emerged from the building, a cacophony of cheers and shouts of congratulations surrounded her. Curious onlookers pressed in, eager to share in the joyous moment and catch a glimpse of the young woman who had been at the centre of it all. Amid the swirl of emotion and excitement, Rose found herself swept up in a sea of jubilant faces, their exuberance washing over her like a tidal wave of relief and happiness. She turned to Sebastian.

"Thank you, Mr Wade. Your support means the world to me, especially given what torment your mother went through."

Sebastian gave her a warm smile.

"Hand on heart, Rose, I wouldn't have defended you if it weren't for Betty's efforts.

She fought your corner tooth and nail and convinced me that you were just as much a victim of Vincenzo as the rest of us. She made me see you were his pawn. She's the one who deserves the most thanks from you."

At that moment, Betty elbowed her way through the crowd eagerly, a beaming smile on her face. As she reached Rose, she wrapped her arms around her friend, giving her a big bear hug.

"Oh, Rose! I knew you'd be alright," she exclaimed, her eyes shining with happiness.

As the crowd dispersed, leaving the friends to savour the moment, Sergeant Parker approached them, his face a picture of genuine relief.

"Congratulations, Rose," he said, extending his hand to her. "I'm so glad the jury saw sense and found in your favour."

"Thank you, sergeant. You were so kind to me while I awaited trial. I will be forever grateful for your support. It was a very dark time for me."

Davy gave Parker a friendly slap on the back to show his gratitude, striking him so hard in his eagerness that the policeman had to take a small step forward to avoid toppling. Betty chuckled as she saw all the buttons on his uniform bounce.

"Might I have a word please, Rose?," said Parker. "I know you must be keen to see your loved ones again, but it won't take a moment."

As Parker shouted out 'excuse us please,' he and Rose wriggled out of the crowd.

"What is it, Ted?"

"Rose, I'd like to offer you the chance to meet Mrs Tanner Carlisle, not now of course, but later on," Parker said.

"Tanner? Never heard of a Tanner before?"

"It doesn't matter, I'll explain later. What's important is she's a journalist who's passionate about fighting for women's rights. I think you two would have a lot to talk about."

"Really?" Rose asked, her eyes lighting up. "That sounds wonderful, thank you."

"Now that the case is over, you have an opportunity to give your side of the story to the press. It's important for other women to understand what you've been through and how you've overcome it."

"I appreciate the offer," Rose said as she nodded, her gratitude evident. "I never thought I'd have the chance to share my humble experience and help others who might find themselves in a similar situation."

As they spoke, Rose was understandably preoccupied with her newfound freedom, her thoughts filled with the possibilities that now lay before her. Parker's heart ached at the thought that introducing her to Tanner might be the last time her ever saw Rose. The policeman couldn't help but feel a pang of longing, as he watched her hug her family as they made their way back to Whitechapel, their lives brimming with joy once more.

*

A few hours later, the O'Shaughnessy family, Rose, Ellen, Davy, and young Billy, along with their loyal friend Betty, made their way to their favourite pie and mash shop on Commercial Road. They were all still in high spirits following the news of Vincenzo's downfall.

"Rose, we're so relieved that you're safe and sound," Ellen exclaimed, hugging her daughter as they walked arm in arm through the cramped and busy streets. "We were all so worried about you."

"Yeah, we couldn't imagine what you were going through locked away all alone," Davy added.

"Thank you so much for being there for me in court, and you Betty, for your visits when

I was in the cells. Your support was my rock."

As they walked along there was the familiar backdrop of the costermongers calling out their wares, children playing hopscotch on spindly chalk grids etched onto the grimy flagstone pavements. The warm glow of street life added to the sense of relief and happiness they felt as they promenaded together.

At Albert's Pie and Mash Shop, the family marvelled at the delicious freshly baked pies on display and the sound of lively chatter from satisfied customers. The shop was a cosy establishment, with padded wooded benches, big communal tables, and a gleaming white-tiled counter displaying the mouth-watering pies. The steam from the vats of mash and liquor fogged the windows, adding to the warm and inviting atmosphere.

"What do you fancy this time, Rose? Steak and kidney or minced beef?" Ellen asked, her eyes scanning the menu.

"I think I'll go for the minced beef today, ma," Rose replied, smiling.

As they ordered their meals, Billy excitedly tapped on the glass counter.

"Can I have a pot of jellied eels too. Please!?"

"Have you got eyes bigger than your stomach again, William O'Shaughnessy?" said his mother as Billy looked up at her with big eyes.

"Please! We are supposed to be celebrating!"

"Aww, of course you can, love. I'm just teasing," his mother said as she pinched his little cheek.

As they sat down and began to enjoy the tasty pies, dripping with liquor, Betty pulled out a folded newspaper cutting from her pocket.

"Here, Rose, take a look at this."

'The Counterfeit Clairvoyant' Found Guilty in Grand Larceny Trial'

By T. Carlisle

After a sensational trial at Bow Street Magistrates Court, the notorious mesmerist and fake psychic Vincenzo Rossi was found guilty of fraud, embezzlement, and grand larceny. Rossi, a former sideshow performer at the notorious Crendon Gardens, preyed on vulnerable widows with his extraordinary powers of persuasion and illusion, convincing them to part with their fortunes by pretending to communicate with their recently departed husbands.

The cunning manipulator's spree of deception began in Hampstead and extended to Islington, starting with heartfelt but fake letters of condolence written during his stay at

Batty Hazlett's Hotel in Shoreditch. Enormous sums of money were exchanged as the fraudster refined his scheme, with one victim, Mrs Wade, mother of the defence lawyer, losing fifty pounds. Fortunately, most of the money has been recovered and returned to the victims.

Miss Rose O'Shaughnessy, Rossi's brave former assistant, and firmly under his spell, was acquitted thanks to heartfelt witness statements. Testimonies from Miss Hardacre (the defendant's long-time friend and confidante), Sally Greaves (Vincenzo's stooge), Mrs Wade (a widowed victim), and Gerald Stubbs (Mr Rossi's former employer), revealed the mesmerist's deceptive tactics. The level of manipulation inflicted on this young woman, including lavish gifts and false promises of a future together, plus his heartless raids on the elderly to steal their inheritances, ultimately led to his conviction.

Vincenzo was sentenced to twenty years in prison, a fitting punishment for his heinous crimes. In addition, he faces a contempt of court charge after losing his composure in the witness box and throwing a punch at his former assistant, which fortunately missed.

The police investigation, led by Inspector Collins and his assistant Sergeant Parker, is to be applauded for their tireless efforts in bringing this malefactor to justice. Mr Wade showed his good nature by waiving his fee and offering to defend Miss O'Shaughnessy gratis.

At the end of the sentencing, Mr Justice Hargreaves warned Miss O'Shaughnessy to be more careful in choosing her business associates in the future. To which the young woman wholeheartedly agreed.

"I better find a new job. Do you think Mrs Ellis needs any extra help with dressmaking, Betty?" Rose sighed.

Betty shook her head as Rose's slumped down.

"No need for that, Rose," said her friend, a mischievous smile spreading across her face. "I've got something even better in store for you."

"Oh dear? Should I be grateful? Or not?" Rose asked, her curiosity piqued.

"Sebastian is going to refer us to his wealthy, philanthropic clients in Hampstead to be their personal seamstresses," Betty revealed. "When the season's taking place, they need extra help, and he says they always keep the best girls on afterwards."

Rose's eyes widened in surprise.

"Sebastian seems awfully kind."

"I don't think he was that kind, Rose. I reckon he offered the post to me to sweeten me up so I don't gossip about being at the arrest if anyone asks!" Betty chortled.

"Yes, I agree," Rose giggled. "And the less said about my criminal background, the better."

The happy group continued to enjoy their tasty meal, young Billy smacking his lips as he savoured the jellied eels first, and was then too full to enjoy his pie and mash.

"Give that here while it's still hot, Billy, if you're not going to eat it," Davy said as he reached over and swiped his dinner.

"Oi!" the youngster protested, but Davy paid no attention and tucked in heartily.

*

On the following Sunday, Parker patiently waited sipping a pint in the pub opposite surveying the front door of a neighbouring home. The lively atmosphere inside was filled with animated conversations and laughter, with the worn wooden tables and warm flickering gas lamps. In one corner, a group of men were engrossed in a heated card game, while others talked of illegal gambling and bare-knuckle fights taking place later that day. The straight-laced sergeant, now aware of the illicit activities, chose to ignore them for once, instead focusing on his much more important objective.

Peering out of the fogged bay window, he spotted Rose stepping out of her home with her younger brother, Billy. Tantalising excitement coursed through the man's skin as he finished his pint in two big gulps, got up from his seat, then straightened his tie and jacket. It was time to speak to Miss O'Shaughnessy one last time and suggest a visit to Tanner at her newspaper's headquarters on Fleet Street was in order. As Parker approached Rose, he greeted her with a warm smile.

"Good afternoon, Miss O'Shaughnessy. It's jolly good to see you again."

Startled to see him, Rose composed herself quickly and responded.

"Hello, Sergeant Parker. What brings you here?"

"Well, I promised you an introduction to the journalist who will be interested in your story. Why don't we go to the newspaper's headquarters? Tanner is a bit of a machine. She works seven days a week, and it should be quiet there today. I know her well enough that it's fine for us to visit without an official appointment."

Upon hearing this, Rose couldn't help but worry about how well Sergeant Parker knew Tanner. She was still wondering how Tanner had acquired such a peculiar name, since Ted still hadn't had the time to explain. Feeling unsure, Rose hesitated.

"—But there's no chaperone."

"I'm a policeman, Rose, and you've just been up in court. If anything, I should be the one who's worried," he chuckled.

His lighthearted response put Rose at ease.

"Go on then, but let's be quick."

Parker bent down to Billy's height and whispered in his ear.

"I shall take the greatest care of your sister and bring her back safely. I promise!"

Satisfied with the arrangement, Billy retreated back inside.

Rose and Parker strolled towards Fleet Street, the heart of Victorian London's thriving newspaper industry. As they walked, they chatted amiably.

*

"Hey, Davy, have you heard? Rose is off to the Beacon's headquarters," Billy said as he burst into their cramped little home.

"What? Why didn't she tell me? Did she go alone?" Davy asked, a note of concern creeping into his voice.

"I don't know. And no, Sergeant Parker is with her." Billy replied, shrugging his shoulders.

"I don't like this. I don't want Rose seeing any more men alone, even if he is a copper. I'm going to follow them and make sure she's alright."

Billy nodded in agreement, and the two brothers quickly made their way out the door.

"I don't think so, young man! In you go!" said Davy, giving his grumpy brother a shove back inside.

Davy stayed well-hidden as he trailed behind Rose and her escort, determined to keep a watchful eye on his sister.

Upon reaching the imposing red-brick façade of the Carlisle Buildings, Rose and Parker entered through the grand wooden doors. The sergeant was stunned. It wasn't quiet at all. The air buzzed with the sound of typewriters clattering away, reporters furiously scribbling notes, the faint scent of ink and paper. Through the soles of their shoes, they could feel the throb of the floor at the entrance as the heavy printing presses churned out reams of newspapers in the huge facility.

Outside, Davy studied the entrance sign then decided to wait in the shadows.

As they crossed the bustling newsroom, Parker spotted Tanner and her husband in her corner office, a sanctuary amidst the chaos. He gestured to Rose to follow him as they navigated the busy floor. Arriving at the office door, Parker knocked gently and called out, "Hello, Tanner! Have you got a moment?"

Tanner looked up from her cluttered desk, a warm smile spreading across her face. "Sergeant Parker! It's always a pleasure. What brings you here?"

Parker engaged in a brief exchange of pleasantries with Tanner before getting to the heart of the matter.

"Please excuse me, Ted. I've got an important piece to finish on the London Dock Strikes," said Sean Carlisle as he made his way to another office.

"Tanner, allow me to introduce you to Miss Rose O'Shaughnessy. She has quite a story to share, one that I believe will captivate your readers."

Tanner appraised Rose with a discerning eye, intrigued by the potential of this new source. She extended her hand and said,

"It's a pleasure to meet you in person, Rose. I was tucked away in the press gallery throughout your trial."

"Yes, Betty showed me the piece you wrote.
I can't believe it, my name in the papers!"

"Well, you better get used to it. I am sure you have some valuable insights into Vincenzo's world. I'm eager to hear more."

After discussing the details, Tanner agreed to interview Rose about her time with Vincenzo and scheduled their first session for later in the week.

"For an exclusive story, I'm willing to pay a pound," Tanner offered, her eyes gleaming with anticipation. "Deal?"

Rose's face lit up, and she gratefully accepted the offer. The money would provide a much-needed reprieve from her family's financial worries. With the agreement in place, Rose and Parker bid Tanner farewell and left the Carlisle Buildings, their excitement clearly bubbling beneath the surface.

Tanner leaned back in her chair, delighted to have secured a meaty exclusive. The memory of Vincenzo's outburst in court only added to her eagerness to expose his secrets. As the couple emerged from the building, Davy gave his legs and arms a shake like a boxer in the ring and prepared to pursue them once more.

"Why don't we take a stroll in Victoria Park, Rose? I've heard there's a brass band playing today. It would be a lovely way to end our afternoon. Go on, say yes? Please?"

Rose, still feeling the glow of their successful meeting with Tanner, shyly agreed. Together, they walked along Commercial Street, heading toward the far side of Stepney and into the beautiful expanse of Victoria Park. Davy, ever the protective brother, followed them closely but discreetly.

*

As they meandered through the park, Parker stole glances at Rose, feeling a mixture of tenderness and anxiety. He hesitated for a moment, then shared his feelings.

"You did exceptionally well today at the meeting, and you seem much happier now."

Rose caught his gaze and smiled, a hint of shyness in her eyes.

"I am, thank you. It really feels as if a weight has been lifted. The chance to clear my name in the public eye, to share my story, is quite incredible. I confess I've had to pinch myself the first few mornings since I was released to make sure I wasn't dreaming."

The faintest hint of a blush coloured her cheeks, making the moment all the more endearing for Parker.

"Here's something else to make you smile, " Ted chuckled as he shared a bit of gossip he had gleaned from a recent conversation with a prison officer colleague at Bow Street. "I thought you'd like to know that Vincenzo isn't faring too well in Wandsworth. Apparently, he's been having trouble adapting to the strict routines and rules, and the other inmates haven't taken a liking to him either. He's finding the experience rather disagreeable, to say the least."

The news brought a sense of relief to Rose, knowing that her nemesis was experiencing the fullest consequences for his actions. As they continued their leisurely walk in the park, the melodious sounds of the brass band filled the air, creating a soothing backdrop for their blossoming friendship.

Unbeknownst to them, Davy continued to observe the pair from behind a tree as they approached the bandstand. He tensed, his eyes widening with what he saw next. Parker took Rose to one side, to a quiet spot between some large trees. Then the man turned to Rose and got down on one knee. Davy darted behind a chestnut tree and peered round.

With a deep breath, Parker looked up into his companion's eyes, his own filled with love and hope.

"Rose, you've brought so much light into my lonely life. It was all police work morning noon and night before. But now, I can't imagine a future without you by my side. So, please, will you marry me?"

He fished about in his pocket then opened a small velvet fancy box, revealing a delicate and understated ring.

Rose's eyes blinked hard, as she nodded, barely able to speak.

"Yes, Ted, I will."

Parker gently slid the ring onto his beloved fiancée's finger, sealing their commitment to one another. The happiness of their special moment would be short-lived as Davy, unable to contain himself any longer, crashed out from his hiding spot and interrupted their privacy.

Davy stumbled over his words, a mix of surprise and bewilderment.

"Has the, err—the thing that I thought I saw happen—just happened?"

Rose, still radiant from the proposal, smiled at her brother.

"Yes, Davy, it has. Sergeant Parker proposed, and I accepted!"

She proudly displayed her engagement ring for him to see.

The awkward trio hailed a Hansom cab to take them back to Brady Street, eager to share the news with Ellen and Billy. Davy, feeling like a spare part in what should have been a private moment between the newly-engaged couple, shifted uncomfortably in his seat.

Rose couldn't help but laugh at the situation, jokingly chiding her overprotective brother.

"Really, Davy, I don't need this much looking after! I'll be turning twenty-one soon, you know!"

Despite the humour, the underlying warmth and affection between the siblings was unmistakable.

EPILOGUE

LOVE'S QUIET TRIUMPH

The long-anticipated day had at last dawned: the wedding of Rose O'Shaughnessy and Ted Parker. The sun cast its resplendent rays upon the world, bathing the ceremony in a warm golden light that seemed to bless the couple as they prepared to pledge their eternal devotion. Nestled in the bustling heart of London's East End, the small church stood as a testament to the enduring nature of love, its ancient stones adorned with a riot of colourful blossoms, their sweet perfume pervading the sacred space.

The eager whispers of friends and kin resonated within the hallowed walls, as all and sundry eagerly craned their necks to catch a glimpse of the bride's arrival. Rose, resplendent in her modest yet elegant gown of fine linen, looked every bit the blushing bride. Her waist was encircled by a delicate ribbon of silk, intricately embroidered with a pattern that echoed the flowers in the church. Her smile was luminous, her eyes alight with joy as she prepared to embark on a new chapter of her life.

Davy, patiently awaiting her at the rear of the church, offered his arm to escort the beautiful bride down the aisle. As Rose's slender hand settled upon his arm, her face radiated happiness and contentment, her gaze fixed upon her future husband, stood beside Collins, who awaited her at the altar.

Ted, beaming with pride, stood tall in his rented second-hand suit. Though the garment may not have been a perfect fit, it bore witness to the young man's heartfelt efforts to honour his bride on this most momentous of occasions. As the couple drew near to one another, a hush fell over the congregation, all eyes brimming with emotion as they beheld the embodiment of true love triumphing over all.

Following the ceremony, the newlyweds and their guests ambled to a nearby pub, where a humble wedding reception awaited them in the small beer garden. A few wooden tables, draped in plain linens, bore a few fragrant flowers arranged modestly as tiny centrepieces. A small platform had been assembled for some folk musicians scheduled to entertain the guests throughout the evening.

Laughter, the clinking of glasses, and well-wishes filled the air as toasts were made in honour of Rose and Ted. Billy repeatedly embraced Rose, while Ellen expressed her pride in the couple. Davy, never one for fuss and small talk, slipped away early, murmuring about matters that needed his attention. The specifics of his obligations remained a mystery to all.

As the sun dipped below the horizon, Rose and Ted took to the makeshift dance floor for their first dance as husband and wife, swaying gently to the soft melody. The guests soon followed suit, their dancing growing increasingly spirited as the evening progressed and the jigs became more lively. The night was one to cherish—a true testament to love and fresh starts.

When the celebrations eventually wound down, the guests bid the newlyweds adieu with raucous cheers, bawdy nods, and heartfelt blessings. Hand in hand, Rose and Ted stepped into the waiting cab.

"Look after her Mr Parker," Billy shouted, holding his mother's hand.

"I will, lad," Ted reassured as he helped his new wife to take her seat.

The driver, a jovial fellow smiled warmly at the couple as they settled into the carriage.

"Congratulations! May you have a lifetime of happiness together!"

"Thank you kindly, sir, we intend to," Ted replied, his face lighting up with gratitude.

"Just remember, love is the glue that keeps everything together. Keep that love strong, and you'll weather any storm."

With a final nod of agreement, Ted and Rose exchanged tender smiles, their hands entwined as the cab set off.

That evening, the couple settled into their new dwelling—a modest police officer's quarters within one of Peabody's model houses. For Rose, this new home seemed a world apart from Brady Street. As they stepped inside, she couldn't help but marvel at their new surroundings.

"Can you believe it, Ted?" she exclaimed, a twinkle in her eye. "This is all ours!"

Her husband chuckled, his eyes filled with warmth.

"Aye, it's hard to imagine. We've come a long way. Especially you—it's a far cry from the cells in Camden, eh?"

"Don't even joke about that!" Rose retorted, playfully swatting his arm.

Hand in hand, they meandered through the small rooms, envisioning their future together and occasionally sharing sweet, stolen kisses.

The following day at breakfast, Ellen, now healthier and well on the road to recovery, and young Billy joined the couple. The family felt complete as they gathered around the table, sharing stories and laughter, their bond strengthened by their newfound happiness.

*

Rose and Parker, united by their love and shared sense of justice, continued to work together to make a difference in the world.

Together with Tanner Carlisle and her husband, they devoted themselves to fighting against injustice and helping those in need, their passion for their mission only growing stronger with time.

Ellen and Rose got some work at the police canteen, thanks to Parker's recommendation and they delighted in catering for the Camden police officers. The bobbies liked it too, as it provided them a welcome change from their previous diet of dry bread and mouldy cheese to keep the sustained during their long shifts. Now, they enjoyed hot tea and wholesome, tasty soups which warmed the hearts and stomachs of the hardworking officers. Life was improving in the constabulary, and their spirits lifted accordingly.

Billy, too, benefited from his new life with Ted and Rose. Embracing the role of a stepfather, he doted on the boy, ensuring he attended a better school. The youngster loved his new environment and eagerly absorbed knowledge. In the evenings, Ted would often quiz Billy on what he had learned, both of them beaming with pride at the boy's progress.

*

Two months later, a battered postcard landed on Rose's doormat, bearing the familiar handwriting of her brother Davy. He wrote that he was enjoying his new life as a merchant seaman and had been sent to the sun-kissed island of Malta. In his message, he confessed that Cupid's arrow had struck him and he had fallen madly in love with a local Maltese woman named Isabella. Davy also revealed that he intended to wed his newfound love and reside in that heavenly corner of the world. He playfully added a postscript: *'P.S. Let us not speak of falling in love with a stranger in the span of mere weeks.'* Rose couldn't help but smile at her brother's news, feeling happy for his newfound happiness.

Betty's skill in designing and remodelling dresses continued to thrive, making her a sought-after seamstress among the affluent ladies of Hampstead. Sebastian Wade had indeed got her the opportunity in return for her promise not to gossip about Vincenzo. As the social season picked up pace, Betty used her charm to inveigle her way into attending days at the races alongside some of the more daring mistresses from the households she worked for.

When she and Rose met for tea on their rare off days, Betty would recount her adventures in vivid detail, painting a picture of a world of glamour and excitement that Rose could only imagine.

Meanwhile, Sebastian found himself presented with a tempting proposition by the Carlisles: to pen a legal column for their newspaper, focusing on the growing rights of women in society and the Suffragette movement. Initially hesitant to put himself in the public eye, Sebastian eventually relented after Rose and Tanner applied pressure, agreeing to contribute under the pen name: 'Alistair Fairweather.'

Occasionally, Sebastian and his mother would cross paths with Rose when they visited the newspaper office. From a distance, they exchanged warm smiles. Mrs Wade was delighted to see the philanthropic life Rose was carving out for herself, actively contributing to the community through her supportive work at the constabulary and collaborating with Tanner on research for new stories to expose injustices against women. There were plenty of tales from the East End to tell, and Rose relished being the busy journalist's eyes and ears.

*

Over a delightful afternoon tea at the charming abode of the Parkers, Betty, Ted, and Rose reminisced about their shared journey and the obstacles they had overcome. The table was adorned with an array of cakes and dainty sandwiches, lovingly prepared by Ellen. As they relished their refreshments, a sense of warmth and gratitude filled the air, a tribute to the beautiful bonds they had forged.

Betty produced a newspaper clipping featuring one of Alistair Fairweather's captivating pieces in the Beacon, and with a playful glint in her eye, she divulged to Rose, 'I know it's Sebastian behind the pseudonym!'

"Do keep our little secret this time, Betty. You know how Sebastian feels about idle tittle-tattle!" Rose replied. "By the way, Davy is coming back soon to visit. I am sure he will regale us with his seafaring tales.

Perhaps he'll bring his lady friend along? That would be such fun. I have no idea what she's like, but she must be quite a catch to have tamed my brother!"

As they chatted and shared laughs, Rose suggested they raise a toast to their bright future.

"What would you ladies like to drink?" Ted asked.

"Anything but sherry, my love," she chuckled, recalling the days when Vincenzo had plied her with endless glasses of the same at the Eagle Tavern.

Ted left to fetch some drinks, leaving Betty and Rose to continue their delightful conversation. When Parker returned, he couldn't resist teasing the women.

"What are you two discussing now? You're like as thick as thieves!"

Betty feigned shock, and Rose playfully scolded him.

"Ted, how can you say such a thing?"

"You know I'm only pulling your legs," he scoffed with a smile.

Suddenly, a light shade swayed, and a door slammed shut, startling the trio.

"What was that?" Rose asked, trying to sound brave.

"It's just the wind," Ted reassured them with a sly wink.

"As long as it's not another departed husband trying to contact us!" Betty joked, quick with her quips as always.

They chuckled at the sheer absurdity of the notion, their hearts buoyant and carefree once again. Lifting their glasses, they proposed a toast to their luminous future and the steadfast bonds of friendship that would withstand the test of time.

"To us," declared Rose, grasping Ted's hand firmly, as the three glasses clinked together.

—

Enjoyed The Mesmerist's Muse? Here are some more books in my 'Victorian Sisters Sagas' series you'll love. Have you read them all?

- mybook.to/VictorianSisterSagas

If you want to know more about how Tanner became a newspaper editor, have a read of 'Forging The Shilling Girl' and 'The Lost Girl's Beacon of Hope.'

Please consider leaving an honest review or rating. It helps get my stories into the hands of people who will enjoy them.

GET THREE FREE AND EXCLUSIVE EMMA HARDWICK OFFERS

Here are three of my books for free for you to enjoy

- https://rebrand.ly/eh-free

Hi! Emma here. For me, the most rewarding thing about writing books is building a relationship with my readers, and it's a true pleasure to share my experiences with you. From time to time, I write little newsletters with short snippets I discover as I research my Victorian historical romances, details that don't make it into my books. In addition, I also talk about how writing my next release is progressing, plus news about special reader offers and competitions.

And I'll include all these freebies if you join my newsletter:

- A copy of my introductory novella, The Pit Lad's Mother.

- A copy of my introductory short story, The Photographer's Girl.

- A free copy of my Victorian curiosities, a collection of newspaper snippets I have collated over the years that have inspired many of the scenes in my books.

These are all exclusive to my newsletter—you can't get them anywhere else. You can grab your free books on BookFunnel, by signing up here:

- https://rebrand.ly/eh-free

ABOUT THE AUTHOR

Emma Hardwick is the author of several series of Victorian historical saga romances. She lives in London with her husband and dogs and makes her online home at:

- www.emmahardwick.co.uk

You can connect with Emma on Facebook at :

- www.facebook.com/emmahardwickauthor

and if the mood takes you, you should send her an email at:

- hello@emmahardwick.co.uk

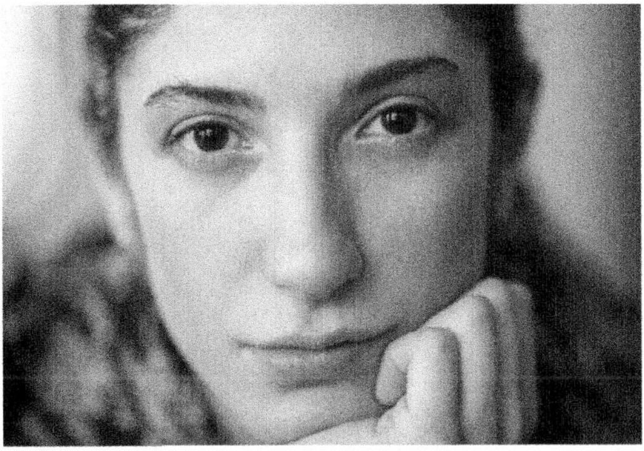

Printed in Great Britain
by Amazon